DRAGON
MARKED

DRAGON
MARKED

Jaymin Eve

SKYSCAPE

SKYSCAPE

Published by Skyscape, New York

www.apub.com

Amazon, the Amazon logo, and Skyscape are trademarks of Amazon.com, Inc., or its affiliates.

ISBN-13: 9781503949782
ISBN-10: 1503949788

Book design by Jason Blackburn

Printed in the United States of America

To my sister-in-law Laura, Aunty Coll, and Marice.
My favorite betas and friends.

DRAGON
MARKED

Chapter 1

My head hit the desk with a loud clunk. I jerked upright, blinking rapidly. What the hell had just happened?

"I'm sorry, Miss Lebron. Am I boring you?" Tall, dark, and deadly was my teacher as he loomed over my desk.

Shit, I'd fallen asleep in class again. Damn those Compass brothers, keeping me out all night in the forest. We'd been looking for the prison again. Another fruitless search.

"Sorry, sir," I said, slinking lower in my seat. I rubbed a hand across my mouth to make sure I didn't have sleep drool on my face.

Like a lot of older vamps, our history teacher, Mr. Vendir Vamissa, hadn't forgotten the last supernatural war—when shifters and vampires had fought on opposite sides—so I wasn't surprised when he hissed before dismissing me with a flick of his bald head. When he reached the front of the class, he leveled another dark look in my direction. I was too strong for compulsion to roll me. Still, all vampires were scary when they locked you in their gaze. Thankfully, he started lecturing again, picking up where he'd left off about the origins of the Slothman. No wonder I'd fallen asleep.

Jacob Compass—one of the quadruplets who were my best friends—nudged me. "Nice one, Jessa, pissing off the vamp before dinnertime."

I narrowed my eyebrows at him, a slight growl rumbling my chest. "You're an asshat. Why didn't you wake me?"

The amusement in Jacob's grass-green eyes was clear. "Hey, I wanted to stay home last night, but everyone follows Tyson when he *reveals* his brilliant plans." He flicked a small orange flame between his fingertips. Jacob was one of the faeries—who we call fey. They have power over the elements, although he was extraobsessed with fire.

Tyson spun in his chair, pointing a long finger at Jacob. "I'm sitting right here, dick."

I knew the brothers as well as I knew myself, and there was no doubt that Tyson, who was a wizard, wanted to punch his brother. The only thing stopping a fistfight was our current awkward seating arrangement. Tyson was in the row in front of us.

Jacob, Tyson, Braxton, and Maximus Compass had been my best friends for most of my twenty-two years. They were quads who—through a quirk in nature or genetics—somehow contained the souls of four different supernatural races.

Our little pack had gone through early learning and special training, and now attended a private supernatural, "supes," college together. Six thousand members of the supernatural community lived in our town of Stratford, Connecticut. Witch magic protected our borders and repelled humans from entering, and there was a very important reason for this. Our town was a gateway, a guardian community, protecting those very fragile and innocent humans from the darkness they never even knew existed. Stratford was a supernatural prison community, the keepers of your worst nightmares.

Maximus, the vampire, was the daredevil of the group. "So are we heading out tonight?"

Braxton growled from my other side. "No. Jessa's tired. And we have a council meeting after class."

Our continued conversation had the teacher hissing in our direction again. In a room this size, vampire hearing didn't miss anything. We shut our mouths and pretended to listen, but it was too late. Vendir's expression indicated that I needed to be taught a lesson in respect. Or fear. Of course he didn't try that shit with the Compasses. Sometimes I hated being small and female. Although, to be underestimated, well, sometimes that was deliciously ironic.

With super speed, Vendir was beside my desk again, the eyes of our classmates following him.

"It's in your best interest to stop interrupting my lesson, Jessa. You don't want to push me too far. I can make life very difficult for you."

Oh shit.

Reprimanding me was one thing, but threatening me in front of the Compasses . . . bad idea. In a single movement, the four of them were on their feet. I followed because my alpha wolf didn't like the men towering over me, although most of them were a foot taller than my five feet four—yep, I was small. My height was another thing that gave me an air of vulnerability, right up until I opened my mouth.

Braxton sounded casual. "You might want to back the hell off of Jessa." But his dark-blue eyes were flashing. "I'd hate to get vamp on my clothes."

"Brax." I laid a hand on his arm, hoping to calm him. Braxton was a dragon shifter, and if he lost control, more than a few supes would die. "Forget it. I'm okay, and more important, my wolf is fine."

It might have been a different story if the vampire had pissed off my inner animal, but her energy had barely even swirled inside. We considered the weaker vamp teacher to be nothing more than an annoyance. If it came down to it, I didn't need the quads to take on Vendir.

The vampire knew when he was outpowered, and lowering his head, he backed to the front of the room. His features were expressionless, but his narrowed eyes flashed fury, fang was showing, and his hands had formed claws that he couldn't seem to straighten. The brothers stood for a few extra moments just to reiterate their point before retaking their seats. The tension that had descended over the thirty students around us started to dissipate. Most of them looked disappointed. They'd been hoping for a throwdown. What can I say? Many of us were predators, and we had a predisposition for the enjoyment of bloody warfare.

Glancing to the side, I noticed how motionless Braxton was in his chair. His face was perfectly calm, but I knew him better than that. He was pissed.

Braxton was the most protective of the group. Maybe it was because we were both shifters, but he had my back even more than his brothers. Yet, all of them could be annoyingly overprotective. Luckily, my wolf thought of them as pack; although as an alpha, she was still annoyed when they tried to control me. I was a dominant shifter through the bloodline of my father, Jonathon Lebron, alpha of the wolf shifters, high council leader of all shifting races, and all-around badass. He was training me to take over the pack. I was powerful, one of the most powerful wolf shifters born in the United States.

This was probably the reason the Compass quads and I were so tight; they were powerful, too, set to be the next American Supernatural Council members. In three years' time they would take over from the current council members.

Maximus was vampire, Braxton was shifter, Jacob was fey, and Tyson was a magic user, a wizard. So they would hold four of the positions on the council. The fifth race was the demi-fey: mermaids, gargoyles, trolls, goblins, pixies, imps, centaurs, and the like. Basically any group who would never be able to blend into the human world. The demi-fey were the only supernatural race that the Compasses didn't have a representative in.

My attention was drawn back to the head of the class and a sudden subject change to a myriad of famous wolf-shifter deaths throughout history, with particular and detailed attention spent on our weaknesses. I silently chuckled; the vampire could not be more obvious. He was probably plotting my murder while he lectured, but was too weak to ever do more than play it out in his head.

Next to me Jacob started mumbling under his breath, singing. The fey love to belt out a ballad. His voice was sweet; I could listen to him sing for days. All four brothers stared off in different directions around the room. The lucky asses were geniuses and never paid attention in class. Truth be told, they were a mystery in the supernatural community. Being the children of two rare hybrids—a vampire-sorceress mother and shifter-fey father—was unusual enough. Hybrids producing offspring: it was pretty much unheard of. But no one had a freaking clue how the quadruplets had come to possess four different supernatural abilities. And in pure-blooded form, no less.

Vendir finished summing up the six strike points for a kill on a wolf—dumb ass—before waving his hand and turning his back on us. "Class is dismissed early today. Make your way to the town hall."

I moved aside as a short, broad troll barged down the aisle. Don't get in the way of trolls; they're like steam trains. Our class was a mix of supernatural creatures. We attended college until twenty-five, and after that we had to choose a career. There were a wide variety of jobs, including many that were connected to the prison. Vanguard was the United States' supernatural prison, hidden, secret, and protected deep in the forest that bordered Stratford. No one knew the location unless they were initiated into the council. Or if your career was within the walls. The boys and I spent a lot of time searching for it, but so far, nada. That's where we'd been last night; Tyson thought he had a lead. They were future council leaders, so it pissed them right off that they were excluded from information about the prison. This was their way of taking things into their own hands.

But since I'd ended up with mud in unmentionable places and a tick on my ass, the wizard had clearly missed the mark. It wasn't the first time the Compass brothers had led me astray, and it wouldn't be the last.

After class I wandered along with the hundreds who were heading toward the town hall. The boys would catch up with me soon; they all had *things* to do. Things I probably did not want to know about. The town meeting was due to start in about thirty minutes, so they would have to haul ass to make it in time.

Stratford wasn't huge, and it was laid out in a circular pattern, everything revolving out from the large towering-into-the-air fountain at the center. The town hall was a stone-and-brick building with old-style architecture that included a pair of large hand-carved stone statues out front and heavy window frames. The building sat off to the right of the fountain, taking up a pretty decent section of land.

My father caught up with me just before I entered the huge double doors, draped an arm across my shoulders, and lead me back to the grassy area off to the side. I smiled as I stared into his dark-blue eyes; they were the same color as mine. His hair was blond though, whereas mine was so black it almost looked blue in the sunlight. My father didn't look much older than me. Supernaturals age very slowly. Most live a good eight hundred years or more.

"Hi, sweetheart." Jonathon leaned down to give me a hug. He wasn't tall for a shifter, but height wasn't important when his power followed him around, ready to deliver a swift boot in the ass. My father ruled our pack with an iron fist, but toward me, he was a fluffy puppy . . . with claws. He placed both hands on my biceps. "I need to tell you something before the meeting. We have some new and disturbing information."

I opened my mouth, but was interrupted by a shout.

"Jessa!"

I spun my head around to see Jacob wave. He was with his brothers, and they were making their way across the paved center arcade. The vamp and shifter girls around me started giggling like morons. For some reason, these men turned cold-blooded predators into silly human females. It was quite amusing to watch as the quads brushed them off. Most of them were just looking to snare the future leaders of the council. We were a bit superficial like that. And while the Compasses were not exactly picky, groupies were not their thing.

I growled at a very blonde wolf shifter. "Get some pride." Damn, she was like three seconds from drooling.

The blonde lowered her eyes, not dominant enough to meet my glare for too long. I turned away with a shake of my head. Silky strands of my straight, inky hair brushed against my bare shoulders. In true shifter style, I was wearing only a tank and short shorts, clothes easy to shed if my wolf needed to run.

"Try and remember, Jess," Jonathon said, drawing my attention again. "You don't see the guys the same way as the other females."

Narrowing my eyes, I turned to observe the four as the crowd parted to let them through. I had no idea what my father was talking about. I saw them perfectly fine. I had outstanding vision, almost as good as the eagle shifters.

The brothers stood heads above everyone else. All of them looked alike, and yet were all so different. They were exceptionally beautiful, with olive skin, chiseled jaws, perfectly straight noses, and dimples in their cheeks. Yes, the smug bastards had dimples, too. But in no way were they cute; they were gorgeous and hard, and you knew they could destroy you if you crossed them.

Braxton stood a little in front. At six-and-a-half feet he was a massive shifter, which made sense for a dragon. His skin was a few shades darker than his brothers' and his hair was as black as night, contrasting beautifully to his eyes, which were as blue as a flawless spring sky. Tyson, the wizard, had brown hair with that hint of auburn threaded through. He wore it a little longer than his brothers, but still only brushing the bottom of his ears. His eyes were a honeysuckle brown, soft and sweet, except when he was using his magic. Then they turned gold and you knew it was time to haul ass. Jacob, the fey, was a little shorter, and finer than his massive brothers, but still big. He had green eyes, like a newly turned leaf in spring, and hair so blond it was pretty much white. Bringing up the rear was Maximus, the vampire, the hugest of the four. His hair was dirty blond, falling into his dark-brown eyes. You knew when he was vamped out, fangs descended, and his eyes turned black.

Yes, they were all exceptional, but if I had to pick the most exceptional, well, Braxton held a little more of my heart than the other three. He was my absolute best friend.

I'd die or kill for any of them in an instant, and I knew they felt the same way. I'd never made friends in my pack. Sure, it was probably because of my sunny personality. But even if I didn't have an attitude problem, being the alpha's daughter inspired fear and respect, not friendship. I was lucky to have the boys.

Jonathon looked calm, but for the first time his wolf was peering out of his eyes. The blue had darkened and yellow threaded around the pupil. "I have to go. Kristoff is calling the council inside."

Ah, that explained the wolf. He hated taking directions from that asshole.

Stratford and Vanguard were ruled by the American Supernatural Council, the very council the boys would take over in a few years. Kristoff Krass was the current head of the magic users, and as I said, an asshole. The tall, thin, and slimy sorcerer was hella powerful and totally in love with his own awesomeness. His daughter, Giselda, was a witch and my BEF, bitch enemy forever. We'd thrown down on more than one occasion. Having Tyson in my corner had probably saved me from her sneaky ways. Magic was underhanded, slow-moving, and hard to detect. Luckily, wolf senses could detect the stirring of a spell, not to mention lies when they fell from forked tongues.

I stopped my father as he turned to leave. "Wait, what did you have to tell me?"

He fixed me in his gaze again. "Right, sorry, I don't have much time, but I can't have you blindsided or your wolf will lose it."

Great, that sounded promising.

"Your mother has returned," he finished in a rush.

I stared at him blankly, before a burning hot flood of lava started in my chest and blew upward to my brain. By the time the fury reached my mouth, I was ready to explode.

Shouts and curses fell from my lips. "How could you let her come back here? She abandoned us! I don't want to see that bitch ever again!"

She was a wolf, so *bitch* was literal. Jonathon met my gaze, and more of his wolf peeked out. I was alpha enough to challenge him, but I never would. Reluctantly—my emotions screaming for further release—I lowered my gaze.

His hand left my arm and cupped my chin, lifting my face to meet his eyes. He was giving me equal status with him in this fight. "I needed her to return. There is much you don't understand, but she's always your mother."

I was shaking my head violently.

"I have to go, Jess." He dropped a kiss on my cheek and took off for the hall.

My hands were trembling as my wolf fought for control. Just thinking that that woman was close by had me wanting to shift and run far away. I didn't care what Dad said; I had no mother.

"What happened?" Braxton dropped one of his large hands on the bare skin between my shoulder blades. The contact was comforting, and my trembles lessened. But I still couldn't answer straightaway.

"Lienda has returned," Maximus said. Score one for vampire hearing.

"Fuck," Braxton growled. "What's Jonathon thinking letting that bitch back into Stratford?"

You needed council permission to enter or leave our town. There were many protections woven around Stratford and the surrounding forest, mainly to stop humans from entering but also to prevent any supes from trying to break their criminal brethren out from the prison.

"He said he had to allow her in for a reason." My choked voice was low and growly. "If she's inside, I think I'm going to need some help—don't let me kill her."

Jacob ran a hand through his hair. "Damn, you ruin all our fun, Jessa babe. We haven't killed anyone for ages."

I punched him once for being a douche bucket. The five of us were relatively nonviolent—supernaturals almost never died around us. The occasional rabbit on the other hand, well, that was fair game.

"Come on . . ." Tyson's voice was relaxed. "We need to find some seats. I feel something of a serious nature is going down tonight."

Wizards found power in nature and from the gods. Tyson *heard* pieces of information from the universe while he was casting spells. Well, either that or he had an oracle stashed somewhere, because he often produced little gems of inside information.

We elbowed and shoved one another, striving to be in front and dominant. In the end, Braxton sent Tyson and Jacob sprawling, and with growling laughter rumbling his chest, scooped me up over his shoulder and charged through the crowd into the massive town hall. Faces turned toward us but quickly looked away again. When Braxton dropped me, I wiped a hand over my heated forehead. It was hot in the room. I was already sweating.

Tyson appeared right behind us. "You're a dick. You know that, right?" His jab landed cleanly on Braxton's biceps; the dragon shifter barely moved. "You better sleep with one eye open tonight."

"I sleep with both eyes wide open. No one gets the drop on me." Braxton was cocky. He called it confident. It was a bit of both.

The five of us found seats in the center of the room. We were some of the few who broke race grouping and sat together. Seated before us on a higher dais were the council leaders. Besides my father, who led the shifters, and Kristoff of the magic users, there was also Julianna Medow, a six-foot-tall and stunning red-haired vampire; Galiani of the Greenlands—male fey—with long, silky yellow hair, feline features, and a graceful stride that made me feel like an elephant shifter instead of a wolf; and the demi-fey leader, Torag of the Eastland trolls. He was four feet tall and the same width. His skin resembled a newly formed tree, a smattering of skin and hard "bark." His nose was long and thin above beady eyes. He was a good troll. I'd grown up with him; he was a longtime friend of my father's and had spent a lot of time in my home.

Wiggling to get comfortable in the padded chair, I kept my eyes locked on the leaders. They seemed to be discussing something serious among themselves. Jonathon caught my gaze and gave me a warm smile, but there was unease in his rigid posture. Was this just about my mother's return? Why would that be influencing any of the other council members' behavior? Unless they all hated her, too. Wouldn't surprise me.

And speaking of . . .

I stood and looked around the mostly seated crowd. I didn't remember Lienda. Funny enough, no one I talked with really remembered anything specific about her, but I'd seen a photo of her once. I knew I could pick her out in a crowd. We looked alike, but she had very blonde hair. God knows where I got my hair color.

It took no time for me to sight and scent that she wasn't in the room, unless she was cloaking herself with the help of a magic user. I slumped into my chair, and suddenly I was crushed by Braxton and Maximus sandwiching me in. The brutes always stole my space, their long arms invading my territory. I was contemplating whether it was worth starting elbow wars when my stomach decided to make its presence known in the form of a loud rumble that echoed throughout the hall. I groaned, dropping my hands to my belly, which of course the boys took advantage of. Now they had much more of their person on my person, squishing the hell out of me.

Surely the meeting was due to start soon. The hall had been pretty full when I'd been looking for Lienda. It seated over two thousand, so about a third of the community attended. I glared up at the council again. Dammit, hurry up and start the meeting; I was freaking starving. I'd missed lunch because I was late for weapons class, and dinner was looking like it would be too far away. The way my stomach was protesting, there was no hiding it in a room full of supernaturals.

And then the ribbing started.

Jacob the jackass was first. "Shit, batten down the hatches and guard your limbs. Jessa's hungry—every man for himself."

"Them there are fighting words, fey," I said as I released my wolf a little and dived across Braxton. Jacob was going down.

Jacob held both hands up in mock distress. "Damn, she's coming at me, Brax! Hand me the emergency snacks." I let free a growl, followed by a solid thump to his chest—which probably hurt my hand more than his body—but I was semisatisfied with my act of dominance.

My stomach growled again, louder than ever. At that point Braxton, Jacob, and Maximus were practically on the floor, they were howling so loudly. Tyson had started flirting with the witch seated next to him and wasn't paying attention anymore.

It's safe to say I copped a fair amount of shit over my love of food. When it came to dinnertime, I could hold my own with any one of these six-foot-plus men. What can I say? I love food. And I'm a shifter—we have a fast metabolism. I wasn't fat at all, but I had plenty of curves and I liked having curves. I wanted them to stay exactly where they were, so I figured it was my duty to eat. The male supernaturals liked my curves, too. I might not have many friends, but I was popular in some ways. What can I say? Wolves are friendly.

The boys were still laughing their butts off, so I decided to give back as good as I got. I rarely acted like a chick around them—sometimes I think if it weren't for the boobs, they would forget I wasn't a man, too—but right now some fake tears were in order.

"You guys are right," I said in a subdued tone. I even lowered my eyes a little, which rankled my wolf, but she understood. "Maybe I could stand to eat less. You know . . . lose a few pounds." Their laughter died instantly as they eyed me with something close to astonishment.

Braxton was the first to recover. "You're fucking kidding me, right?" His eyes flashed as he straightened in his chair. "You do that, and I'll follow you around with a goddamn steak . . . day and night." His voice lowered on the last word of his threat.

"And ice cream," Maximus added. They knew I loved dessert of any description. Sugar was my weakness. "You lose one inch off that delectable ass, and we can't be friends any longer." He crossed his arms over his chest, which at least freed up some space on his side.

I internally rolled my eyes. Braxton and Maximus's responses were not a surprise. The predator supes were pretty earthy and sexual.

I stared at the three Compasses. Their unwavering attention was locked on me, their faces scrunched up and all of them frowning. The morons looked really worried. Then I couldn't hold a straight face any longer. My lips curved up as laughter burst from me and I flipped them off.

"Like I would give up food for any man." I followed the middle finger with another rude gesture that shifters were fond of.

Their retaliation was cut off as the council members stood, ready to start our meeting. Braxton leaned in closer to me. "Just for that, no sharing of my dessert tonight."

Ouch, that was mean. He always got extra for me; I could never fit enough on my plate. I turned sad eyes on him, but he just shook his head. Damn, the girlie act wouldn't work twice on him tonight. Problem was, it wasn't really an act, I was genuinely sad without cake.

Kristoff was center stage, where he liked to be. "Quiet now," he said, and the room fell silent. We all knew disobeying your council leaders was bad news, no matter your own personal power levels. "Thank you to all that take the time to attend our monthly meetings. We have much to discuss. You will remain patient until we finish explaining all the details to you. There is some news that you will find shocking, but rest assured you will understand . . . mostly everything."

Yeah, everything they wanted us to understand. Our council operated the same way as all powerful groups. Control worked best when the rest of us were kept in the dark about things. Like where the prison was that we were supposed to be laying down our lives to guard. And speaking of the prison system, it seemed there was some news.

Julianna started us off with a bang. "Prisons in Romania, Greece, Japan, and Scotland have been infiltrated in the last month." Her beautiful face did not change expression despite the symphony of gasps that blasted through the hall. "There were numbers of prisoners broken out. The filtered-down information we're receiving seems to indicate this is a worldwide strike against our system."

I shifted forward to the edge of my seat. There was an entire network of secret supernatural prisons around the world, at least one on every continent. Supernatural numbers were much smaller than those of humans, which is why, despite the size of America, we needed only one prison. And like Stratford's hidden Vanguard, we knew very little about the different prisons. I had never heard of a mass breakout like this.

"Sounds like an inside job," I heard Braxton mutter.

I turned and met his gaze, the fine skin around my eyes tightened as his words penetrated my brain. I agreed with him, and surely that circumstance would narrow the pool of suspects considerably.

Jonathon spoke then. "We don't want you to panic. We've had no word that Vanguard is to be hit, and our hold is strong." He sent out some calming vibes, which, for an alpha of his power, worked on everyone, even those not shifter. "We've tightened up security, and we urge no one to run by themselves in the forest for a little while."

He leveled his warm gaze on me. I kept my expression calm, eyes wide as if I were innocent. Nothing escaped my father's attention. He knew what the Compasses and I had been doing. He'd turned a blind eye, but there was a subtle warning in his tone now. No more night runs searching for the prison, which would rankle the boys. Something about being denied their rights to view it really pissed them off.

Jonathon finished his speech. "We'll keep you apprised of what happens. Our belief is that we'll soon bring those involved to justice, and they'll join our prison system in a different manner."

The next lot of news came from Galiani. "The body of one of my brethren was discovered on the edge of the forest this morning."

Gasps and curses rang out again. Shit, they were hitting us with the serious news this afternoon. A dead fey. The element wielders were damn hard to kill, so what had happened? I glanced at Jacob. It was always terrible to lose a member of your supernatural race. I could see his chest vibrating, his anger palpable. He sat rigidly next to Braxton.

Galiani was still speaking. "At the moment we're investigating, and it's pretty clear that this was no natural death. We don't take kindly to supernaturals killing each other. I suggest if you were involved, turn yourself in before we find you. If you have any explanation, well, the punishment might be a little less severe."

I doubted that; the fey could be the most hard-assed. They had a cold, clinical approach to many things. Which was something that separated them from the rest of us. Vampires, shifters, and the demi-fey contingent were more animalistic, the magic users very earthy and grounded.

The council members were still looking around the hall. Did they really think someone was going to jump up and say, "Yeah, it was me. I killed your fey"? I noticed they hadn't named the victim. I wondered if they were keeping the identity secret for a reason.

"Fine," Galiani spat out after a few tense moments. "The magic users are working on it, and there will be no place on earth you can hide where we won't find you."

My father cleared his throat, and I could see the apology in his eyes as he opened his mouth. Great, seemed we were ready to move on to my mother—that is, Lienda. I had no mother.

"We have welcomed the wolf shifter Lienda Jackson back to the community," Jonathon said. "She has journeyed far and is resting now. She brings with her a daughter." He turned his head to the side. "Come out, Mischa, and say hello to everyone."

Wait, what?

My ears were buzzing, and there was some sort of weird fuzziness descending over my eyes. What was happening? Was I having a breakdown, or was this just shock? Had I heard him correctly?

Pain knocked the disorientation from me. I looked down to notice I'd half shifted my hands to claws and they were cutting into my palm, drawing blood. I heard Maximus grunt as the scent hit him. He'd told me on more than one occasion that my blood had a very distinct scent, one he'd never encountered from any other supernatural. Easy to recognize.

The black-haired female was hesitant, head down as she crossed the front stage. She looked small and nervous, shuffling across the floor to stand beside my father. As she lifted her face, I gasped. What the hell? She was a carbon copy of me, but instead of blue eyes, hers were a light turquoise green.

Jonathon spoke over the murmurs from the crowd. "This is Mischa, my daughter and younger sister to Jessa." As the second bomb was dropped on me, I barely noticed the multitude of faces that had turned in my direction.

Holy hell, knock me over with a feather. How was this possible? She wasn't just Lienda's daughter, she was also Jonathon's. I had a sister he'd never told me about. Her wide doe eyes scanned the crowd before landing on me. We stared at each other for an indefinable amount of time. Tearing myself from her gaze, I let out a howl and took off from the room.

Chapter 2

My wolf washed over me, and I was shifted before I hit the edge of Stratford. I didn't think, I just ran and ran, tearing through the fallen and decaying undergrowth. I was not big for a shifter; my wolf was the size of a large human dog. My coat was the same blue-black as my hair, and since the sun was setting, I blended right into the dark of the forest—the forest that my father had just laid down the law about running alone in.

Good thing I didn't care for his rules. The canopy was thick in this wilderness. It was against our laws to tamper with our forest; it was allowed to grow free on its own. But the magic users and fey often poured their energy into the land, which led to some unusual flora. As I dodged and darted through the dense undergrowth, the landscape was flashing in shades of black, gray, and green. When I'm in wolf form, my senses are sharper, and I always rely heavily on scent and sound. Sight is almost secondary. Before my very first shift, I'd had fears of what it might be like to turn into an animal, but even though I was guided more by instinct, the animal was still me. I didn't lose Jessa to gain the wolf; we coexisted and were really the same being. Two sides of the same coin.

I'd been shifting for over six years, and now didn't even have to think about the process. It just happened when I called on the energy. My wolf stayed curled inside of me until I reached for her. On occasion she fought her cage, but mostly we lived in harmony.

Still, there was another small part deep inside that I didn't touch, an energy that frankly scared the shit out of me.

I called it the demon. My wolf and I had lived with the demon my entire life. When I was seventeen I'd tried to explain this dark energy to my father. I'd hedged around my awareness that it was a large, unknown power hidden deep below my wolf. He'd had no idea what I was talking about. Despite my fear of this unknown energy, I treated it like my wolf, although I kept it caged permanently. So now the three of us sort of coexisted.

Dysfunctional-Relationships-Are-Us.

For the first time in a long while, though, I was struggling. My shock and energy were fuel for the demon. It was beating at the cage. How could my father have kept this from me? I had a sister out there. A more innocent-looking pup I'd never seen. She'd been terrified in the hall. I could smell her fear and I wasn't the only one. They were going to tear her apart. I wondered where she'd grown up. Had she known of her shifter abilities? Surely our bitch of a mother had at least clued her in. The first change was rough, and if you didn't know it was coming, well, it would probably feel a lot like dying.

When I'm in wolf form, my thoughts and emotions are simpler, which meant I knew without any doubt that I hated Lienda and was pissed at my father. But I wasn't sure how to feel about the sister, Mischa.

I needed more information.

A familiar scent flooded my nostrils, and even though I couldn't see anything, I knew he was out there. Vampire was distinct, sort of a mix of dark, rich spices. Tantalizing with a hint of danger. Then as I rounded the corner, there he was, leaning casually against a tree.

Maximus Compass.

"You about done yet, Jessa babe?" His pose still looked relaxed, but tension was radiating off him.

I knew that with his vampire speed, he'd have caught up to me immediately. He'd been letting me have my run.

He straightened. "Time to change back, Jess. You're needed in town. We're having a little trouble with Brax. You might have to stop him before he kills your parents and burns Stratford to the ground."

Shit. Braxton didn't lose it much, but when he did, well, things got messy fast.

I decided not to shift back yet; I was quicker in my wolf form. I circled around and took off back the way I'd just run.

Maximus kept pace with me. "It'll be faster if you let me carry you," he said.

He was right, and the only reason he hadn't just scooped me up was my wolf would have attacked him. Something he knew from experience. But it was okay if he gave me the choice. Without breaking stride, I jumped into his arms. I decided not to shift back, no need to be naked. Sure, I wasn't shy of my body—I was a damn shifter, we were always naked—but I didn't need Maximus carting my naked butt around.

I closed my eyes as he took off, his speed fast enough to blur us to anyone watching. I always got a bit motion sick when traveling at vampire speed. The journey into the forest, which had taken me fifteen minutes, was over in seconds. Back in front of the town hall, Maximus dropped me to all fours, before turning his back—in deference to my own personal preference for privacy. I called on my energy and shifted back to human form. I stretched out my limbs and shook off the moment's disorientation as colors and light flooded my vision.

I strode ten feet to reach one of the many clothes bins that littered Stratford. Reaching in blindly, I grabbed the first couple of things my hands touched. Looking down, I nodded; this would work. I shoved the white T-shirt over my head and pulled on denim cutoffs. They were a little big, but I just rolled the band over once, exposing a line of tanned midriff.

I hurried back to Maximus. On the way, I noticed the main double doors were blocked by a large scaly tail. Black with hints of blue tipping the edges. Braxton was the size of a house in his dragon form, and he was wedged in the entrance. Dragons were the most powerful, rare, and scary of the shifter forms. By size alone they dominated the supernatural races.

As I reached Maximus, I grabbed his arm. "We're going to have to use the side entrance."

We moved fast. I could hear screaming from inside, but the lack of magic in the air told me it hadn't escalated too far. Yet.

Reaching the door, I scrambled with the handle; the damn thing was locked. Maximus reached around me and snapped the silver clasp before cracking the whole door right off the hinges.

"I could have done that," I shot out as he threw the metal aside. He just grinned, flashing a little fang. Show-off.

It was chaos inside. The weaker were pushing back from the drama, and as soon as they noticed the exit we'd provided, they started scrambling to get through. Which of course made it damn difficult to go in the direction of the dragon. Maximus stepped in front of me and used his bulk to bulldoze us through the crowd. I gripped the back of his shirt so as not to lose him in the panic. I was grateful he was in front. It would be easy to get crushed in this crowd, especially by the trolls and gargoyles. When they hit you, it felt as if they were made of wood and stone, which was not surprising, as those were their other forms.

As we made it farther into the hall, I noticed that the council leaders—some elders and other powerful members of the five supe races—were standing around Braxton in a semicircle. It was some type of standoff. The dragon wasn't attacking yet, but smoke poured from his huge snout and nostrils, and the rumbling roars that were shaking the ground told me he was reaching the end of his patience.

Some random supernatural hit me hard from the side. With a shriek I went head over ass and landed on my face. Smooth. My wolf was real proud of that graceful move. Before I could pull myself up, Maximus lifted me without effort and hauled me over his shoulder. Wasting no more time, he started barreling through the crowd.

Increased growls and rumbles flooded my ears. Braxton's long snout had shifted direction and was now roaring at us. *What the heck?* Slowly, Maximus lowered me to the ground.

"She's fine, Brax," he said, holding both hands in the air. "No one is touching her."

Right. Dragons were possessive, and in this form Braxton had less control over his base instincts.

I pushed my way around Maximus and glared at the deadly but visually stunning dragon. He was massive; he'd had to tuck his wings in at his side to have room for movement. The black and blue of his scales shone even in the dying light. His bright-yellow eyes surveyed the room before locking me in their gaze. He roared again and I decided to take a stand. In general I didn't think much before I acted, and my plans were often considered to be brave or stupid. Usually both.

"Braxton Compass," I scolded him, moving right up into his strike zone, my hands on my hips. "Your scaled dragon ass is blocking the doorway."

Jacob, Tyson, and Maximus crowded behind me. They were ready to snatch me up if their brother made the wrong move. But I knew it would have to be pretty exceptional circumstances before Braxton would lose enough of himself to hurt me.

The massive beast lowered his head until we were eye to eye. He would scent trickles of my fear, but despite my body's involuntary response, I wasn't really afraid of Braxton. His dragon was a little unpredictable, but he was strong enough to keep both of them controlled. I knew he'd pulled this stunt to remind the council where the real power lay and that he didn't like secrets being kept, especially when they personally affected us. I wondered for a second then where Mischa had ended up in the crazed exodus from the hall.

The dragon and I continued our stare-off, my dark-blue eyes locked on his yellow. "Let's call it a tie," I finally said, grinning and raising my eyebrows at the same time.

With a huff of smoke that enveloped my entire head, he lifted his long snout full of razor-sharp teeth away from me. There was a pull of power, and with a bit of a light-and-energy show, he started to shift back to human form. I let out the breath I hadn't even realized I'd been holding, my heart rate finally slowed, and when Jacob moved to grab Braxton some clothes, I turned to find my father right beside me. My smile faded out to a glare. Jonathon was far too close for my liking right now.

"I'm not talking to you." I pointed a finger, uncaring that he was my alpha and council leader. "How could you have lied to me all these years?" I hated that my voice trembled on those last words. My anger sometimes turned me into a hot mess of tears.

He opened his mouth, but I wasn't in the mood to hear more lies, so I held up a hand.

"Don't. I'm going to need some time to process my feelings on this. Right now I'm about five seconds from losing my shit. I might not be as big as a dragon, but I'd do my damn best to tear this place to the ground." And I would. My energy was rolling inside of me, threatening to free the demon.

Maximus dragged me under his arm. "Jessa will be staying with us tonight," he said.

I shook him off. I needed to stand on my own two feet right now; independence was keeping me from dissolving into tears. Although if the lump in my throat continued to grow in size, it was going to choke me soon.

Braxton moved to stand at my back. I could feel the heat and his unique spicy scent wrapping around me. When I rolled my head to the side, blue-and-yellow eyes captured me. He was back in human form, but his dragon was still riding him.

"Don't ever do that again." His voice was low and deadly. "I could have killed you."

I shrugged. Maybe . . . maybe not.

He shook his head before turning to the others in the room. "We're the future leaders of the American Supernatural Council." His tone was guttural. "This is the last time I will say this. Stop lying to us—and before more bullshit falls from your lips, omitting information is the same damned thing."

The council leaders were changed every quarter of a century or upon death. Positions went to the most powerful in that age bracket—simple but effective. The Compass brothers were coming up to their time, only a few more years. At twenty-five, they would be blood-bound to their supernatural races. No one knew who would lead the demi-fey—they were more secretive, only revealing their choice the night before the crowning.

Kristoff stepped toward us, his hard gaze locked on Braxton. "What did you say?" His voice was a whisper of disbelief. A hand on his shoulder had him pausing. Jonathon had halted him. The sorcerer sneered before throwing off my father's hand. "Don't touch me, Jonathon. Deal with your shifter."

My father tensed but didn't engage the magic leader further. He turned to us. "Don't forget that we're still the rulers right now." Since Jonathon was council leader to all shifters, Braxton's show of dominance was his problem. "If you pull one more stunt like this, we're going to have serious problems."

If the low growls from the Compasses were any indication, we already had a problem. I was not interested in this happening tonight. Jonathon was still my father, and no matter how angry I was with him, I didn't want a fight to break out. I suspected he'd lose to the powerful dragon shifter.

Time to defuse the situation.

I stepped between the groups. "We're going to walk away right now . . . with no further repercussions." I was ensuring they wouldn't revisit this situation to punish us at a later date. "And next time you might want to think about imparting a little more information before dropping a freaking house on me."

Jonathon's blue eyes softened. "We need to talk about Mischa. There are reasons we didn't know of her."

What? He hadn't known of her either. Lienda was so going down when I got my hands on her. I had noticed my father's words were deliberately mysterious. Which was annoying, but I understood. This wasn't the best place to be airing our dirty laundry. Too many here could use it against us.

"It's best if you leave and calm down, but make sure you find me in the morning." He held my gaze until I nodded, lowering my eyes just slightly.

"I love you, Jessa," he said as he turned and stormed out the door in a wave of power.

He was probably going to find Mischa and make sure she was okay. Damn sister taking my father already. Sure, I'd pushed him away, but that wasn't the point. I didn't like to share.

Tears were still burning a trail all the way from my gut up through my throat and were trying to force themselves free from my eyes. I refused to cry in front of the council members. Those bastards would destroy me if they scented weakness. I turned and followed my father's path from the building. Stepping out into the cooling air, I saw no sign of the alpha wolf. He'd disappeared fast, even for him. Many of the supernatural races were milling around the fountain. Curious faces turned in my direction, but none were game to ask anything of me. I moved through a group of tiny fluttering pixies, their firelight shining up and down the street.

Footsteps sounded first and then Braxton's arm came around me, his scent enveloping me. "Come on, Jess, let's go to our place." And just like that, all the curious faces were suddenly busy doing something else.

"Dammit, it's not fair," I growled. "Your dragon has them all cowering like rabbits." One of the weaker shifter animals. "Why is it that no one shows my wolf her due respect?"

He laughed. "It might be a dog-eat-dog world, but . . . a dragon eats everyone."

He made a fair point, but still.

"You better have food," I said as my stomach grumbled again.

The rest of the Compasses fell in beside us, and we made our way through the streets of Stratford. There was no need to rush, besides my want for food; it wasn't a very long walk to their house. The boys lived on their own near the edge of the forest line. Their parents loved them but had kicked them out not too long after they came into their race powers. They'd had a little trouble putting up with the long trail of women drifting in and out of their *friendly* sons' rooms.

It was to be expected, supernaturals were hot-blooded, highly sexual beings. I had similar trouble with my father, who refused to realize his little girl was all grown-up. But thankfully my sexual escapades were fewer than the boys' and they usually took place outside of my family home. Whether parents were supernatural or human, I got the feeling they were always parents and they didn't want to see their babies smacking nasties with someone.

With that in mind, I gave my usual warning. "If I'm staying over tonight, please, please try and keep your ladies out of my room." I had, more than once, woken to their extras climbing into bed with me. Of course one swift wolf bite to the ass took care of the problem, but really . . . it was just wrong on so many levels.

Maximus swung me onto his shoulders. "Tonight we're all yours, Jessa babe." The vampire was so tall I swear the air was thinner up there.

He rounded the last little section of free land, and as he moved up onto the massive wraparound deck of their house, he dropped me to my feet.

"You better mean *all mine* in a completely nonsexual, unkinky way, Max." I knew all about vamps and their freaky sex requests. "I have stamina, but the four of you might possibly kill me."

Tyson and Jacob started snorting out their laughter, and before I knew it a plethora of *sharing* suggestions were being tossed around.

"I'm going to miss you two," I said. There would be bloodshed soon if they didn't shut up.

Braxton moved then and, before I could blink, had the two brothers locked in under his muscled arms. "You two have six seconds to stop talking or you're going to stop breathing."

Called it.

We walked across the front deck. Their house was a huge dwelling. The boys had built it together using blood, sweat, and a bit of magic. I noticed that one of their black Range Rovers was parked out front, probably still there from last week when Jacob had headed out of Stratford to help the other fey round up a few imps who had been causing trouble in New York City. Most families had cars, but they were only used to leave town or if there was a call for a mass evacuation. Within Stratford, we walked everywhere.

I followed Braxton into the house and through the long hall that opened to their spacious and open-plan living room. Everything in this place was built to cater to large men. The rest of them tumbled through in a wrestling heap. I dropped onto the soft leather sofa, trying to switch my mind off. I couldn't believe what had happened tonight. I had a sister. A freaking sister. Not something you expected to find out at twenty-two years of age. I cursed my mother and father. Mainly my mother, though. I just knew this was mostly to do with her.

"Are you okay?" Braxton's warmth wrapped around me, pulling me from my worries. "Want to talk about it?"

I wrinkled my nose, my eyebrows scrunching as I glared at him. "Do *you* want to talk about it? Why did you go all *Dragonheart* on us back there?"

His features hardened and all of a sudden he looked so fierce. I almost wanted to drop my eyes at his show of dominance, but I managed to stay where I was. "The look on your face when your father made the announcement," he said, "was one of complete betrayal." His blue eyes were not as hard as the rest of his face when he locked me in his gaze. "And pain, I could literally feel the hurt and pain bleeding off you. My dragon decided that no one hurts his Jessa."

"Not to mention the council continues to feed us bits and pieces of information," Jacob said, flicking his fingers out to light the large hearth fire that was the center of the room. It was icy this time of year, early November, although most of us didn't worry too much about the cold. "I'm starting to think we've been a little too lenient with them. They should have already started training us, passing along the information we'll need to be council leaders, but they aren't. What sort of leaders will we be if they just hand us our mantle and throw us to the sharks at twenty-five?"

They had a point, and it was something I knew my father was uncomfortable with. "Dad said Kristoff doesn't want to spread the network of information too far at the moment."

Jonathon had never really been clear about what the council's worry was, although after the meeting today, it probably had something to do with the prison breakouts and dead fey. Suffice to say, something was whacked-out in our world at the moment. Something we had no idea about. I had that tight feeling low in my gut. Prison breakouts, dead fey, mysterious sisters . . . what the actual fuck was going on?

"That's the shit we're talking about," Tyson said as he used his magic to smash a bowl against the wall and then re-form it back to perfect. It was his stress reliever when he was upset. His eyes were flashing with threads of gold but were still mostly brown. "We're not just anyone. Spreading information to us is what they're supposed to do."

Jacob grinned then. "So, Jessa, your sister's kind of hot, don't you think?" The jackass struck again. I knew him well enough to know he was simply trying to release some tension.

She was hot, in an innocent I'm-still-a-virgin way. But I was so not having this conversation tonight. "For that you will get me some food now, or I'll tell Stella that you were with her and her sister on the same night." Stella was the most competitive fey I'd ever known. If she found out, he would never hear the end of it.

"Damn, that's low." He got to his feet and moved toward the kitchen, calling back to me. "And for the record, your sister has nothing on you. You're as fucking gorgeous as they come. It's a shame you're off-limits, but I'd rather be your best friend forever than your lover for a moment." *Truth.* Jacob was not giving me a line. His sincerity was clear, and I could scent truth. This was not a skill every shifter had, but I was very good at it.

The Compasses were the love-'em-and-leave-'em types. Most supes were, unless we found our true mates, but that was a rare occurrence. We'd all decided long ago it wasn't worth it to risk a hookup; we had too many years of friendship to put in jeopardy for one fun night. And I was standing by that, no matter how often they flashed those dimples in my direction.

Funnily enough, though, you found your mates through sexual contact, once you passed the age of maturity. It could happen from something as simple as a kiss—if it was hot enough—right up to that moment during sex when you can't even remember your own name. So far all of us were minus mates, and we were okay with that. We were still young, and forever with one supernatural was a long time.

The boys must have sensed I wasn't in the mood to go over the events of the day. Instead, they busied themselves doing other things. Except Braxton. He stayed by my side, his hot thigh pressing down the length of mine as he crowded me. Maximus chose a movie for us. I was sort of paying attention; it was something with lots of action and explosions. Tyson was busy manning the front door. One would think it was a nightclub from the number of freaking girls he had to turn away. Although his responses brought a true smile to my face.

"Fuck off, we're full tonight," I heard him holler to a few very persistent shifters. He was shaking his head when he walked back in. "The witches are so sensitive. I only have to hint that their ass is too big and they run for the hills. But shifters, you guys are tough as nails. I can't even insult them away from the front door."

"You're a bastard, Ty," I said as I snuggled down into the sofa, my lack of sleep and emotionally trying day getting the better of me. If my stomach weren't trying to eat itself, I'd have been flat out snoring already.

"It's not my fault witches' metabolisms are not as fast as the other supes," he said, flopping down on the other side of me.

I was rolling my eyes under my closed eyelids. Tyson loved curves of all descriptions; he was just talking his usual shit. And speaking of metabolism, my eyes flew open as the scent of food tantalized my senses. Jacob was pushing in the buffet sideboard, and on it was a ton of food. Generally we ate in the large dining hall with everyone else; it was a place of bonding for the supernatural community. But on nights we didn't want to mingle with the masses, the boys had a service that provided them with meals. My body rose off the chair of its own accord. I was angling to be first in line for food.

"I tell you, if I can find a woman who looks at me the way Jessa looks at food, I'll be a lucky man," I heard Maximus murmur to Braxton.

Masculine laughter echoed around, but I was too hungry to care. It was Italian night. Be still my beating heart.

I started muttering crazily to myself before grabbing a plate. "Food, get over here so I can eat you."

Walking the length of the sideboard, I piled the plate high with pasta, pizza, and breads. I'd be back for dessert. Crossing into the next room, I sat at the dining table. It was a hand-carved masterpiece: thick dark wood, turned legs, and long bench seats on either side. It was made from one of the big red oaks that had come down in a massive storm; the colors and patterns that threaded its length were almost mesmerizing. Braxton had spent weeks painstakingly stripping it back and carving the ornate legs. Even on the odd nights when some of the Compasses ate in front of the television, I always sat at the table. And so did Braxton.

Tonight everyone joined me. Braxton on my right and Maximus on the left. Jacob and Tyson were across from us, and our five trays were piled high enough to feed a small country. I started without words, or breathing. The food was inhaled into my stomach.

Jacob was grinning at me. "The way you eat is a work of art."

I flipped him off before resuming my pleasure.

When I slowed a little, I took a moment to peer across to Braxton's tray—damn, he had meatballs—he always found food I missed in my haste. Reaching out with my fork, I stabbed one. Braxton never batted an eye; he was used to me stealing from his plate.

"Anyone else would lose an arm." That was a mutter from Tyson.

Braxton and I ignored him. I swiped a few more bits and pieces from him, and then he finished off my lasagna and pepperoni pizza. We had a routine, and there was no point messing with a good thing.

Jacob took away the plates and was back in moments with a tray of desserts. I had my knife and fork in my hands, prepared to use them if necessary. The chocolate cake and ice cream were mine. It felt like the world held its breath just before the tray hit the wooden table, and then it was on. I dived across Braxton, kicking Maximus in the face. Jacob had jumped back. He had the least sweet tooth of any of us. The fight was pretty fair right up until the point when Tyson's eyes glowed gold. I leveled a finger in his direction.

"Don't do it, Tyson Compass."

Apparently I wasn't scary enough, because the tray levitated high into the air.

He changed his tune, of course, as Braxton and Maximus recovered from my surprise attack and also fixed their gazes on him.

"Oh shit," Tyson said. Although he didn't really look worried.

"Not your smartest move, wizard." Braxton was grinning lazily. "Jessa has that look on her face. You're about to lose an eye."

In reality, I was judging the distance to the tray, wondering if I could make the jump. Maybe if Maximus gave me a boost. Before I could launch off the chair, though, the plate with the cake and ice cream drifted down to rest in front of me. Tyson winked at me.

"You've had a hard night, Jessa babe. The cake's yours." The rest of the tray lowered. "And I'd like all of my body parts to stay attached to me." He ran a hand over his left ear.

"It was an accident," I protested. "As if I would cut your ear off on purpose."

A couple of years ago I'd been giving Tyson a haircut when someone burst into the room and startled me. Let's just say it's lucky we heal fast and have regenerative properties. Or he'd have been a little lopsided.

The others divided up the remaining desserts and silence prevailed. I finished mine, one delicious bite after another. I was full, but that didn't stop my head from swinging side to side. Maximus and Braxton inched away, large arms curling around their plates in a protective manner. I huffed, leaning forward on my elbows. Another plate appeared in front of me, the baked caramel pecan pie. My second favorite. Braxton didn't glance in my direction, but I knew it had come from him. I saw Jacob and Tyson exchange grins; I didn't even want to know what they were thinking. First nutty bite was almost as good as sex.

Damn, I loved food.

Chapter 3

The food had given me a new burst of energy, but not enough that I wanted to explore the forest. Jacob and Tyson were itching to get out and look for the fey kill spot. Jacob, especially, was taking this death hard. On top of that, they often searched for the prison. I didn't really understand why the council continued to deny the men their right to view it. In a few short years, they would have the responsibility for its protection. Since the council wouldn't tell them anything, they were determined to find the prison and test its security. Considering we'd been searching on and off for about six months and hadn't found anything yet, well, its security seemed pretty good to me.

I stretched out on the couch again. Jacob was still musing about the dead fey.

"I don't understand why they didn't announce his name." He paced the floor. "I hate thinking I might be looking for a friend."

"Maybe they'll wait until after their investigation to reveal the identity."

Fey and demi-fey used to be separated from the supernatural, living in an alternate dimension of earth in an undying land. Something happened to their world a few thousand years ago that resulted in masses of them migrating into the human world. They didn't speak of the event, and it was not safe to ask the elders. Naturally they gravitated toward our communities, fitting into the niche of supernatural creatures, though they were really the most alien, never quite adapting to the human world. The faerie lands were still there, but the assumption was that their fading magic and energy were not a fit for inhabitants any longer. Although some diehards persisted in trying to survive there.

"Do you think the fey was from the hidden faerie lands?" I asked Jacob.

He shrugged, pushing back strands of his white-blond hair. "Hard to know when they haven't given any idea of who it was." His green eyes looked reflective, like his body was here but his mind not. "I haven't heard of anyone coming through the portal in many years."

I flipped open the footrest so I could stretch out. "Well, you four can go out searching, I'm totally fine right here. I'm gonna nap and watch a movie." It wasn't late, but I felt like relaxing. I wouldn't call it moping. Wolves do not mope.

The other three looked at Braxton. "She speaks *truth*. She's fine with us heading out to patrol."

Maximus lifted my chin so he could meet my eyes. "Okay, keep your cell on you, and make sure you call us if anyone bothers you."

I pulled my face free and waved them away. "Guys, I'm fine. Stop worrying like four hulking mothers."

With laughter and a few elbows, they finally tumbled out the door. But not before Maximus waved his phone at me again. Reluctantly, I pulled myself up to search for the cell. I'd left it at their place earlier and had no idea where it had ended up. I wasn't a big fan of technology—I was an outdoors girl, but I had a phone at the insistence of my father. It took me a while, but eventually I found it wedged behind the sofa. Sliding my finger across the screen, I laughed at the first text that flashed at me.

Maximus: When you finally find your phone behind the sofa, let me know you're all good.

He missed nothing. I quickly texted back. I'm fine.

The second text was from my father.

Jonathon: We need to talk and I'd like you to meet Mischa. Find me in the morning. I'll be in the dining hall for breakfast.

I hesitated over the keypad before replying: See you in the morning.

I wanted to say more, but didn't trust my emotions right now. I did love my father, and he deserved a chance to explain this mess. I hoped he knew better than to invite Mother Dearest along; otherwise, the dining hall would get a front-row seat to a bitch fight. And I'd bring more than claws. After making sure the phone wasn't on silent, I threw it aside again and then reached over to grab the pillow and blanket that was draped across the chair. The original, and in my opinion best, *Transformers* movie was playing on the huge flat screen. I snuggled down and enjoyed a few minutes before my lids started to get heavy.

A loud knock rang through the house, startling me from my comfortable slumber. Ignoring it, I squashed my face deeper into the pillow. Whoever it was could come back later. I wasn't in the mood to deal with any of the women. But of course the knock continued, over and over until I couldn't ignore it any longer.

Stumbling on the blanket, I got to my feet and crossed the room in a few angry strides. I yanked at the door. My mouth opened, preparing to blast the shit out of whichever desperate girl was outside. Sure, I could have had more sympathy for the women who thought they'd finally be the one to tame a Compass, but their weakness annoyed me. Maybe I'd change my tune if I ever found myself in love. But I doubted it.

I froze as I came face-to-face with a pair of green eyes that sat above a small, straight nose and full rosy-red lips. Nose and lips exactly the same as mine.

Mischa stood there, more fire in her face than I'd seen in the hall. She was scowling, another thing we had in common. Closing my mouth, I took a moment to examine her up close. We were eerily similar, and yet not identical. I had the smallest smattering of freckles across my ivory skin. Hers was clear of any marks. Her eyes were a little wider spaced than mine, forehead a little smaller. But all in all, there was no denying our familial relationship.

I opened my mouth, but she spoke first. "Jonathon told me where you were. Don't be mad at him. I badgered him until he broke." I doubted that; her power was nothing compared with his. He was trying to get us together. "All the years I dreamed of meeting you, I somehow thought it would go differently." Despite the bite, her voice was soft, sweeter than mine had ever sounded. And why the hell had she been privileged enough to know of my existence?

The way she continued to lower her eyes as she spoke told me everything. She had not been raised in a pack; she did not know anything of dominance. She was unknowingly giving me the upper hand in our relationship. I opened my mouth to say something. I actually didn't know what would come out, so we both looked a little surprised when I said, "Do you want to come in?"

She nodded, her fine black brows drawing together as she stepped around me and into the Compass home. I shut the door firmly behind her and led the way into the living room. We sat facing each other, a three-foot gap separating us.

"So you knew about me?"

She stared at her hands as she twined them over and over. "Yes, Mom told me I had a sister, that we'd had to leave for both of our safety, but that I'd meet her again someday."

Well, damn, Mother Dearest seemed to be a hell of a lot more honest than Dad had been with me. Although his last words to me seemed to indicate he'd been in the dark as much as I was.

She was still speaking: "I've been alone a lot of my life, and I always imagined the fun of having a sister and a friend. Of course, I was like ten at the time, but it has stayed with me."

I pushed my hair behind my ears. "Until a few hours ago, I had no idea you existed." I pulled my gaze from her eerily familiar features. I kept wondering if I did the same little things that Mischa did, like chewing the corner of my bottom lip when I was upset or wrinkling my nose to stop tears. "Why have you returned now? What did you do about shifting if you had no pack?"

Shifters could change at will, and only had a mild call from the full moon. But we still needed to free our animals regularly. If we didn't, they would force the change on us.

She shrugged. "I've never shifted. I knew about you as my sister, but not as a shifter. Mom decided to wait until we were almost here to inform me that our new town was full of supernatural creatures." A short laugh escaped her, and she was doing that lip-biting thing again. "And that I was a part-time wolf. Let's just say I was a tad disbelieving . . . right up until we crossed that magical border."

I leaned farther back into the soft cushions. She had to have been spelled to prevent her shift. I opened my senses, allowed the wolf to rise to the surface a little. I knew my eyes had changed by the way she shrank back from me.

"Don't move," I warned her. "I won't hurt you."

With my heightened senses, I noticed the energy binding her body. It was heavy, especially over her chest. I could scent no wolf on her; I would have thought she was a regular human if she hadn't been coated in magical protection.

I tucked my wolf away again. "You've been spelled to suppress your wolf and hide your shifter energy. Is Dad . . . Jonathon . . . going to lift that from you?"

"I don't know." She dropped her head in her hand, her voice thin. "I'm not sure how to process all of this. I'm a shifter . . . what does that even mean? I don't understand why we didn't grow up together." I could tell she was crying a little. Shit, I was terrible with sympathy. Shifters love touch; it's comforting to us. I wondered if she'd received much over the years. I decided to treat her as I would a hurting pack member.

I leaned in close and wrapped an arm around her shoulders. Dropping my head into the crook of her neck and shoulder, I breathed deeply, hoping she'd act on instinct and do the same. Instead, she freaked out, shrieking and diving away from me. I landed on all fours on the floor, low growls rumbling in my chest. It took me a few moments to calm down.

"What the hell were you doing?" She was still shrieking. I resisted the urge to punch her out and quiet that racket. I have sensitive hearing and her shrieking was grating. Lucky for her I didn't act on my instincts. I simply picked myself up and sat back on the chair.

"Touch and scent are comforting between shifters," I bit out through clenched teeth. "Especially wolves." I massaged my temple. Not enough sleep and too much stress were giving me a headache. "I was trying to be nice." Last goddamn time, too.

She studied me for a few seconds before tears pricked her eyes again. "I'm so sorry, you must think I'm a mess." I kind of did, but knew better than to say anything. "I just have no idea of this world. I'm not sure I'm cut out for this life." She slouched next to me, closer than last time.

Her reaction was the reason we didn't interact with humans. They couldn't handle the supernatural. They needed their world ordered, and we went against their laws of nature.

She was still talking. I forced myself to pay attention to her.

"So . . . you never leave this town?"

My head tilted to the side as I examined her. "Some do—the hunters who search for the criminals, others who take jobs in different communities—but most of us never leave." I shrugged. "It's not that bad. We have about nearly a thousand acres of forest that we use to run in and hide the—"

I broke off. Was she supposed to know about the prison?

"Vanguard . . . the supernatural prison." She nodded her head, as if pleased she finally knew something. "Mom hinted it was something about this jail that forced her to flee with me when you and I were babies."

I got a strange punch-in-the-chest feeling whenever she mentioned our mother. I was so not ready to explore that emotion. I changed the subject. "What are humans like?"

I was curious. We had human studies twice a week, and I watched television. On paper I knew all about them, but had never met one. It struck me that despite her naïveté about the supernatural world, she would be a hell of a lot more knowledgeable about the rest of America. She'd been out, traveling around, going to normal school. Sometimes I longed to spread my wings and fly—I know, weird analogy for a wolf shifter. Stratford for all its wonder was still a cage.

She scrunched her forehead as if I'd asked the stupidest question ever, although at least the tears had stopped. "Well, humans are just . . . normal."

I sighed, and was proud that I didn't growl at her. If my question was stupid, her answer was even more so. Apparently she wasn't finished though.

"There are so many different types, funny, petty, cruel, evil, sweet, and honorable. I've never had many friends—we moved around a lot—but there are great people in the human world. I've loved, lost, had fights and more fun than I'd ever dreamed I could." She was studying her hands again. "And through all of my experiences, I still always felt different, living on the outside a little." She met my gaze. "Guess I finally know why."

Humans sounded like supernaturals, just with shorter, more fragile lives. We had plenty of drama here also, but maybe not on such a grand scale. We were more patient. Say if we wanted to exact revenge, well, sometimes that could take ten years to play itself out. We had a lot longer to think it through.

"Can you tell me about your world?" she asked, as she studied her fingers. It looked as if she didn't care, but I knew better. I could see the slight tremble of her hands.

As if they'd been timing their entrance, the front door slammed open.

Maximus's voice led the way. "Jessa, you okay?" There was a dark warning in his tone.

The four of them prowled their way into the living room. Judging from their expressions, they'd come in expecting the worst. I guessed they'd heard voices and wondered who else was in their home. The room seemed smaller as they moved into a semicircle around my back, towering over me and Mischa. She looked a combination of freaked out and awed as she shrank back, her gaze drifting around their four faces.

"Guys, meet Mischa, my sister." Yeah, I was acknowledging the relationship. Seemed stupid not to. As far as I knew, she was just as much a victim of our parents as I was.

A slight smile crossed her face and her eyes lit up, the green so bright, with those fine traces of blue. Damn her for having awesome turquoise eyes.

"So you wanted to know about the supernatural world," I said, waving a hand behind me. "The Compasses might just be the perfect examples, since they represent four of the five races."

The quads hadn't said anything more; they were standing in their "intimidation" pose, faces expressionless, except for the locked-on gaze. No wonder Mischa was cowering like a lamb thrown to the lions.

"Okay, firstly, as I said, there are five races. The one not represented here is the demi-fey." I listed out the creatures that fell under this banner. Mischa's face went a sickly white color as she realized the true extent of our world. "The demi-fey only live within the protected supernatural communities. The few times they have made themselves known to humans, well, let's just say things went a little haywire."

I was the queen of understatements. Think Loch Ness, Bigfoot, and gargoyles.

"We have a lot of trolls here. They mine underground for gold and gems. Subsequently, everyone in Stratford is filthy rich—not that we have any need for money. Most of the demi-fey are from the dying lands of Faerie." I stood and moved next to Jacob. He smelled of forest and cold night air; his white-blond hair had a few leaves in it. "And so is Jake. He's a full fey, descended from faerie."

"Pleasure to meet you," he said, smiling at the stunned girl. He flashed two straight rows of very white teeth. Mischa probably didn't recognize the threat in them.

It wasn't unusual for the quads to be so protective, but I was a little surprised they viewed any threat in Mischa.

"Fey have a special affinity for nature and the four elements," I finished.

Jacob quickly demonstrated his skills by calling—one after another—fire, wind, water, and earth. The ground rumbled as he shifted the rock beneath us. I was glad he didn't feel the need to create a full-blown earthquake.

I touched the smooth silkiness of his shirt. "The fey are quite alien. Jake's been domesticated by his brothers and me, but generally they stick closely to their own kind and spend lots of weird group-bonding time in the forest." Jacob cuffed me gently behind the ear. "You're dismissed." I lifted my hand and waved him away. I felt his chest rumble as he moved back to stand behind the couch.

"Ty," I said, and raised my eyebrows at him. "Front and center."

I didn't shift my head. I could smell the magic coating his skin. He'd been casting spells in the forest. "Tyson is a wizard, a magic user. A male is a wizard, female a witch, and if they're particularly powerful and advance to the next level, they're known as sorcerer and sorceress."

Tyson saluted her, his hand touching the brow of his auburn hair. His honeysuckle eyes watched closely, but he didn't say anything.

"Magic users gather power from nature, from the energy within the earth. They're the closest to humans, and have fewer 'supernatural abilities' than the rest of us. They use words and spells to direct their energy. And they are scary and sneaky motherfuckers."

She flinched a little at my cursing. I hid my grin, but the Compasses didn't bother. All four of them cracked dimpled smiles.

"Max," I said, ignoring them.

The massive vampire stood at my back, his distinct power wrapped around me.

"Maximus is a vampire."

Mischa's hands went over her mouth, but instead of the fear I expected, there was something else in her gaze. She didn't smell afraid, she was reeking of . . . interest. I met Maximus's eyes and raised my eyebrows at him a few times. He was damn attractive, but poor Mischa had no idea she was letting him and the rest of us know her feelings. I continued speaking, hoping to distract her amorous thoughts.

"Vamps are like the legend, but also not. They're blood drinkers, but also require food. Sun does not harm them, and they have super senses. Speed, sight, taste, touch, and smell. They can compel any weaker being—don't let them lock you in their gaze. If they're stronger than you, they'll own your mind."

I was pretty sure she wasn't even listening to me, because she was still staring him straight in the eyes. Luckily, Maximus didn't take advantage. Braxton replaced him before I could call for the dragon.

"Braxton you might have seen in the town hall. He's a shifter of the dragon persuasion—which is rare and dominant. There are many different shifter forms. Our family is wolves, the second-most-dominant form, but every group argues about the power ladder." Lions in particular were real snooty about thinking they were at the top. "Generally, shifter children are the same animal as their parents, but if you have a split mating, then the animal can go either way. But never more than one animal. Shifters have earth energy also. We're strong, heal incredibly fast, can detect truth from lies through the fluctuation of scents and hormones—"

"Can you really have only one shifting form?" Mischa asked. She had scooted forward on the couch.

I blinked a few times at her.

Braxton spoke before I could. "Why do you ask?"

She shook her head. Her hair, which was much longer than mine, fell around her face. "It's just that I always dreamed about being able to shift." She looked between each of us. "But in these dreams I wasn't a wolf . . . I was a dragon."

I couldn't speak, so Braxton answered her. "You can't have more than one animal. There are no dual shifters, but since you've never shifted before, well, maybe you are a dragon."

Chapter 4

Braxton's eyes were as wide as mine when he met my gaze; we were almost having a silent communication. *Could she be a dragon shifter?* I was asking him, knowing that would make Mischa the only known female dragon shifter in existence today. Braxton nodded his reply, his blue eyes reminding me that dragon was an anomaly, a random quirk in DNA or something. It was not passed from parent to child. Braxton's father was a lion shifter. I was kind of pissed off. I tried to sort through my feelings, but I couldn't halt the growling trembles that were racking my chest.

"What does this mean?" Mischa backed up a little, which probably was because my lips were half-curled into a snarl and my hands were in a clawed position, but I hadn't shifted them yet.

One of the boys started to explain to her about dragons and their power. Meanwhile, I was trying to contain myself, my wolf, and the demon. Why was I reacting so violently? Did I not like the thought that my sister would be so much more powerful or revered than me? I turned the thought over and over. It might have been a small part of that, but something else was riding my emotions hard. As I met a pair of stunning sky-blue eyes, I recognized the origin of my fury. I was jealous—not of her power, but of what a female dragon would mean. Shifters tended to stick with their own for mating and companionship. Every male dragon in the world—who were very few—would want Mischa. Including the man standing before me.

My eyes roved over the hard features of Braxton's beautiful face, his bronze skin, and hair as black as my own. I couldn't lose him. Once he was mated, his female would steal him away. We are possessive like that, and none would tolerate our close friendship. Even my sister would have an issue with it. It was our nature.

Braxton captured my hand. "You will never lose me," he murmured, reading the agony on my face. "A hundred dragon females could exist—you're my number one. Best friends for life. I haven't forgotten my promise."

His words and soothing power wrapped around me, calming the wolf and the demon inside. I knew one day the Compass brothers would settle down, find true loves or mates, but we were way too young now. I was not prepared to give them up yet. They were my pack, and I loved each and every one of their crazy asses. I knew my fear that the women in their lives would not accept our friendship was justified. Like I said, possessiveness is common in supernatural groups. I would never expect the boys to choose me over their loves. I shook off my melancholy; no point creating worries for what tomorrow would bring.

I stumbled across to my shell-shocked sister and sank down next to her. Even though I had said I wouldn't be nice again, I decided to give her one more chance for some Jessa comfort. My arm dropped over her shoulders, and this time instead of flinching away, she grabbed my tank and pulled me closer. She buried her head into my shoulder. I widened my eyes as I stared at the top of her head.

"I'm thinking we need to speak with Dad," I said, running a single stroke of my hand over her silky hair. She smelled flowery, like her shampoo or lotion was scented. But it was very light, and had none of the chemical undertones I always smelled in commercial products.

I heard grumbles and muttering among the quads. I knew they wouldn't be happy if a dragon shifter had been hidden from the community. But what had Dad actually known of Mischa?

"Did you find anything in the forest?" I asked as I held Mischa. I could feel her calming under my touch.

The Compasses started moving around the room, dropping off weapons and their packs. Except for Braxton, of course. He was his own weapon and took nothing with him.

Tyson growled. "They have the prison hidden from every one of my spells. Jake couldn't even get a read from the trees on the prison or fey kill. Whoever did the original security on Vanguard did a goddamned thorough job."

Mischa's head flew up. "You're looking for the prison? Why?"

Jacob kicked off his boots before answering. "We're to be the next council leaders. In just under three years. At this stage, according to our studies, we should be starting our initiation and training, learning all the aspects of leading the American Supernatural Council."

"But we aren't learning a damn thing," Maximus bit out, staring into the fire. "Kristoff—the leader of the magic users—assured us that we will know everything in time. But he's generally shown himself to be a liar, so his word doesn't mean shit."

"Yep," I added. "A few months ago we decided to do our own exploring and investigating, to stop blindly accepting everything the council spews at us." I needed her to be aware of what she'd been thrown into. "I don't know what Lienda was like, but while Dad . . . Jonathon . . . is a brilliant father, he's also a cagey and powerful man."

Braxton spoke from where he leaned against the far wall. "He would never hurt Jessa, but sometimes he thinks he's protecting her for her own good by withholding information."

And it was no secret that I told the Compasses everything. We did not lie to one another; it was part of the pact we'd made many years ago.

"I might be mistaken," Mischa started to say, her words slow and drawn out. "But I was under the impression, from some of the things that Mom said, that the prison was underground. Her brother was imprisoned a long time ago. She used to tell me about the weird bunker he was in. Of course, I never knew he was a supernatural when she spoke of him, but now I've put the information together, well, I'm pretty sure of what she was telling me."

I think every one of us froze into a statue at her words. Had she just handed us the breakthrough we'd been looking for? Information on the prison was so scarce. It wasn't that supernaturals didn't gossip—they were like the housewives we'd read about in human studies—it was more that there just wasn't information out there. Only a select group knew anything about Vanguard, and they were all spelled to keep these secrets. And had she said Lienda had a brother?

I furrowed my brow. "We have an uncle in the prison?"

She shook her head. "I'm not sure what happened. Mom wouldn't really go into details, but . . . I think he died."

I sucked in a deep breath. I wasn't sure how to feel about that— probably better not to think about it right now. I would lock that away in my emotional safe box, where I put all the things I didn't want to deal with. We needed to focus on the prison.

"No wonder the trees didn't reveal anything to me," Jacob growled. "I should have been asking the earth. Or the roots. That's where the essence of disturbance would lie."

I shook my head. "The prison's been there so long it has become one with its environment. I don't believe we'll find it that way."

"What made you think it was hidden in the forest?" Mischa asked.

Braxton answered lazily. "The reason Stratford exists is as a gateway community to protect Vanguard. We all know it's in the forest, and we had it on reasonably good authority that it was hidden within an *invisible* dimension near the back of the east quadrant."

A friend of theirs claimed to have been there. He was the one giving out the information.

Suddenly Braxton's tone was a lot less casual. "Seems we might have to have another little chat with our friend."

Mischa stood then. "I should go. I didn't even tell Mom I was leaving." I stood also.

"I'll see you in the morning?" she asked me, although her eyes also flicked across to Maximus. We all pretended not to notice.

"Yep, I'll be in the dining hall around nine." The night was half-over and I was tired. I needed extra time for a nice sleep-in.

She started toward the hallway.

I halted her before she got out the door. "Hang on. Max will walk you home. It's not always safe to wander alone at night."

Especially when she was the council leader's daughter and had no supernatural abilities to call on. She was now a weak link in the Lebron house, and we needed to keep our vulnerabilities protected.

I grinned at Maximus as he passed me. His expression was one of resignation. I was about the only person in the world he let order him around. Not even his brothers would try it.

Mischa's eyes widened as she moved to Maximus's side. He was so large and she looked tiny. I hoped I didn't look that small and delicate against the Compasses. I moved across to her, and leaning in, gave her a hug good-bye before whispering in her ear: "He can scent your interest. I'm not sure if you care that he knows, but if you do . . . try and tone down the arousal."

She hugged me harder. "Thank you," she whispered back, although her cheeks were a pretty pink color when she pulled away.

I waved as they left the house. "See you in the morning."

I shut the door firmly behind them. I made it six steps into the living area before I was surrounded by large men.

"What?" I growled, pushing through them. I hated their dominance shit.

"You didn't answer your phone, and then we come back to check on you and you have ignored our rule about letting people in while we're not here." Tyson followed me, practically stalking my ass. I spun around and planted my palm firmly on his chest. I opened my mouth, but my tirade was interrupted.

Braxton tilted his head as he spoke. "We were worried about you." As always his words tugged at my heartstrings. The angry reply I'd been about to hurl at Tyson fell away unsaid.

"Shit, I'm sorry; it was my sister. I figured she didn't mean any harm."

Jacob playfully scooped me into his arms. "We know nothing about her." And with a laugh he tossed me through the air and across the room onto the couch. I hit it pretty hard—luckily I was a shifter. "She might not even really be your sister. Her energy is cloaked. I'm getting zero read on her."

Braxton growled. "A little more care next time, Jake."

He dropped down next to me, his big hands coming around to rub out the tension in my shoulders. I groaned, closing my eyes as he worked out the knots I didn't even know I had. His strong hands paused as I groaned again, then the rubbing motion started up again.

"Stop doing that, Jessa babe." Tyson's voice sounded strangled. "We made a pact, no inappropriate thoughts of you. You're making it a little hard right now."

I caught the double entendre there.

I stuck my tongue out at him, my eyes still closed, but I did halt the groans that wanted to emerge. Shit, Braxton was a god with his hands.

"Mischa has never shifted," I said, when I could finally speak again. "I can see that she's been spelled, her abilities cloaked . . . plus, she looks exactly like me."

Braxton moved, his hands digging deeper. "She looks similar to you, which could be achieved through a spell also."

I started to squirm, moving until his hands were on the spots I'd just decided needed some more work.

I bit back another moan. "They would have had to deceive the high council. I'm sure they do some sort of test to detect truth from lie."

There were nods all around.

"They definitely do that, but did you ever stop to think someone on the council might be out to get you and your father? It wouldn't be the first time."

Julianna was a replacement leader, brought in after Derk, the last vampire councilman, was discovered plotting to destroy the Lebron line. Of course, someone removed his head the day before his trial, and no one knew who. The Compasses had been questioned, and they'd had this amazingly detailed alibi. I'd listened hard to their version of events, and my senses had told me there was both truth and lie in their story. I just couldn't figure out which part was which.

I had accepted long ago that one of them had done it, and that made me love them just a little bit more. True friends have your back no matter what, and in our world, which was fraught with danger, sometimes that meant getting your hands dirty. It might seem a little harsh, but we lived in a kill-or-be-killed world, and I had no problem with death if it kept my loved ones safe.

Jacob came back in from the kitchen with a thick brown-bread sandwich clutched in his hand. "So what is our plan to find the prison now?"

Tyson leaned forward. "It's taken us months to properly scour the forest. It would take just as long to find the right underground area. We need more information." The wizard reached out and in a swift movement snatched Jacob's sandwich before throwing out a shield spell to stop his brother from pounding him into the earth. By the time Jacob broke through the barrier, the food was gone.

"Focus." Braxton halted their bitch fest before it started.

Jacob continued to look murderous as he stared down the grinning Tyson.

I blinked a few times, willing my eyes to stay open. "We need the trolls. They rule the underground and they'll know, either it's spelled or off-limits, or because trolls are part of the secret keepers."

There were a few nods. Tyson started swirling magic in front of him. "First thing tomorrow, we will see if we can snag ourselves a troll to *chat* with." The wizard sounded a tad creepy when he spoke like that. I'd been saying it for years, but if there was ever another supernatural war, the Compasses were definitely going to be the cause.

"I've got to get some sleep." I was plenty relaxed now after the truly orgasmic pleasure Braxton had induced in me with just a simple massage. "I'll see you all in the morning."

Three sets of eyes followed me as I started to drag myself down the hall toward the room that was unofficially mine. I expected to be out the moment my head hit the cloud-soft pillows, but it was then that all of the worries piled in on me. How would the talk with my father go tomorrow? Would Lienda be there? Could I truly accept a sister after all of these years thinking I was an only child? What was with the dead fey and all of the council's secrets? Could Mischa be a dragon shifter?

Eventually I had to call on my wolf for help. Animals don't sweat the small stuff, acting mostly on instinct, and right now she knew we needed sleep. Within moments my worries fuzzed away and the blissful release of sleep claimed me.

I wasn't one for dreaming. I usually slept like the dead and had no memories of anything from the moment I closed my eyes until I opened them. But tonight I seemed to be mimicking my sister and was plagued with dreams of dragons.

The dream started out with my wolf running across a field, sunlight glinting off her midnight-black fur. The area didn't look familiar, but I wasn't afraid or curious. Then out of nowhere a dragon appeared above my head, circling me a few times before coming to rest right in my path. I had no choice but to stop, skidding to a halt about twenty feet from the massive animal. It was a light-blue color, the sun reflecting off the scales, and more delicate than Braxton's dragon form. I shifted back to human. I wasn't surprised by this appearance. Instead, anger flooded me.

"What do you want?" I yelled, hands on hips.

A thump behind had me spinning around. Another dragon was coming in at my rear. One more thump, and I was surrounded by three massive dragons. Shit, this was not good. The dreamworld kept the panic at bay, but still every beat of my heart seemed extraloud as I tried to figure out what was going to happen.

"You must join us or die." In the spot the original aqua dragon had stood was Mischa.

I shook my head. "I cannot be a part of this. I refuse." I took a step closer, both of my hands held aloft. "You're wrong; there's no way this can come to pass."

"The shifter law is truth and you know it. They're an anomaly and must be stopped. We need you." My sister tried again, but I shook my head, my hair bouncing on my naked shoulders.

"I can't let you go, Jess. You know that. I'm oath bound."

"Find a way around it," I warned her.

"Shift to dragon and we'll decide this in the old manner." One of the other females, a short, curvy redhead, transformed long enough to speak before turning back into a black dragon.

I simply stared at her, and then in a heartbeat I felt the energy consume me, but instead of my wolf . . . I became a dragon. My scales were the blue of my eyes, and as I spread my wings, the other two dragons launched into me, except for Mischa, who was still human. I clawed and bit back, but was vastly outdragoned. The pain felt real as they proceeded to tear me to shreds.

Screams pulled me from sleep, and I realized they were my own, my fear so very real and pungent that the scent coated the inside of the room. Before I could blink or pull the sweaty shirt off my body, there were four men in my room in varying stages of undress, holding weapons. Tyson had magic energy gathered in his hands.

"Jessa," Braxton said, as he lifted his head and scented the room. He moved in a blink across to me. In the same moment, I was in his arms.

I struggled against him, tears pouring down my cheeks as I fought the fear overwhelming me.

Maximus was growling as he reached the side of the bed. "What the fuck? Is she crying? Who do I have to kill, Jess babe? Tell me what happened."

I almost laughed; they would die if they knew it was only a dream. Right now they were still talking over my head.

Braxton had started barking orders. "I can't scent anyone else in here, but her fear is real. Check the perimeter and I'll search inside."

"Wait," I stuttered out. "It was just a bad dream."

Braxton's arms tightened around me, his warmth helping to quell the final shudders of paralyzing fear. In the human world, this relationship the five of us had would probably be viewed as odd, but they were my pack. Supernatural packs always stayed close together. It calmed our souls.

"A dream?" Tyson sounded dubious. "You never dream, and even if you did, you were reacting to something physical. That wasn't just your mind, that was your entire body."

He was right. Weirdly enough, I'd reacted as if I'd really been there, not merely mentally creating the situation.

Braxton lowered me back onto my bed, and when I started to shake and hug my legs, the four of them crowded onto the soft surface and comforted me with touch.

"Tell us what happened." Jacob held my hand tightly. I could feel soothing fey energy seeping into me.

I quickly detailed the dream. As I was putting it into words, well, it didn't sound scary. But something within that event had created heart-racing fear. I just wish I knew what it was.

"Do you think it means anything?" I asked. "Or was it simply a by-product of Mischa mentioning her dreams of being a dragon?"

"So there was more than one female dragon?" Braxton asked.

I nodded. That's why all the dragons had seemed so delicate; they'd all been female.

"There were three and . . . myself." Because apparently I was also a dragon shifter.

I felt like such a moron. "I'm being stupid. It was just a dream," I said, waving my hands agitatedly. "Just a dream."

I forced myself to calm down, but the moment the quads moved off the bed, panic flooded through me again. I hadn't realized how much their presence had been keeping it at bay. I bit the inside of my cheek. I wouldn't ask them to stay. I'd shown enough weakness tonight.

"We'll stay with you until you fall asleep," Braxton and Maximus said together. Again it was as if these men could read my thoughts.

Jacob grazed my cheek with his fingertips. "Just close your eyes. The boys will keep you safe, even from your dreams."

Tyson landed a kiss on my forehead and then those two left the room.

My vampire and dragon shifter sprawled out their large bodies on either side of me, and with a sigh I slithered down under the sheets and closed my eyes. Trust me when I tell you, nothing makes a girl feel safer than a Compass on either side of her. I challenged any scary dream to try to get me now.

The heat woke me. I was so . . . damn . . . hot. I tried to move out from under the boulders holding me to the bed. Not a chance in hell of that happening. My eyes opened. Small streams of light were filtering through the large single window. It was morning, and not that early judging by the light low on the wall. A thick arm rested across me, and that's when I remembered the dream and falling asleep with Maximus and Braxton. No wonder I was so damn hot, those two threw off heat like the roar of a fire. Maximus had rolled away. Vampires didn't sleep like a pack. But Braxton was all over me, one arm and leg thrown across my body, and his head buried in the crook of my neck.

"Ugh," I groaned, "get off, you hot, heavy-ass dragon."

I tried shoving him, but by the lack of movement I'd have had more luck moving the house we were in.

"Go back to sleep, Jess, or I'll bite you," Maximus grumbled.

I used my free hand to pinch him. "You wouldn't dare."

I'd never shared blood with him, although he had tasted my blood when he'd healed a cut or two. But for feeding, he used his vampire women or other volunteers. There was something quite intimate when a vampire fed from you. Apparently the feelings it spread were, well, inappropriate toward a friend. Even a best friend.

"What's the time?" I tried to squirm free again. "I have to meet my father."

"It's just after eight." Braxton's voice was low and husky. I had no idea how that man always knew the time, but he was scarily accurate.

"Shit." I lifted my head and without thinking bit the muscled arm over me, my teeth leaving marks in his dark skin. Just blunt human teeth. I wouldn't shift to wolf on him; that would leave more than a mark. "I've got to shower. I stink from my run last night."

Braxton slowly lifted his head, hooded eyes locked onto my face, black hair tousled all over the place. How did the Compasses look so good when they first woke?

"Did you just bite me?" he said, his tone low and hypnotic.

Both of his eyebrows raised, and his lips lifted in a half-curved smile. I immediately felt like prey, and I had to fight the urge to run. Braxton could be a scary mother when he had you caught in his sight.

"Um, no, it wasn't me."

"*Lie.*" He growled, dropping his head back into my neck. "You're lucky I love you. And you smell fine."

He moved his body then, letting me escape to the bathroom. I rolled free. Three minutes later I was blasting myself awake with a freezing cold shower. I had clothes everywhere through this house from all the years of staying over, so I wasn't surprised to reenter the bedroom after my shower to find a stack on the end of the bed. The bed that was empty of men.

I dressed quickly. I was starving. This stupid talk with my father better not ruin breakfast.

That was something I wouldn't forgive.

Chapter 5

The dining hall was packed. Supernaturals were everywhere. The groups were distinct, each sticking to their own race. Vampires were in the back right corner, shifters to the left, magic users outside on the open deck, with the fey close by them, but the demi-fey scattered throughout. The council members, along with other advisers, chiefs, alphas, the head mage, and so forth, were in the center of the room. All that power in one spot was quite a shock if you walked too close.

I grabbed a tray and started moving through the buffet, making sure I checked under each hot cover. Before I'd even reached the end, my plate was overflowing. I glared at the three covered dishes I hadn't gotten to. I refused to look under them, just in case they were better than what I had. Nothing worse than seeing what I couldn't fit on my tray.

I mused as I moved toward my usual spot: *Were they making these plates smaller?* I swore I used to be able to fit more on them. I took a seat at my usual table, close to the council but not within hearing distance, except maybe for the vampires. My father would find me here. A tray landed next to mine. I grunted and flicked my eyes to the left, but I'd already scented who it was.

"Seat's taken," I mumbled, having started eating a piece of toast.

The lion shifter ignored my reticence and rested his hip against the side of my table. "I thought you would come over last night." Jerad, who had been my bed partner last month, leaned closer and looked at me with his golden-brown eyes. I swallowed loudly, before meeting his gaze.

He was a big alpha shifter, tall, with wild sandy hair a shade lighter than his eyes. I'd been trying to get rid of him for weeks now, but he was like a recurring virus. Just when I thought he'd taken the hint to leave me alone, he'd pop back up again. Sure, our hookups had been fun, but I was done. Our little dalliance had run its course. He was . . . five shades of needy, wanting me over all the time. I already had too many demanding men in my life.

"I'm sure you heard about the family drama." I reached for my coffee. The way I felt right now this cup was nowhere near big enough. I gulped a few large mouthfuls of the sweet, creamy liquid. Ah: gift from the gods. "And I've told you before, I'm no longer interested."

On top of his neediness, lion shifters liked it rough and ready. I was sick of claw marks on my butt. Not that wolves didn't occasionally leave them, too, but lions were the worst. Claw-happy bastards.

I waved my coffee at him. "If you don't mind, I'm meeting my father," I said. "I'll catch up with you later." I had no real intention of meeting with him later, but my words didn't scream lie because I knew, in a town this size, we'd run into each other eventually.

He brushed back his mane with both hands. "I'll be a little busy. You don't show up, I replace you. You know the rules, Jessa."

He had to be kidding me. Was insanity part of lion shifters' DNA?

I narrowed my eyes as I slowly dropped my coffee onto the table. "Well, then what the fuck are you doing over here interrupting my breakfast?"

He'd better go away now.

Tyson fell down into the chair beside me. "I believe the lady's had enough of your shining personality, lion."

I'd already lost interest in Jerad. Now I was trying to figure out how Tyson seemed to have even more food on his tray than I did. Must have used magic. Damn wizards were so lucky.

Tyson bared his teeth at the lion. "Time to hurry home and groom your mane."

Lion shifters were not only delusional but really proud—kings of the jungle. It pissed them right off that the council leader was a wolf shifter. They hadn't had a representative for at least the last four councils. Jerad straightened, the affable personality disappearing under the storm clouds crossing his features. He was striding toward Tyson right up until Braxton's hand landed on his shoulder. "Move."

It was enough for Jerad to grab his tray, turn, and stalk away.

Braxton dropped down on the other side of me. "You need better taste in men," he said.

I glared before reaching across him and stealing his coffee. I needed more caffeine. Somehow my cup was empty. I didn't even remember finishing it. "You know I gave him the boot ages ago; he's just having trouble understanding how anyone could not want him." I flicked my free hand at Braxton. "And you make it hard to find good men. You scare away any but the most alpha shifters, and they're always arrogant dicks."

"We alphas are confident, not arrogant," he said, as he picked up another cup off his tray and waved it in front of me. "Now give me back my coffee."

I moaned as the scent of hot chocolate hit my nostrils. I love chocolate in any form. It was at the top of my food pyramid. In reality, it was pretty much my entire food pyramid.

I reached out my hand that wasn't clutching the coffee. "Give me," I said, waggling my fingers. "Don't make me chase it—you know that only ends in tears."

"Coffee first." He held the cup just out of my reach.

Boys are mean.

I reluctantly parted with his coffee and was rewarded with heaven in a glass.

"Forget sex. I'll just have hot chocolate," I moaned again.

"Keep eating chocolate like that and sex will be the last thing anyone wants from you, fatty."

Giselda Krass, BEF, strolled past my table. She was tall and that anorexic-looking skinny, which I found unnatural and repulsive. She had long red hair and deathly pale skin; I had a sneaky suspicion that she was one of the dangerous magic users, those who dabbled in the darker side.

She was sneering so prominently I couldn't help but laugh loudly. "I know you're confused, Krass, considering you weigh about the same as an eight-year-old with the curves to match, but I have hips and boobs." I tapped my chin. "Who knows, it might happen for you one day, too."

With a huff and glare, she stormed past with the rest of her witchy coven of evil crows.

Tyson clenched his jaw. "Giselda's friggin' creepy. And she stinks of death."

I tightened my fist around my fork. "If she starts talking about animal sacrifices again, I'm going to kill her." Shifters didn't take too kindly to the disrespect of any species. We shared a soul with our animals and rejoiced in their intelligence and beauty.

The three of us were quiet as we finished our breakfast. The boys let me pick bits and pieces off their plates. They knew it was easier than fighting with me. In the end they'd finish my leftovers. If there were any.

I glanced up from my tub of yogurt as the chair across from me scraped. Maximus stood there with a pale-faced Mischa beside him.

"Look who I found," he said, before pulling out a chair for her.

She set her tray down. My eyes widened as I took in the dismal selection. There were only like . . . five things on her plate, and one was granola.

"Where's the rest of your food?" I asked.

She shrugged as she sat. "I don't eat much for breakfast."

I'm sorry, what? Who was this crazy lady? Breakfast was the most important meal of the day, closely followed by lunch and dinner and three or four snacks in between.

Tyson's dimples appeared as he smiled. "Are you sure they're sisters?"

I ignored him. "Where's Jake?" I asked Maximus.

I was a little worried about him. He was taking the fey death very personally. I didn't want him going off half-cocked trying to find the killer.

"He's over at the council table," Maximus said. "Trying to get some more information out of them."

That reminded me. "We need to have a chat with a troll today, too."

Mischa's green eyes widened as she glanced around the room. My words seemed to have reminded her of Stratford's various inhabitants. Many who did not appear even close to being human. Because they weren't. Today was her first full day in the community. It must have been a little overwhelming.

I closed my eyes then as a sweep of power washed over me. My father had arrived and he wasn't alone. Rumbles were trying to burst from my chest, but I forced myself to stay calm. After a few rounds of counting to ten, I could even open my eyes and pretend the new arrivals weren't there. From the corner of my vision I was locked in on everything that was happening. I wrinkled my nose when Lienda took the seat next to Mischa, laying her delicate fingers onto my sister's shoulder. Jonathon took the chair beside her. They were both nursing coffee, but I'm guessing they would've had breakfast hours ago.

Lienda swept her gaze around the table. "I'm very happy to see you all eating together," she said. "I appreciate you helping Mischa adjust to her new life." Not that I was looking at her, but it was hard not to notice that the woman had really weird eyes, like they couldn't make up their mind. One minute they looked blue, the next green.

Her long blonde hair was stylishly cut, in layers with a sweeping side fringe. She looked young, early twenties, but we all did until we reached at least a hundred years of age. Then we looked about thirty in human years. It was a slow aging process. I wanted to stare at Lienda, examine every tiny detail of the mother I'd never known. I forced myself to stare at my hands instead.

No one at the table said anything. The Compasses were not giving her particularly friendly glances.

"I know this is difficult, Jessa." Jonathon's voice was even, but there was something under the calm tone. I scented the air. It was very subtle; he was nervous. "But you need to hear the entire story before you judge either of us and our actions. Lienda and I made the decision together; there were no other options."

So he had lied to me in the hall. He had known.

It hurt deep in my chest when he admitted he was part of this entire scheme to keep me in the dark about my family. When I was a little girl, I asked him all the time why Mom had left us, but he would never say anything. It was from others in the community that I'd heard the multitude of rumors of why Lienda abandoned us. I figured Jonathon was too heartbroken to speak of it. They were a true-mated pair, and losing Lienda would have felt like losing his heart and soul. I'd never understood how she could leave her mate; hence, my immense hatred for her. Jonathon had been a dark man for my younger years, but over time he seemed to heal a little, until finally I had a father again. Still, for a long time I was alone, except for the Compasses. The way they rallied around me, keeping my spirits high, nurturing my wounded soul—not to mention their stupid shenanigans—gave me countless opportunities to laugh my ass off. For all of that they had my eternal gratitude.

Jonathon's voice was low as he continued. "This is not the place for this discussion though."

There was definitely no hiding anything in this hall. We were under more scrutiny right now than the human president at election time. Yeah, we didn't vote, but we watched television.

Lienda leaned forward. "Let's take a walk through the forest."

I tilted my head to the side, still not meeting anyone's eyes. "I'm not quite finished with breakfast."

I heard a few cleared throats. Tyson was actually squirming as he tried to contain his laughter.

Jonathon was either hiding a grin or fighting the urge to throw me across his knee and smack me, but since I wasn't a kid anymore he was going to struggle with that. "I'm sure you've had enough, Jessa."

What was he talking about? Okay, yes, there were three empty plates, numerous scattered tubs, three mugs, two glasses, and two dessert bowls stacked in front of me. But . . . breakfast was important.

With a sigh I stood, slamming back my chair with my calves. It screeched across the floor, drawing even more attention in our direction. "Let's get this over with. Then we can all resume our normal viewing stations." Something told me I was kidding myself. These interruptions were permanent, and my life would be forever changed.

We walked in silence, just the four of us. I'd made the boys stay behind so they could finish their food. Braxton had shot me hooded eyes; he wasn't happy. Oh, well, he'd give me grief when I got back, but that was okay: I knew how to handle him. Although the quads were my pack, I knew Dad wanted to do this with just the four of us. His wide grin when I stopped the Compasses was a bit of a giveaway there.

The deeper we went into the silence of the forest, the easier it was to breathe. The cool, earthy scent surrounded us. The canopy was thick in some places and let in beams of sunlight in others. Wolves don't like crowds—too many avenues for attack, too many scents disturbing our sensitive noses. Out here felt right and safe. Reaching a small alcove, Jonathon stopped and, reaching out, linked hands with Lienda. I chose to be a mature person and ignore it.

I sucked in a deep breath and almost had myself convinced that I could handle anything that came out of his mouth. Right up until he said: "You two need to know the truth. You're not just sisters, you're twins."

My mouth fell open. Well . . . that was unexpected. Why had he not just said that when he'd first introduced Mischa?

He continued before I could ask: "No one knew we had twins. The moment both of you were born, Lienda and I recognized that we had to protect you." Jonathon didn't fidget, except for his head swiveling in my direction. "Twins are rare in our world, about one per a hundred thousand supernaturals." He already knew what I was thinking. "Quads are almost unheard of. It has happened only one other time in our history. That's how we know the Compasses will be the strongest, and the leaders." Lienda was silent, letting Dad do the talking, but I could feel her examining me.

"So what if we're rare?" Mischa said. She'd moved and now stood side by side with me, facing our parents. "Why would we have to leave? I've spent my entire life running from city to city with Mom, all the while thinking I was a freak. Just to hide the fact we're twins? That makes no sense."

Yeah, what she said. Because the quads hadn't had to run or be separated. Why would we have to just because we were twins? I crossed my arms over my chest, my bare feet scuffing at some of the dead leaves.

Jonathon continued to move his head, listening and scenting, making sure it was safe to keep speaking. "It wasn't just that you were twins, it was that you were twins born with the dragon mark." The last two words were said so softly I barely heard them.

Mischa didn't react, but I couldn't stop from gasping. I raised a shaky hand and covered my suddenly dry lips. "What?" My voice was a strangled whisper. "You're mistaken. I've never seen the mark." Yeah, stupid seemed to be falling from my lips today.

Mischa's voice hardened. "Wait, what's a dragon mark?" She had her hands on her hips as she leaned her upper body forward.

I liked that she had some fire. It made me think she might actually be my sister . . . uh, twin.

I started to explain. It was either talk or go quietly crazy in my head. "It's a legend in the supernatural community," I said. "Like a thousand years ago some crazy-ass dragon shifter tried to rule all five races. He gathered a dragon army and a major war erupted." According to the history books, it had been bloody. "When they finally captured him, they found out why he was so powerful—he was a hybrid sorcerer and dragon shifter." I cleared my throat. "Just before his head, and the heads of many of his followers, were removed, he cursed the supernatural world. He said that the dragon marked would rise and they would finish what he had started."

Jonathon added more details. "Nothing happened immediately, but our history records indicate that within a month of the king's death, supernaturals of all different races started to be born with the mark. They have been killed off ever since."

This was also why dragons were so rare. Many dragons died in that long-ago battle, and for years the rest were hunted. Kind of like the human witch trials, but supernaturals targeted dragons. Thankfully, that shit had halted a few hundred years ago; otherwise, I wouldn't have my Braxton. Well, the *dragon*-slaying part had halted; the dragon marked, on the other hand, were still hunted.

Lienda hugged her arms tightly around herself. "Any child born with the mark . . . they were taken from the family and never seen again. We would not let that happen to you two. Jessa was born first, and the moment we saw the mark, we knew we had to hide it. Then Mischa came next and she also bore the mark. It didn't matter that your father was a council member, they would have taken you . . . killed you."

Jonathon rubbed at his temples. "We pretended Jessa was the only one born—twins are thoroughly examined for the marks, since almost all twins have them. A very close friend of mine—a sorcerer—spelled the marks, and Lienda disappeared with Mischa. Everyone thought she ran away because she didn't want kids, and I did nothing to discourage the rumors."

At some point during this conversation, tears had started running down my cheeks. I'd hated my mother for so many years, cursing her existence and her abandonment of me and my father. But she'd run to save our lives. I should have known this story. I was half-sad and half-pissed off. I hated being kept in the dark. I slapped at my cheeks, removing the traces of moisture.

"Why is it okay for us to return now?" Mischa asked, her voice husky. She had a few tears, too.

Lienda walked forward and wiped a tear off her daughter's cheek. "You turned twenty-two last month. The spell keeping your wolf contained is due to wear off soon." She turned, and with the slightest hesitation, gently wiped at my cheeks also. I closed my eyes at the featherlight touch. "You need the community to help you; you need a pack." She glanced at Jonathon. "We figure most of the danger of detection has passed."

Not to mention that anyone with eyes and a heart could see that she and Jonathon could not stay apart any longer.

Jonathon moved to her side. "Your wolf will break free, Mischa, but don't worry about the spells muting your marks. They are much stronger, and should last your lifetime."

I wondered then if the dragon mark had something to do with my demon. Could the mark be something I felt inside just waiting to explode? Was it only the spelling to hide and mute its energy that was keeping it contained?

There were still so many things I didn't understand. "Why did you announce that we were sisters?" I knew why he hadn't said twins, but it might have been better to pretend there were no familial ties.

He bestowed a gentle smile on me, a familiar twinkle in his blue eyes. "Because there was no hiding your similarities, we decided to stick as close to the truth as we could. But no one knows that you're twins. Mischa is twenty according to her identification." Jonathon moved even closer until the four of us were in a tight circle. "I told the council that I left Stratford once and found Lienda."

"And that from our union came Mischa," Lienda added. "They think Jonathon didn't know of the second pregnancy, and that's why he didn't demand I return. I'm a pariah in the community, but I don't care. As long as you two are safe, it's all worth it."

"What are the dragon-mark abilities?" I asked.

They both exchanged glances before shrugging. Jonathon tried to explain. "We don't know. There have been none that we know of to make it past the age of one. A few parents managed to hide their children until then, but they made the mistake of only spelling the mark, not the abilities also. There are trackers trained in the arts of detecting the dragon-mark energy. They are strong and lethal and will stop at nothing."

He paused and my heart froze in my chest. His eyes shimmered as he met my gaze, and I knew bad news was coming my way. He crinkled his eyes, and his lips thinned to a single line. "You can't tell anyone about this, Jessa, not even the Compasses."

I just stared at him. He knew I told those boys everything. I trusted them with my life a hundred times over. Finally I shook my head. "I can't promise that. Why would you even ask me to? What do you know?"

"Remember how I said there had been one other set of quads born to the supernatural community?"

I nodded. Mischa also bobbed her head a few times.

"The Craiz men, which the supernatural world call the Four. They are the first quads, and are the most vicious dragon-mark hunters in existence. Even though they're very old and powerful, they still actively hunt." His eyes bore into me, and I felt he was trying to warn me.

"What are you saying?" My voice was barely above a whisper, and my eyes widened at a sudden thought. "That based on one other instance in history, all quads become dragon-mark hunters, and the Compasses are going to hunt me one day? That they'll want to kill me and Mischa?"

Nothing in this world would make me believe that.

Jonathon's features tightened. "I don't know. Part of the reason I've always encouraged your friendship is the hope that your love for one another would keep you safe. That if they did become dragon-mark hunters—because that seems to be the calling of the quads—the boys would protect rather than hunt."

My head was hurting. I reached up and rubbed my temples, hoping to relieve the tension. I was on information overload and honestly wasn't sure I could process one more thing. Quads became dragon-mark hunters; twins were always marked. This was confusing and heartbreaking and . . .

"I need to go," I mumbled, not even caring that Jonathon was there and he had forbidden running alone. Lucky for him, he didn't say anything.

I had my shirt halfway over my head when I noticed Mischa's wide eyes on me. I halted. "Do you want to see me shift?"

I felt a kindred spirit in Mischa now. The circumstances of our birth had shaped both of our lives. But somehow I thought she'd gotten the worst, never knowing who she really was and never having her animal to fall back on. It made me kind of sad to think about it.

She swallowed loudly. I could see her throat working as she attempted to speak. She looked at our mom. "I'm going to be forced to shift soon?" Her voice was low and breathless.

Lienda nodded.

Mischa moved closer to me. "Does it hurt?" She stared at me. My nose was telling me that she was nervous and excited.

"The first time it does." I gave her a half smile, tilting my head to the side. "It's like the magic has to learn how the cells change, the way we will be different in wolf form. The first shift takes a while, and you'll probably pray for death."

"Jess, come on," Jonathon groaned. "Stop scaring her. I'll help you," he said to Mischa.

"But after that, when your wolf calls, or when you need her, you'll be able to shift without effort or thought." And with those words I stripped naked. Bringing up my wolf energy, I let it wash over me. Dropping to all fours, the power was visible as it coated my naked skin, and then I shifted. It wasn't instant, but within two beats of my heart, I was a silky black wolf.

The world changed. My senses were stronger; my brain morphed into that place of instinct. I hadn't noticed before, but there'd definitely been some recent sex going on in this spot. Two shifters and a vamp if I was correct. I sneezed a few times to rid myself of the scent.

I realized three sets of eyes were locked on me. Mischa took a step away when I approached. My lips curled up at the thought of chasing her. I liked chasing.

Jonathon placed a hand on Mischa. "Don't back away. Wolves like to stalk and chase weaker prey."

"Does she know who I am?" she asked him.

"You don't lose the person to become the wolf. We are one and the same. She knows you."

I was sick of this now. I needed to run. It felt good to be wolf, to forget about my worries for a little while. I spun around and took off into the forest, leaving all thoughts of the others behind.

Chapter 6

I ran for a long time before returning to Stratford. I'd passed others in the wolf pack, but I'd stayed solo for this journey. It was almost lunchtime, and I'd more than burned off breakfast. As I shifted to human form, my worries flooded back in.

I was at the front of my house. I wanted to wear my own clothes for once. We lived in a bi-level bungalow-style residence, two blocks from the Compass boys. I loved my home. It was all wood and slate inside, everything very earthy and natural.

Climbing the stairs, I pushed open the door to my room. Stepping inside, I was so consumed with my thoughts I never noticed or scented that I wasn't alone. Not until the shadow zoomed across the room and to my side.

I shrieked. "Braxton, what the frick? Are you trying to give me a heart attack?"

His head was sweeping awfully close to the ceiling as he stared at my face, which was good considering I was butt naked. I quickly grabbed underwear and clothes, slipped into my bathroom, and slammed the door in his face.

"Can't a girl get some privacy?" I grumbled, knowing he'd hear me.

"I've been worried about you, Jess." I could tell by the muffle of his voice that he was resting his head against the door. "You disappeared with your parents hours ago to hear this bad news, and, well, let's just say I was worried."

How could anyone as caring as Braxton be meant to take innocent children and slaughter them? I could not believe that. Stupid dragon mark, stupid hunters. I examined myself in the mirror, wondering where the hell this mark was hidden. My body looked the same, but now I felt as if I didn't know myself. As if there was something hidden on and under my skin.

"Jess?" His husky tone washed over me, and I shook off the melancholy and dressed quickly.

As I opened the door, he pretty much fell in on me. He must have had all his weight leaning on the poor frame. He steadied himself—thankfully, because I'd probably have died if he'd actually landed on me—and reaching out, gripped a big hand around each of my biceps.

"What the hell happened, Jess? You're as pale as anything and I can feel your sorrow."

I shook my head and pulled myself free. "Please don't. If you're nice to me, I'll cry, and I don't want to cry."

"I'm always nice to you," he said, bunching his eyebrows together. Then he smiled, flashing both dimples at me.

For a moment he looked like a little boy, the same little boy who'd been with me my entire life. So beautiful and innocent he'd been as a child, and now he was beautiful and hard. All man. But still my Braxton.

I attempted to smile. "Come on, I'm starving."

For once I actually wasn't hungry, but I needed to do something normal.

"Can you tell me anything?" he asked, as we walked toward the dining hall. I should have known he wouldn't leave it alone.

"Um . . ." I thought about it. "Well, Mischa is my younger sister." Not completely a lie, just an exaggeration—a really big one—our age gap was about two minutes. "Apparently our parents have had a few rendezvous over the years. It was a mutual decision to be apart, and now they've decided to try and be a family." I wasn't certain when I would tell them the truth. I was heeding Jonathon's words for now, but it would come out eventually. I sucked at keeping secrets.

Braxton's features were hard as we continued to walk. "Still sounds like Lienda's a selfish bitch." His voice was low. "I don't understand how anyone could leave their child behind. At least she had the decency to raise Mischa."

I guess you could leave your children to save their lives. It was actually a very good reason, as reasons go. I wished Braxton knew the truth; I didn't want people to hate Lienda anymore. Did I agree with what my parents had done? I wasn't sure, to be honest. I guess it's hard to know if they had stayed together whether I'd have been taken and killed. In that case, they'd definitely made the right decision, but maybe simply spelling the marks would have been enough. I'd missed so many years with my full family. I wanted those years back.

"No point dwelling in the past," I mused. "I can't change that. All I can change is the future and how I decide to handle the return of my mother and sister."

Braxton laughed. "Gee, that's very rational of you. Did some sort of mind meld happen in the forest?"

I punched him; it was like hitting a rock wall. Dammit, why did I continue to punch these men? It was killing my hands. He laughed again, shaking his head as if I were the funniest thing he'd ever seen. I needed a better way to smack some sense into them.

Braxton suddenly shifted directions, steering me off the main road and toward their place. "Let's stop in and grab the others. They've been worried, too."

As we neared the front door, my sensitive ears picked up the sounds of cursing and shouts.

"Great." Braxton started moving. He had the front door open and disappeared inside faster than I could track.

I followed his path inside. Exiting the hall, I ground to a halt at the sight of Tyson and Maximus fully going at it. The four boys didn't fight a lot; they were as close as any siblings I'd ever met, but they were hot-tempered men and on occasion, disagreements erupted.

"Don't talk about her like that again," Maximus bellowed as he slammed his big fist into Tyson's jaw. "This was not her fault."

Maximus was bigger, but Tyson was a brilliant fighter, fast and strong. Tyson spun once and elbowed Maximus across his cheek, knocking the vampire back a few steps.

"I don't trust her, and if you'd stop thinking with your dick, you'd realize I'm right." He launched onto Maximus, knocking him down. "Her arrival couldn't be more coincidental . . . fey dead . . . prison breakouts." He was punching his brother in between each word. "And it's not just us to worry about, Jessa is right in the thick of this."

With a roar, Maximus jumped to his feet, sending Tyson flying backward across the room; then using vampire speed, he followed.

Braxton was leaning against the wall, all casual-like. "Don't make me break you up," he said.

He wouldn't get in the middle unless it got further out of control. Which it easily could. They'd let their inner hunters free and probably wouldn't stop without serious bloodshed. Both of them had cuts and bruises, but nothing major yet.

Maybe it was because I was so out of it over the dragon-mark revelations, but I decided to do something I'd never done before. I darted across the room, and with barely a moment's hesitation, jumped between the brawling men. If my sudden appearance didn't shock them into stopping, I was going to be in a world of hurt.

"Jessa!" Braxton roared. He was reaching for me, but I was too far away.

The world seemed to hold its breath as the air swirled between the two of them. It almost seemed to be in slow motion as Maximus's fist swung toward me. He'd been aiming for a body shot on his brother. Horror and fear crossed his features as he realized it was going to hit me and not Tyson. I closed my eyes and prepared for the hurt.

Silence descended over the room. I flicked my lids up to find a trembling fist right in front of my face.

Somehow he'd halted his punch a hairbreadth away from me. My heart was pounding rapidly, and my fear flooded the room, so potent I could taste it.

"Don't fight, please." I was begging. I had so much turmoil inside that I just couldn't see them smash each other to pieces right now.

Maximus's hands were still trembling as he reached for me. "Jess . . ." His voice wavered. "I could have killed you." Then he was shaking me and roaring even louder than Braxton had. "I could have killed you! Don't you ever do anything like that again. Don't ever get in the middle of a fight between us."

I closed my eyes, willing my pulse and heart rate to slow. Then his strong arms were around me and Maximus's scent was everywhere. "I'm sorry, Jessa." He held me tight enough to cause discomfort, and I knew by the way he continued to shake that he was full-on freaking out.

"It's okay, Max." Braxton was behind us. I could feel him. "You stopped; you didn't hurt her."

"I could have killed her," he moaned.

I opened my eyes, meeting the deep brown of Maximus's. His anguish was visible.

"Stop," I said. "It was my own stupid fault. I know better than to jump in between you all fighting."

"Yes, you're in big fucking trouble, Jessa." Braxton's voice had that edge; he was close to losing control again. "And you are going to tell us what happened with your parents. Clearly, it was something bad enough to make you suicidal."

Maximus still hadn't put me down; he seemed unable to let go.

Jacob burst into the room then. All of our heads swiveled in his direction.

"There's been another death," he said. "Someone killed a vamp."

I exhaled. The quads might let me get away with my hedging on what had happened with my family in the forest. Murder was a pretty big distraction.

As the five of us ran toward the gathering in the forest, Braxton quizzed his brothers hard, trying to determine the reason they'd decided to use each other's faces as punching bags. The most we got out of them was that Maximus was defending Mischa's honor, and Tyson was feeling a little distrustful toward the new arrivals. Our stilted conversation halted as the stench of death reached us. We were still a hundred yards from the scene. As we moved closer, the crowds came into view; already there were onlookers.

I found it a little odd that there were so many people around the corpse. Generally, the council would have cleared the evidence by now. I pushed through the masses of supernaturals who were gathered in a circle around the kill zone. I cursed as the scene came into focus. What the hell was going on? Vampires were notoriously hard to kill. The constant influx of new blood gave them amazing healing and regeneration abilities, but someone had cut off the victim's head. The body was slumped against the large roots of the redwood, and a long machete had been speared through the skull, pinning it to the trunk.

"Is that Markus?" Jacob cursed. "Shit, he was like a hundred years old."

Which meant that whoever killed him had been strong and powerful, able to resist his vampire compulsion. Not to mention crazy as hell, judging by the scene we were looking at. Which was a scary concept.

"No blood and no bite marks." Braxton was sidling closer for a better look. "This is not the kill scene. He was moved." He lowered his head close to my ear. "Do you scent anything strange?"

I closed my eyes and tried to focus my nose on the scene, filtering out all of the scents that had nothing to do with the murder. The most demanding smell was still that of death. It was a recent kill, so there wasn't an overpowering smell of decay and excrement, but death was still there. I wrinkled my nose, moving past that to anything else strange. Forest smells and . . . coconut.

"I smell coconut oil and something flowery," I murmured as I opened my eyes.

Braxton nodded, "Yes, coconut and lavender."

He was right—those were the underlying scents.

Why was that ringing with some familiarity in my head? That combination was something I'd smelled before. I turned and saw Tyson. "Didn't one of the spells you used—to find the prison—use those two ingredients?"

"Yes," Tyson bit out. "And it's a spell I created. The scented oil was designed as a trail marker to take us to the prison."

I twisted my head back to the morbid scene. "Does that mean someone has left us a trail to lead to the killer? Or are they trying to implicate Ty as the killer?"

"Fuck!" Braxton clenched his fists. "Those marks on the tree, do they look like claw marks from a rather large animal?"

I'd been so focused on the head speared to the tree, I hadn't noticed there were two large gashes out of the bark. I examined them, and they were definitely a familiar shape and size. I didn't need to be an evidence magic user to know those claw marks would probably line up perfectly to Braxton's dragon. There was no reason for the Compasses to have killed Markus. Note I did not say they weren't capable—they were more than capable, but they would need a reason. Someone was staging this scene to implicate them.

At the moment of that realization, arms grabbed around me, tightening across my chest and yanking me backward. I was dragged ten feet away before the boys realized I was gone. They spun as one, coming at me, but in unison stopped when they saw who held me. I hadn't scented him at all; he'd cloaked himself so he could take me unawares. But the large ring on his middle finger was familiar enough that already my skin was starting to crawl. Kristoff.

The sorcerer had one hand wrapped around my throat. "We left this scene here to draw you Compasses into public. The four of you need to come quietly." He almost sounded gleeful. "I will keep a hold of Jessa until you allow the council guards to cuff you."

Where the hell was my father? My eyes darted around the crowd, but none of my family was here.

When Jonathon found out about this, he was going to be pissed. He would not appreciate the council using me as leverage to arrest the boys. I noticed Jerad off to the side, but the way he spun his head and walked away spoke volumes. Spineless dickwad. I was so well rid of him.

I didn't struggle against Kristoff; I could feel the strength of the spell under his hands. He would only have to let it loose and I would most probably lose my head.

"You can't kill her." Maximus sounded confident, but he wasn't stepping closer. "If you kill an innocent, then you're a murderer and will lose your leadership and freedom. Right after I torture you for life," he added, no change in tone but the fires of hell in his eyes.

Kristoff laughed. "The five of you are implicated in the murder of Markus. Jessa would simply be killed resisting arrest." He waved his hand at the scene. "I've been examining it for hours. All the evidence points to your group."

Shit, there must be even more than we'd noticed, and Kristoff was a master at deception and manipulation. It would not be hard for him to convince everyone of his word. Our standoff was starting to draw a crowd.

"I've been waiting a long time for you to make a mistake." The magic leader's lips curled into a sneer. "You think you're untouchable, all-powerful. You show no respect, not even to the council members. But you made an error in not cleaning up your kill site."

"Come on, Kristoff, doesn't this seem a little convenient?" someone shouted from the back of the crowd. It sounded a lot like Torag, the demi-fey council leader. "No one would be this stupid, and we know the Compasses have the power to hide anything they want."

Kristoff growled. "That's up to the investigators and the trial. For now the men need to be held in our cells at the prison." He straightened. "As an added incentive, I'll wipe Jessa as a suspect if you promise to go quietly and behave in Vanguard."

I wanted to shake my head at them, but I couldn't move. I had to keep fighting my wolf, she wanted to rip Kristoff's face off. But attacking a council member would be a very bad move. Even if he'd started it.

All four pairs of Compass eyes were locked on me, and one by one they placed their arms behind their backs. From the crowd, ten wizards emerged, as if they'd been lying in wait for this movement from the quads. I recognized the red bands they wore around their right biceps. These were our magic users skilled in offensive powers, like supernatural police. It took no more than ten seconds for the unbreakable magic cuffs to be slipped around the Compasses' wrists. They were threaded with silver and gold links, and then infused with spells that cut off our access to the energy inside, rendering the boys as close to human as they could ever get.

Kristoff released me. I coughed a few times, finally free to breathe deeply. I didn't think or pause, I swung at him, throwing my shoulder and full weight into it. Okay, so I said attacking him was a bad idea, but really, who gave a shit? The sorcerer clearly had not expected for one second that I would hit him. He never even raised his hands. My shifter strength flooded down my arm, and as I connected, bone crunched under my fist. He flew backward and slammed into the ground. I heard his yells and knew I'd broken his jaw. With one last sneer, I turned away from the pathetic lump.

Braxton called my name. They were already leading the quads away. I ran to catch up. They were being marched along at a rapid rate, but we had enough time for a few murmured words.

Braxton held me in his gaze; there was something cold in his dark-blue depths. "Jessa, this scene is complete bullshit. There's no way for this to make it through a trial. I'm not sure why, but watch your back." The cold changed to a hot fire in his gaze. "If someone is gunning for you or Jonathon, now would be the perfect time."

"Remember your training, Jessa babe." Maximus was leaning toward me. "We'll get out soon and come for you."

All four of them looked pissed, but I was also picking up tendrils of fear. And from men who were never afraid—that was the most worrisome. They were trying to tell me that this whole setup was probably just to get them out of the way to get to me or Dad. And they didn't even know about my dragon mark. If they did, I doubt they would have gone as quietly, because all of this seemed to be happening conveniently right after I found out about my heritage. It felt like too much of a coincidence. My heart ached as I followed them all the way to the edge of town, where they were thrown into the back of two Hummers. I didn't know where they would be taken—all I knew is that they'd be gone at least a week.

"Stay safe!" I screamed as the doors slammed on the vehicles. I raised a shaking hand to cover my mouth. I didn't know what to do. Who knew what was going to happen to them?

Kristoff's words kept running through my head. They'd deliberately left that scene there, using my presence and the crowds so they could publicly arrest the boys. My heart felt as if it were going to burst from my chest as I watched the cars disappear. The Compasses were gone. I must have stood there for a long time. Eventually I found my feet leading me back to the scene. I had no idea what I was looking for—evidence, a clue of who might have created the murder scene.

The crowd was still gathered around. There was much noise and chaos as I stumbled into the forest area.

"Jessa?" Jonathon ran up to me, his strong arms wrapped around my shaking torso. "I was showing Lienda and Mischa around Stratford when I heard."

Kristoff stormed across in a wave of power. "Your daughter broke my jaw." I could see the healer behind him. His face had been mended. Bastard. "I want her punished."

Jonathon swung around and in one movement wrapped a hand around the sorcerer's throat and lifted him into the air.

"You used my daughter as leverage to falsely arrest the Compasses. You held a decapitation spell to her throat. You're lucky I don't kill you right here and now."

At least Dad believed in their innocence.

Kristoff was not strong physically, but his magic was. With a blast, he shot my father back. "You would be lucky to kill me," he sneered, as he straightened and smoothed down his black dress shirt. "See you at the trial, Jessa. I hope you're okay without your protectors."

I bared my teeth but didn't reply. I took the warning for what it was.

"Jonathon . . ." Lienda's panic was clear as she came up to us, Mischa by her side. "This is what you were talking about, the start of an assault on our family."

He nodded. "Maybe. It's too soon to tell if it's about the Compasses, the girls, or just another attack on my position on the council."

It was late at night and a small group was gathered around our living room. Jonathon, Lienda, Mischa, and myself on one couch. Across from us was, well, I almost couldn't believe it . . . Louis. The. Sorcerer.

This had to be the man who had spelled our dragon marks. He was the strongest sorcerer in Stratford, probably in the entire supernatural community. A legend. He looked about twenty-eight, which meant he was old in supernatural years, and he was absolutely striking. Honey-blond hair with caramel-colored skin, almond-shaped eyes that I swear were so blue they were purple, and straight, aristocratic features. He wasn't as tough-looking as, say, the Compasses, but you only had to meet him once to know he was scary. I'd seen him from a distance a few times, and I couldn't believe he was sitting here in my living room. Our privacy dome was courtesy of his spell, so we all knew it was more than safe to speak freely.

I was doing everything I could not to think about the boys. I kept having some sort of panic attack as my brain conjured up images of what might be happening to them in the prison. Sure, they could look after themselves, but for all I knew this entire setup was to take them off and kill them.

Shit. *Stop thinking, Jessa.* I focused back on the room.

Sitting next to Louis was Torag, the council member of the demi-fey and loyal friend and supporter of my father. It had been him in the crowd to call Kristoff out. And lastly were the Compass parents: Jo, their very tall, black-haired, and stunningly beautiful vampire sorceress mother, who was tightly gripping the hand of Jack, their very blond lion-shifter fey father. He was built like a tank, and it was easy to see where the boys got their size. Yep, Jo and Jack, simple of name but huge of presence and power.

"We have to get them out." Jo's voice floated softly around the room. Her pale, creamy features were scrunched. I could scent her desperation. "They have enemies in there, criminals they've detained." Jack pulled her closer, his hands running soothingly over her.

She was right, although the boys weren't officially hunters—we hadn't even finished school yet—they'd been involved in a few arrests. As future council members, they were not *supposed* to take part in risky missions, but hey, they were the Compasses, they lived for dangerous shit. Generally, they didn't hear the word *no* much. So all of them at one time or another had left the protections of Stratford. I'd been waiting to reach twenty-five to be able to head out with them. Jonathon had laid down the law. I couldn't leave Stratford until I was legally a supernatural adult.

The Compasses used to go out together, but the last time all four of them left the community, the vampire had tried to usurp my father from the council. It was then we realized their presence added some protection to the Lebron home. They never left me alone again; at least two of them were in Stratford at all times. Which made it doubly hard right now. I felt their loss like a missing limb or organ. No wonder my chest hurt. It felt as if my heart had been ripped from its cavity.

I jumped to my feet, both of my hands flying to my hips. "You have to tell me where the prison is." I was trembling as I raised my chin at Jonathon.

He shook his head. "I won't. Firstly, it's forbidden and I'm spelled to prevent unauthorized location revelation. And secondly, I will not enable you to get yourself killed trying to free them."

I huffed in and out. Each breath felt strained, as if my lungs weren't filling. I narrowed my eyes. "I can't leave them there. I will find the prison. Don't you think for a moment you can keep me from helping the boys."

Jonathon and I locked eyes, neither of us backing down. I could not let him dominate me this time. I loved and respected my father, but if he didn't fight for the Compasses, then we were going to have a big problem.

He finally sighed. "We'll get them out, Jessa, but we have to be smart about it. Going in guns blazing to one of the highest-security prisons in the world is foolish."

His words had my heart rate slowing a little. Was he saying they weren't giving up, they were going to get them back?

"What do we do first?" Mischa seemed almost as anxious as me, which I found odd, but was too stressed to really think about.

Louis spoke then, and like magic, everyone froze and stared at him. "They'll hold the trial in six days." His voice was low, and energy seemed to float through the air following each note. "We know it will be a farce. I have no doubt that Kristoff is involved. His craving for power is reaching dangerous levels, and he knows his time on the council is almost over. He doesn't want to lose the boost from his people."

Jonathon nodded. "Desperate people do despicable things, and right now Kristoff is more desperate than I've ever seen him."

To become council leader you had to be the most powerful of your race at the time of choosing. Then, on top of already having incredible power, the leaders also received small portions of energy from everyone under their lead. Which, as you can imagine, increased their power monumentally. This was what Kristoff was afraid of losing. Louis had been the mages' council member fifty years ago, and now he was a chief, an honored place for those who had served as leader.

"I will defend the men," he said, his voice calm and smooth, and it seemed he was staring right at me when he said it. "I have gathered evidence from the scene and have no doubts that this was a staged murder."

"I will also defend," Torag said. "The trolls not like this deception."

Ignoring the sorcerer's probing gaze, I strolled across the room and hugged the small, robust troll tightly. "Thank you . . . thank you."

Over his shoulder I met Louis's eyes. I didn't know him well enough to hug him, but I gave a single nod. Which he returned with a wink . . . which was curious. His features definitely softened and he looked . . . friendly. Was he flirting with me? I couldn't scent interest, but he would only reveal what he wanted to.

Jo was on her feet, too. "Where are they holding them? Will we be able to see them before the trial?"

Jonathon attempted a reassuring smile. It fell far short of the mark. "The prison has a special cell for those awaiting trial. They boys won't be in with the rest of the sentenced criminals. The trial will be in the town hall, and you're permitted to attend. The morning of the trial, we'll meet here at 8:00 A.M.; the doors will be secured at 9:00 A.M. That gives us plenty of time."

I felt a little better knowing that the Compasses weren't in with all the hard-core criminals. I could only imagine the fights they could get into there.

After an hour or so of discussion and comforting for Jo and Jack, everyone left.

Except Mischa and Lienda.

Louis said the privacy dome on the house would last until the morning, so we continued speaking freely.

Jonathon stepped over to Lienda, reaching out and linking their hands together. "Your mother and sister will be staying here from now on, Jessa."

Even though I thought it was for the best, I still bristled. I hated being told things instead of asked. But I couldn't begrudge him his mate back, and to be fair, the four of us needed time together to try to learn to be a family. If that was even possible.

He was still speaking: "The more I think about it, I doubt this has anything to do with your . . . special abilities. But still, it's better to be safe, so try to be cautious. Don't find yourself wandering through the forest alone until after the trial."

"So you think it's usurping of your position on the council?" I asked, tilting my head to the side as I waited for his answer.

My parents exchanged a look, but before I could get a good read, he answered me: "No, I think the Compasses are wrong. The more I look at the evidence, the more I'm convinced this is not about our family at all. I think it's about them."

My eyes widened. "So what's with all these secret meetings and shit, making it look like we're afraid?"

My father grinned, showing all of his teeth. "Just in case someone wants us to think this is about the Lebrons, I'd hate to disappoint them. I want them to keep up appearances for a while."

I growled so loudly, it seemed to shake the foundation of the house.

Lienda finished his sentence. "So we can't tip them off yet. We're hoping they'll trip themselves up. They just need to make one mistake."

I flexed my hands, forcing the change down. "I don't like this plan. You know where they're being held. Let's break them out." I wouldn't take the risk that they would end up in the prison. There were thousands of criminals in there; they could so easily be killed.

Jonathon shook his head. "Then all of us will be considered criminals, and the entire supernatural community will be looking for us. How long do you think we could run before they captured us?"

Fuck. Fuck. Fuckity. Fuck. We could not escape the entire supernatural world. They were everywhere, on every continent, and those who searched for criminals, well, they were damn good at their jobs.

I lowered my head as I continued to fight for control; my wolf and the demon inside were warring for me to free them. It was as if a tearing sensation were ripping through my chest, but I managed to hold the seams together. I wouldn't lose it now. Braxton, Maximus, Jacob, and Tyson needed me, and I would not let them down.

Eventually I calmed enough that I could sit with my family and go over our plans for the next few days. After that, I went up to my room and attempted to get some sleep. I couldn't help the dark thoughts as I lay in a tense huddle under my cover. Only last night I'd slept between two of my favorite people in the world, and now

I was alone. A few stray tears dripped from the corner of my eyes, but I refused to let any more fall. Just as I had not let go of my wolf downstairs, I would not fall apart yet. I would fight and I would kill anyone who tried to stop me.

Chapter 7

The next few days passed in a blur of suspicion and pain. I was struggling, worrying myself stupid about the four of them. I wasn't sure I believed they were just waiting in a cell by themselves. Someone wanted them in there for a reason, and that wasn't to throw them a birthday party. So far, Mischa and I had had no trouble in their absence, besides the pitying looks and some nasty smirks from my BEF. So it didn't look as if someone got them out of the way to knock me off. Which meant it was about them. Which, for me, was far worse.

The morning of their trial we had our first snow for the year. Since I loved it when the world was dusted with fresh powder, all white and clean, I was taking it as a good sign for the quads. For once I was the first downstairs and was sitting at the table in our dining room, staring at the piece of toast in front of me. Under usual circumstances my lack of appetite would have me thinking I was dying or at least very ill. Jacob would have already thrown me over his shoulder and charged me to the medical building. I flung my fork down. Damn, this week had sucked balls.

Minutes later, Mischa entered the kitchen. Her hair was free, curling down her back, and she was wearing jeans and a black sweater. Simple.

Like my own jeans and long-sleeved underwear. Although Lienda and Mischa had ended up here because of the imprisonment of my best friends, I really liked how full our house felt. Before this, Dad and I'd rattled around in here; it had been a bit lonely. Now I wouldn't feel so guilty about hanging with the Compasses, knowing Dad wouldn't be alone. When I got them back, of course.

A smile crossed Mischa's face when she saw me, and for a second I thought she was going to hug me. But she refrained. "Did you get any sleep?" she asked, examining me.

I shook my head, raising my eyes to meet hers. "Nope. I've been too pissed off all week to sleep."

Especially last night. I'd spent it fuming and planning elaborate ways to kill whichever assbucket was responsible for the incarceration of the Compasses. I noticed Mischa flinch again as I cursed.

"We're twenty-two," I said, unable to help a slight grin, "and you seem afraid of a swear word."

One corner of her mouth curled up. "Mom never let me curse. Guess it's just instinct to cringe. I keep thinking a walloping is coming my way."

Interesting. Sounded like Lienda might have been a tougher parent than Jonathon. At least in some ways.

Lienda strolled into the room. "It's a terrible habit." She was dressed in a severe black suit. It wasn't hard to tell she'd worked as an executive assistant to a CEO of a huge multinational business in the outside world. I felt claustrophobic just looking at her clothes. "Ladies don't curse, even if they are wolves in their spare time."

"Morning, Mom," Mischa said, raising her cheek for a kiss.

Lienda complied before moving toward me. She hesitated behind my chair. I tensed, wondering if I could handle any overly familiar contact. We'd kind of been skirting around it for days, trying to find our middle ground. In the end, she just ran a light hand over my loose hair. I relaxed. I wasn't sure I could handle a kiss, but I liked the sense of having a mother. Even if it did continue to take me by surprise.

Jonathon joined us, and when he kissed Lienda gently on the lips, I averted my eyes. I just wasn't used to seeing my dad show affection for a woman. It kind of freaked me out a little. But I wasn't a complete selfish ass; they deserved some happiness after all of their years of sacrifice. I didn't know, of course, but I could imagine the torture and pain they'd felt not being with each other for the past twenty-two years.

We were quiet for the rest of the morning, each lost in our own thoughts. The front door opened at 8:00, and the very punctual sorcerer entered. Louis was dressed in ripped designer jeans, a white ribbed long-sleeved shirt, and black boots, which added an inch to his already impressive height. He looked like a model, not a hundred-year-old powerhouse mage. Jo and Jack followed him, both dressed formally. I hugged them. Jo squeezed me extrahard, and I could sense her nerves.

"We will get them out," she whispered to me. "Even if this does not go the way we hope today."

I loved the Compass parents. They were some of my favorite supes, having put up with me over the years. I'd spent as much time in their house as my own. It was a huge comfort to have them there, no matter which way the trial went.

We sat and waited for Torag, who arrived about ten minutes late, which for a troll was almost early. As a group we left the house and strolled toward the town hall. Somehow I ended up at the back with the intimidating sorcerer.

"So which one of the Compasses is your mate?" His voice seemed to vibrate when he talked, as if he had so much power inside that it even coated his words.

I blinked rapidly a few times, catching his gaze. His purple eyes were stormy today, not to mention unusual and hypnotic. "None of them. I don't have a mate," I said, pulling my attention from his compelling force field.

"Right."

I swung my head back around. That one word had said so much. "What?" I had to ask.

"You act the same way as a mate. Maybe you just don't realize it yet."

I snorted, the air whistling out through my nose. "Those four have been my best friends for twenty years. I'd die for any of them, but still we're only friends . . . pack."

His eyes hardened then, the purple shifting to almost black. "All true love stories should start as best friends, because that's the minimum foundation needed to survive the tumult of a relationship."

There was the echo of years and layers of experience in his wise words. He was trying to teach me something, then the moment was gone.

"If you are not with any of them, I'd be interested in spending some time with you."

My feet shuffled and then proceeded to trip over themselves. He caught me before I took a face-plant in the road.

I stared up like an idiot as his arms tightened around me.

"What . . . why?" I stuttered, before slamming my mouth shut.

I sounded like a freaking starstruck idiot. Sure, Louis was famous in Stratford, and I'd bet all over the supernatural world, and right now he was . . . asking me out, but still, I was acting like one of those girls.

He continued to hold me, the corner of his lips shifting as if he were refraining from smiling. "You interest me, have since your . . . unusual birth." He set me back onto my feet. He made the task seem effortless.

We started walking again, and I mulled over his offer. Of course he knew of my marks, his spell had been keeping me safe. But still, his words were resonating in my head. For my fun dalliances, I tended to stick with shifters; it was just easier. They understood the way I liked to keep things casual, and they feared and respected my power.

Louis was different, but I couldn't deny my attraction to him. He was mesmerizing.

"If you make sure the Compasses are freed, I'll consider your offer," I murmured, hiding a little behind my loose hair.

He laughed. "I do like a challenge."

I shivered again at the energy strength of his words. He was one scary, interesting, sexy-ass mage. I'd just never imagined sleeping with a magic user. Well, for Louis, I could surely make an exception. Rounding the corner, I forced my hormones under control and focused on the task at hand. Jonathon wanted us to take note of who was present at the trial. He said the supernatural we were looking for would want to see the trial. In fact, that supe was probably involved in the process.

"Stay close to your father," Louis said, his hand brushing along my arm, and then he was gone.

I took a deep breath and stepped into the darker room. There were about twenty people milling around. I moved across the space to join my family, Torag, Jo, and Jack in the front row. Louis had moved to the raised dais across from Kristoff, who was presenting the evidence against the Compasses.

Supernaturals don't get a trial by jury. The evidence is offered to our *Book of Guidance*, a large tome that rests in the center of the dais. This magical guide absorbs all the information and acts as an impartial judge. I've never trusted it myself. It's archaic and seems open to magical manipulation. Plus, it views all crimes as purely black and white, and we all know there are an awful lot of gray areas in the world. But what was the alternative? To have supernaturals act as a jury left the process open to mass manipulation. There seemed to be no truly fair way to judge these crimes.

I sat up straighter in my hard-back chair before scanning the room. "Where are they?"

"They'll be here soon," Jonathon said.

The area behind us, which seemed to be the unofficial Compass support zone, was starting to fill with females. Lots of teary-eyed, overly primped females. I sighed.

"Is it always like this?" Mischa was warily eyeing the sobbing supernaturals.

I narrowed my eyes. "Yep, unfortunately, hanging with the boys equals dealing with their *ladies*, and I use that term loosely. Most of them are groupies, hoping to get noticed."

The Compasses were pretty picky, but they were still men, and there were plenty of supernatural females to go around. They were the top dogs in this meadow, so generally all they had to do was look in the direction of a female for a little longer than a heartbeat, and they were surrounded. Surprisingly enough, Braxton was the most circumspect. In fact, I didn't know of more than a handful of his hookups over the years.

Damn, I missed the boys. My chest tightened, and I gripped the bench in front of me so firmly I could see the white of my knuckles. Mischa reached out and wrenched my fingers free one by one and took my hand in hers. I was struck by a strange sensation. My heart flip-flopped a little. I had a sister, a twin. Somehow just knowing that made me feel less alone in the world.

"I'm really glad you returned," I said. I stayed facing forward to hide my emotional leaking.

"Me too." She squeezed my hand harder, and we sat in companionable silence. I knew our parents were watching us; I could feel their stares, and . . . I scented the air—they were happy. Insert some sort of wolf-pack-love analogy here, and you get the gist.

Lots of glances were being thrown toward our group. Some covert and others very obvious. So far I wasn't seeing many viable suspects for the murderer, too many weaker powers in here. It was someone who was smart, strong, and evil. Which at the moment still had Kristoff as my number one. It was ten minutes until the start of the trial. Once the time ticked over, the doors would shut and nobody else could enter or leave until the spell was lifted. As a shifter, I chafed at the sensation of being caged, but I would deal.

Right before the doors were about to close, a hush fell over the room, and then the first of the red-band wizards entered. Five led the way, and my breath caught in my throat as I got my first glimpse of the Compasses. The boys were brought in one by one in a straight line, their hands again secured behind their backs with the magical cuffs. They were surrounded by magical security. I examined the four of them closely, but they looked the same. A little scruffier maybe, and a whole lot less fashionable—dressed in gray sweats—but there was no damage to them that I could see.

Mischa's grip on my hand was the only thing that stopped me from rising and running toward them. Maximus, who was in the front, bore no expression, but there were firestorms burning in those dark eyes. Braxton wore his trademark smirk, the one he used when he was preparing to beat the living crap out of someone who'd been stupid enough to run their mouth. That look worried me. It was his dragon that gave him the strength to throw himself into risky situations. But I didn't want them being reckless.

Not today.

As far as I was concerned, they'd better not do one thing to jeopardize their release from Vanguard.

They stopped moving when they reached the center of the dais, standing between Louis and Kristoff and facing the room. All of their gazes touched on me—I was surrounded by chattering idiots who thought they were looking at them—and smiles crossed their four handsome faces, full dimples gracing the room. Damn, I was pretty close to joining the pathetic souls behind me and fanning my face to lessen the heat.

Instead, I blew them a kiss, and my eyes leaked for a split second before I pulled myself together. I was just so happy to see them alive and not hurt. Louis was also staring at me, a knowing smile across his face.

Which I was kind of wanting to slap. He should keep his opinions to himself. I did not need anyone coming in and upsetting the status quo.

The clock ticked over, and the doors were slammed shut. The securement spell washed over the room in a haze of yellow. The trial started out normal enough. Kristoff started laying out the evidence against the four of them. There was something from each, including Tyson's spell, dragon-claw marks, a flaming circle from Jacob, and apparently the murdered vampire and Maximus had had a raging argument last week outside the training hall. That was probably the motive. Seriously, the Compasses argued with everyone . . . it was not a killing offense. Of course, Kristoff then dropped the main bombshell.

"The argument in question, of which I have six witnesses who testified under truth . . ." His slimy voice gave me the worst feeling in my gut, like period cramps, only a zillion times worse. "Was about Jessa, and whether she was free for Markus to pursue. This upset Maximus Compass to a visible degree, and we believe at the time of his death, the victim was on his way to the Lebron home. It was at this point he was intercepted by the four Compasses."

Ah, shit damn. Not good, everyone knew the Compasses were hot-blooded over me; it was starting to look more like a real motive. Kristoff had a few more bits and pieces of evidence, such as the magical trace forensics that found proof all of them were at the scene. Hair, scent, even a fingerprint. Of course, that was to be expected—we all were there eventually, we'd gone and gawked like morons when we should have stayed home. But too late to worry about that now.

When Kristoff was done, it was Louis's turn. I could see Jo and Jack tightly gripping hands as they watched their boys. Each of their sons had touched his brow and saluted two fingers to his parents upon arrival, a supernatural sign of respect. They followed that with a wink for their mother. Their confident swagger did not seem to have lessened Jo's worry.

I'd always known that Louis was impressive, but today . . . damn, he was unbelievable. Piece by piece he tore the previous argument to shreds. His voice was calm, his stance relaxed, and, as always, the power that rode his words spread throughout the entire room. He had alibis for three of the four—Maximus was keeping that day's events to himself. Probably involved a woman. Louis then pointed out the obvious regarding evidence at the scene, which wasn't even the kill spot. I could see Kristoff's face darkening as each of his points was turned around. If the quads were cleared of charges, he would look like a fool, since he was the one who had made the huge scene and arrested them on trumped-up charges. Finally, after a tense fifty minutes, all the facts were in, and all we could do was wait for the magical verdict.

It took forever. I fidgeted, twitched in my chair, and drove Mischa crazy by knocking into her.

Finally, the book delivered the folded paper. Kristoff reached out and took it. He looked down for a second before flipping it open.

No expression crossed his features. He lifted his head.

"Not guilty," he muttered, before throwing aside the white slip and storming off the stage.

The hall erupted with delight and uproar. I wanted to jump up and down and scream a little, but before I lost my shit, I turned and took in the room. My eyes alighted on the many faces. Most looked excited, but there were a few with neutral or unhappy stares. Kristoff, obviously, and Giselda, who'd been near the back of the room; also a troll, two pixies, and another vampire—who was vaguely familiar, but I couldn't remember his name. Strolling closer to them, I tried to scent the emotions, but there was so much going on in the room, I couldn't get anything clear. There were traces of guilt and anger coming from someone, but the mess of emotional resonance made it impossible to pinpoint who.

Finally, I decided to just catalog each face closely, for future reference.

As I turned around, the guards were removing the cuffs to free the quads' hands. I strode back to where my family was excitedly waiting. Jo was practically vibrating on the spot, and only Jack's hold on her kept her from flying off into the ceiling.

Then they were in front of us. Jacob and Tyson gathered their relieved mother into a hug. Maximus got to me first, wrenching me up and crushing the life from me, along with a few ribs and some happy tears. He handed me over to Braxton, and as his spicy, masculine scent wrapped around me, I felt the constriction in my chest finally ease. I wasn't alone anymore. I buried my face in his hard chest.

"We have a shitload to tell you." Braxton's words in my ear sent ominous shivers down my spine. I could tell that this was going to be bad. "And don't lose it, but I have to go back into the prison."

He'd better be freaking kidding me. I just got them back from there. Pulling away, I narrowed my eyes at him, followed by my eyebrows. He just flashed me some dimple before turning away to join the celebrating crowd. With a huff, I focused on the pair next to me. This wasn't the place to start demanding answers. Maximus and Mischa seemed to be having some sort of intense, silent conversation, using only strange facial expressions. I watched them closely for a few moments. What the hell were they doing?

"Looks like you owe me a date." I swiveled to find Louis at my side. His enigmatic features were relaxed, but a lot was going on in his eyes.

I crossed my arms across my chest but didn't move away. He was close; I could feel the power surrounding him.

"Looks like I do," I murmured.

"I'll collect soon," he said, running a single fingertip along my cheek. His touch left the slightest burning path in its wake. And then he was gone, leaving via the now-open doors.

I blinked rapidly, clearing the vapidness his mere presence had created in my head. That sorcerer was way too powerful.

Braxton left his mother and was at my side. "What was that all about?" he said.

Jacob and Tyson were right behind him.

The boys hugged me, distracting us from his question. Well, distracting me—Braxton never moved. He had me locked in his blazing blue eyes. I knew he would wait forever for me to answer.

I waved my hands at the stubborn ass. "Louis asked me out, and I said I'd go if he got you four out of prison." I shrugged. "It's just a date."

His nicely shaped black eyebrows narrowed in over his eyes. "You shouldn't promise shit like that for us."

What was his deal? It wasn't like I sold a kidney. Which I would have.

"It's no big sacrifice; he's hot and powerful. Sure, I hate picking magic from my teeth, but I'll cope." I dismissed the conversation with another swish of my hand.

I heard an exhalation of breath, but he didn't say any more.

After the trial, we convened back at our house. Jonathon had called a meeting. Maximus was explaining what had happened during their week in Vanguard. Finally, he reached the moment of this morning where they were led from the cells and thrown into a magical step-through—a portal that joined two places—and ended up at the hall for their trial.

"I wouldn't be surprised if they tried to have us imprisoned again," Maximus finished, leaning forward from where he sat on the bottom step. "We met a sorcerer who converses with the dead, and word on the other side is that we're a threat and someone will stop at nothing to keep us from taking over the council."

Tyson was grim-faced as he stood near the doorway. He hadn't spoken much, but I could feel the rage he was working to conceal. "Apparently if you're convicted of a crime, you automatically revoke your rights to being council leader." He sucked in deeply. "But that's not really the most important part."

Damn, what could be more important than someone trying to strip them of their rights to be council leaders?

"There were these rumors flying around the prison that the breakouts from all over the world, well, it was to do with the dragon marked. That they're being freed, and the dragon king is going to rise again. Word is Vanguard is next. Supposedly there are marked in there, members from all different races and . . . even kids."

I was actually shocked to hear that the marked were imprisoned. I'd always thought the marked were killed. But I couldn't remember if I'd ever actually been told that. Had I just assumed it? I raised my hands and rubbed my eyes as I worked to conceal the astonishment I felt.

Silence descended over the room. Lienda had excused herself a while ago, but there were still plenty of us there to be taken by surprise. Could this be true, and wouldn't my father have known? He was on the council and had information on the prison. Plus, he had two pretty big reasons to be interested in the dragon marked.

"Dragon marked . . ." Jo broke the silence. "We were led to believe that you were just in a holding area." She was agitated, shifting in her seat. Jack tightened his arm around her. "Are you telling me the entire time you were in the main supernatural prison?"

I could understand her dismissing the rumors for the more important fact that her sons had been hanging around with dangerous criminals.

Maximus strode across the room and knelt in front of her, taking both of her hands. "Don't worry, Mother, we were perfectly fine. We were in the main prison, but for the most part we could stay together and watch each other's backs."

"With all the criminals," I blurted.

"Yes," Jacob said, from his position against the wall.

Jonathon interrupted. "Back to the dragon marked. What makes you believe that could be true? I've been to Vanguard many times, toured the different sections. I've never seen anything like that. And there are no children in there. You know we don't imprison our young."

Truth.

In America, if a supernatural under the age of twenty-two committed a crime, that supe was tried and punished but did not enter the prison system. Instead, they served house detention, rehabilitation, and various spellings, depending on the severity of the crime.

Braxton rested his arms along the back of the couch. "There were these vampire transfers from Europe. They had all of these stories about the breakouts, that those freed were all marked, and that the escapes were orchestrated by two females."

Girls? For reals? A part of me thought that was kind of awesome. Two females taking on all of those prisons. And if they were freeing the marked, well, I was all for that.

"They were sure there are dragon marked in Vanguard . . . somewhere," Braxton said.

I hadn't forgotten his words from before. "Why do you want to go back into the prison?" I'd heard nothing in their story to indicate a reason for this insanity.

He took a deep breath. "Okay, I don't know if this is off topic or part of the same thing, but despite the fact we don't imprison children, there *was* a kid in Vanguard. A little boy . . . his name was Nash." I could feel my face tightening as confusion flooded my body, and I wasn't the only one with a scrunched-up face. "He used the sewage system to move around the different areas."

I exchanged a glance with my father. Really, how was it possible that a child could be in Vanguard? Could there really be dragon marked in there somewhere, hidden away? And if so, how did the boy get free?

Braxton was still speaking, his words picking up in urgency. "He's six years old. He wouldn't tell me much about himself or why he was in there. He just said he was small enough to fit places that others couldn't. It took him a couple of days, but he started to trust me. He told me how to get into the area where he lives, and I promised that if I could, I'd try to break him out."

Great, Braxton's need to be a hero was probably going to get him killed.

Jack sat straighter in his chair. "You think he's marked? You can't free the dragon marked." He usually didn't pull rank on his sons, but it looked as if he might now. "There is a reason they're locked away."

I kind of saw red on that one. "That's bullshit. A stupid scary story from over a thousand years ago is not a good enough reason to lock away children for their entire lives."

It was hitting close to home now. I apparently bore this stupid mark. It didn't make me want to go out and gather an army. So I assumed the rest felt similarly. Although the murder and imprisonment of dragon marked was not going to make them particularly sympathetic to the supernatural community. As always, people created their own enemies. These extremist actions would probably be the reason the marked rose up against the supernaturals.

"I never saw a mark on him, Dad." Braxton's voice was low. "He was just a little boy; he deserves a damned chance to run in the sun and play with kids. Vanguard is not the place for children."

"So how are we going to get in and free this child? Do you know the way back?" I asked, my eyes fixed on Braxton. I knew nothing was going to change his mind now. He had that stubborn look on his face. All I could do was tag along and make sure he didn't get himself killed.

Mischa jumped in. "I want to help," she stuttered. Her nerves were palpable; I could smell her sweat, see it beading her forehead. But she spoke truth—she did want to help. I wondered why. Maybe she had a soft spot for kids. Or was she wondering, like Jonathon and me, if there really were marked in there.

Maximus growled. "Personally, I never want to set foot in there again. But I always have Braxton's back, and this is something he needs to do."

Braxton's voice went really low. "I won't leave him behind."

I'd never noticed that Braxton had a particular affinity for children, but I could see that this one boy had made an impression.

Jack rubbed at his temples. "How is it that your Nash has evaded detection from everyone but you for all these years? What if it's a trap?"

Jacob laughed a few loud barks. "He probably sensed a kindred spirit in Brax. Neither of them stay where they're supposed to."

Braxton was on his feet now. "Nash said he'd been running around in there since he was a young child. If he hadn't figured out how to move undetected, he'd have been killed or starved. He discovered a way to use the sewage system, most of which an adult would not fit into." He ran his hands through his black hair, leaving a spiky disarray. "He's a little wild, and I smelled him before I saw him the first time."

"How do you plan on releasing him?" Jo said, still gripping Maximus's hands.

Braxton clenched his fists as he continued to pace. "The hardest part is finding the entrance to the prison again. But once we do, there's apparently one small weakness in the outer perimeter, something incorporated into the original design so that there was an exit for the water mains. All the prisoners know about it, but there's no way for them to get to it from the inside. But we would be coming from the outer zone. With a bit of magic, we can create an opening. After this, we'll follow the main thoroughfare in the sewer, which leads to Nash's room."

Jonathon tented his hands in front of him. "You do know that the prison is hidden for a reason." His voice was low, echoing around the room. "If you're caught, you'll be locked away for a long time. And I'm oath sworn, I cannot reveal the location to you."

Jacob nodded. "We know the entrance to the underground shifts every forty-eight hours," he said. "We became sort of friendly with one of the guards."

Tyson snorted. "And by sort of friendly, he means that we scared the ever-living shit out of him, and he spilled lots of information."

Sounded about right.

Braxton growled. It was deep, not human. "We will find it. This time we won't be wasting energy looking in all the wrong places. We know a lot more now."

I joined Mischa in the center of the room. "I want to help, too."

They were going to get themselves killed or locked up again, for life. I was either going to save them, or I was going down with them. Plus, I was curious to see whether I could sense anything in there about the dragon marked. I wanted to know if I would feel some sort of kinship with others like myself.

The Compasses immediately vetoed the idea.

Tyson was first to jump in. Time for the overprotective bullshit. "It's much too dangerous for Jessa and her sister to go. The prisoners are not to be messed with. There are some hard-core crims in there. If we get caught, it's better if they aren't with us."

Maximus stood and towered over the two of us, his standard brand of intimidation. "Not to mention the guards are all outfitted with silver and iron bullets, and they're a little trigger-happy."

Bullets hurt supernaturals—can kill us if you hit the right spot— but if you just shoot us in the leg, you'd better run because we heal fast and will be coming after your ass. Silver is more deadly for shifters and vamps, poisoning us. Fey and many of the demi-fey are allergic to iron; the element does weird shit to their blood. Witches are not weakened by either, but in general they heal slower, so it evens out.

I took a step back from the black-eyed vampire who was trying to use his will to influence my decision. I could feel my eyes changing as my wolf pushed to the front, and my shifter power rose up from inside of me. The demon whined to be free, but I shut it down.

"I'm only going to say this once, Maximus Compass. Don't try that vamp bullshit on me again. If you try and stop me from going, I will do something bad enough to get myself thrown in there."

"Jessa," Braxton said slowly.

I spun and pointed my finger at him. "I'm an alpha wolf; I don't need any of this overprotective crap in my life. I'm not letting some little boy rot in prison. End of story." I tilted up my chin.

I felt only a slight guilt that it wasn't just this factor that propelled me. The rest of my guilt was reserved for the fact that I couldn't explain my real reasons because I was still keeping my dragon mark secret from my friends.

Braxton studied me carefully, his eyes roaming over my face. He must have seen something there, because his right cheek lifted as he half grinned. I was blinded by white teeth and dimples, but I held his gaze. I couldn't back down now after such a bold statement.

"You can help." He nodded firmly. "But until Mischa has control of her wolf, she's too risky."

"What?" she blurted, opening her mouth to say more, but Maximus cut her off.

"I'll take responsibility for her."

His words hung in the air, weirdly suspended there as everyone stared at him. He'd just done a complete about-face not two minutes after declaring it was too dangerous for us wee womenfolk. What the hell was going on with those two? Maximus had no time for weakness in others, and besides me and his family, I'd never seen him give two shits about any supernatural. If anyone loved-and-left-'em with vigor, it was the vampire.

He hurried to answer our questioning stares. "She's Jessa's sister, and if she wants to come along, well, we're not her father to say no." He shrugged it off, but the slightest red was staining his cheeks. Interesting.

Jonathon cleared his throat. "Well, I am her father, and I'd really rather you didn't go, Mischa. I've trained Jessa; she knows how to fight and she's tough, with full control of her shifting abilities. You would be vulnerable."

Mischa crossed her arms. There was the slightest tremble to her lips as she stared into the corner of the ceiling. I could tell she wanted to cry, and I was kind of feeling sorry for her. But she didn't argue, which of course made me want to argue for her.

"What about a compromise?" I found myself saying. "While we search for the prison, Mischa can be learning her abilities. If she shows enough power to control her wolf and look after herself, she can come with us to break out the boy."

We locked eyes and an understanding passed between us. A sense of twin kinship.

"I don't need any heroes," Braxton said. "I know I can't stop you all from coming—no one ever listens to me. But when it boils down to the actual breakout, you will all do everything I tell you."

I almost snorted, but managed to keep it to myself.

It was weird. From the moment the quads had returned and spoken of the dragon-marked rumors and Nash, I'd felt this strange urge to go into the prison. Not to mention there was this fear deep in my gut, a fear that it was only a matter of time before something tore all of us apart. It was as if some sort of strange magic were floating around, and I knew I was being influenced. But I couldn't bring myself to care.

Chapter 8

"Mischa!"

I attempted to lower my voice, but it had been at least forty-two failed attempts at shifting, and I was getting a tad growly. I was cold and hungry; someone should be feeding me while I was slaving away. It had been a week since the boys were released. They'd narrowed down the section of forest that had the prison beneath it, so now it was all about searching for the entrance. Since it moved every two days, they searched constantly, taking turns. The rest of us waited for the signal to infiltrate, and until then I was trying to help my useless sister. Yeah, I'm a right-old bitch when I'm hungry.

Mischa was struggling big-time. Her shifter abilities were unlocked, but her fear kept her from being able to relax and let the transformation happen. Sooner or later, her wolf—or dragon—would force her, but for now the most we'd achieved was hairy arms. Not a huge success. Maximus appeared over my shoulder. He'd been off feeding, I could tell by the extra flush in his cheeks. He dropped a kiss on my cheek.

"How's our girl doing?" he asked.

We both stopped and stared at her writhing on the forest floor. Tyson had used a spell to clear the remnants of sludgy snow from this area, and Jacob had a fire lit nearby. But Mischa still looked frozen.

"I think this pretty much speaks for itself," I said with a lift of my brows. "We've reached the stage where she needs a good wax, and that's about it." I hoped the hairiness indicated that she was a wolf and not some sort of furry dragon. Which would be ridiculous.

"Fuck you," she snarled at me.

"Oh, and we've advanced to cursing, and our hearing has improved monumentally."

Maximus strode over to where Mischa was now in the fetal position. Bending down, he started murmuring to her, and no matter how I strained my ears, I could not hear the words. Spoilsport.

Jacob was jogging toward us as well, his face glowing, leaves scattered in his blond hair again. I took a step toward him. "Everything okay?"

He scooped me up and spun me around. "Everything is fine. We're free of the prison, and there have been no attacks. I'm not going to complain."

I was set on my feet again. "Personally, I'm finding it a little unnerving that no one has attacked or tried to frame you again. The last time was so sloppy, it makes me wonder what the hell the point was."

I crossed my arms over my chest before turning back to watch Maximus and Mischa. The vampire had his hands wrapped around her biceps, and I could see he was trying to coach her. He wasn't a shifter, so he couldn't know the exact process, but he understood how to channel power.

"I'm confused also." Jacob settled in next to me, arm around my shoulder. "At first I thought it was about getting us away from you, and then I thought it was about locking the four of us away so we couldn't take over the council. But you're right; it was sloppy, a reckless mess. So what the hell was the point of us being in there for a few days?"

I straightened, his arm slipping down off my shoulder. Was the point simply to have them go in long enough to find Nash? Had it been a setup? We needed to figure out who this Nash was and if there was any connection to him and someone on the outside. Or was it about making sure we discovered there were possible dragon marked in the prison? Had this been aimed at Mischa and me?

The list of people who knew we were dragon marked was short: Jonathon, Lienda, Louis. I couldn't imagine it being any of them. Of course, Louis would be the most obvious. I didn't know him very well. Maybe he had an agenda here? But still, what the hell would that be? I was supposed to go on a date with him tomorrow night. Maybe I could ask a few pertinent questions.

"Yo!" We all spun around to see Tyson and Braxton coming at us.

Braxton's voice was flat. "A and D starts in ten minutes, and we can't miss it again."

Right, we had an attack-and-defense class at 9:00 A.M. Braxton looked tired; he'd barely stopped searching since they had returned. His need to find Nash was eating away at him. Unfortunately, we had to keep up appearances, and college was not going anywhere. We still had three years left of classes. And it was important for Mischa. She needed to learn about the supernatural world more than any of us. Despite having gone to human college and holding a degree in arts or some bullshit, she was woefully uneducated in the important things. Maximus helped Mischa to her feet. She straightened her shirt and brushed the dirt and leaves from her hair. All right, time to book it, or we'd be in shit again.

We were quiet as we made our way through the streets and across town to the schooling block. We had to move at a fast jog; it was a fair distance. All of the different schooling levels were housed in this zone. The area was massive, and the college spread out over most of this space. The buildings were old architecture, large wooden structures that had plenty of space. We weren't big on changing what still worked, and most had been standing for a very long time. I loved the character in each building, the scars from shifter fights, the black marks of misspells. History was recorded in and on the walls.

"I'm really not looking forward to this again," Mischa said as we opened the door to step into the gym.

The smell was the first thing to hit me. I was used to it, of course, but old sweat and blood was never my favorite. There were padded mats scattered around to stop some of the hurt that was about to happen. In Mischa's one and only A-and-D class since she'd returned to Stratford, well, she'd been a little dominated. Most of us had been fighting for years, and on the outside she'd been a cheerleader . . . which was in no way helpful here.

I couldn't halt my smile. "Hopefully, Lincoln—the teacher, big horse shifter," I added at her confused look, "teams you up with someone less . . . vigorous . . . this time."

She returned my smile with a narrow-eyed glare. Jacob and Tyson snorted with laughter as we crossed the room. What? It wasn't my fault she'd gotten stuck with a jackrabbit shifter. The little critters were . . . enthusiastic. She was lucky it was fighting and not sex. There were some things that would never be a turn-on. Rabbits were one.

The room was already filled with various supernaturals. Everyone was out on the floor, and most already teamed up.

"Jessa, you're with Candice," said Lincoln with his bald head and perfectly white, but a little bucked, teeth.

With a half eye roll, I shook my head at the Compasses before crossing through the room to stand in front of the female vampire. Candice was taller than me, broad and strong-looking. Her skin was tanned, and her hair was golden blonde. She had silent, watchful brown eyes, and I knew it would be a mistake to underestimate her. Rule number one in battle: always watch the quiet ones.

I didn't know any humans personally, but I'd watched their television shows, and it was clear that something set us supernaturals apart from them. It wasn't just that most supernaturals were exceptionally good-looking—even the demi-fey with all of their differences were still incredibly mesmerizing. More than that, it was this energy that was infused into us. We glowed with it, and the shine of our skin and the gleam in our eyes foretold how we differed from regular Joes in the human world. A few humans seemed to have a glow to them—from my television watching, anyway—and were probably half-breeds, but the majority faded to nothing beside us. I wasn't being vain; it was simple fact.

The demi-fey, who would be considered ugly by human standards, weren't. They were just different. But if you truly studied them, the knobby knees, the foreign features, you found a uniqueness. Humans thought the stranger demi-fey were ugly because they did not understand them. And like all creatures, they feared what they did not understand.

Mischa ended up next to me, on my right side, against a pixie. Her partner was one of the demi-fey who could change her size at will. She had very big, round eyes, and her nose and mouth were small, fading into the rest of her features. Her hair was coarse, standing up in spiky twirls around her head, and her skin the color of a sunset. In the past, demi-fey had been hunted almost to extinction by the very humans that we tried to protect. Now I was glad the supernatural communities provided a sanctuary for them.

Lincoln was at the front of the room, his voice loud and bellowing. Typical horse. "All right, we are on rotation today. Hand-to-hand."

Usually we trained with all types of weapons. I was able to hold my own with pretty much anything, but was particularly proficient in crossbow. I liked the power and ease, although it lacked accuracy when used while on the run. I sized up my opponent. Candice was vampire and would be quick, strong. I needed to use my shifter strength; otherwise, she'd crush me. She came straight at me, her arms elevated in front of her and her strides strong. I didn't hesitate, ducking her first blow and using my elbows to clip her unguarded chin. She was an offensive fighter but not great with keeping her guard up. I was distracted by Mischa hitting the mat next to me. The pixie had zipped around behind her and planted both feet into her back, slamming my twin face-first into the stinky, squishy floor.

Of course, my moment's distraction was all Candice needed to crash into me and, using a wrestling hold, flip me over and then twist my arm behind my back. She held it at the point that the slightest exertion of pressure would break the bone. I would be pissed, because even for me a broken bone took twelve hours to heal—unless I called in a healer. Luckily, I was sneaky, and she'd left my other arm free. Stupid move, really. Pushing down for leverage, I bucked, which loosened her hold. Seems she hadn't had a true grip on my wrist. Swinging my legs around, I twisted my body for enough leverage to uppercut her. I followed through with my entire weight—well, the best I could from my position on the ground. Her screech was cut off as she slammed back onto the mat. I was up and moving, but the whistle sounded before I could beat on her some more.

"Move to your left," Lincoln shouted.

This continued on and on, each opponent with a different advantage depending on which supernatural race they were from. Vampires were so fast and superstrong. Shifters had unparalleled senses; our speed and strength not far behind vamps. The magic users had extra energy and the ability to use spells if they were quick enough—although Lincoln didn't encourage spell casting in hand-to-hand. It was supposed to be more about physical abilities. The fey were magical without needing any spells. They could blur themselves and almost act chameleon-like to blend into their surroundings. They were so in tune with nature that the very air itself whispered, helping them gain advantage. In Stratford, we were low on female fey, who we called sirens. They had the ability to enthrall the mind with their *calling* song. It seemed to mainly affect males . . . go figure. Probably a reason we had so few. Men did plenty of stupid things without additional help from a clouded mind.

Lastly, the demi-fey were all different. The pixies could fly, zap with energy, and bespell with pixie dust. The trolls were like brick walls. You could hit them, and they wouldn't even move. Sometimes I wondered if they even noticed me hitting them. There were about twenty different demi-fey, but Stratford only had six species. While others had come and gone through the years, I'd met most of them. The mermaids were the strangest. They preferred places with large bodies of water, not forests, so despite our large tanked area, we never had long-term mermaid residents.

We continued to rotate. I was starting to feel the bruises. There'd been a few lucky hits in my distracted state. Maximus had somehow maneuvered himself next to Mischa and was helping her out. Which, luckily for her, resulted in her opponents going easy on her, thinking her vampire bodyguard might pound them into the ground. He'd done that for me before, and I kind of felt a little put out that I no longer had him watching my back.

Damn sisters, always stealing your favorite toys.

I groaned when I saw my last opponent for the day—Melly, a six-foot-six, muscle-bound dickface. And I say that with no love at all because he was an ass who had tormented me for many years. For some reason, the bear shifter had a hate-on for me that would not disappear, no matter what I did.

"Well, if it isn't the wolf princess." Melly's shoulder-length red hair was always scraggly. His skin was spattered with red freckles, and his eyes were moss green. He spent most of his time in the forest. His family had left Stratford last year, and, unfortunately, he'd decided not to go with them. I'd felt sorry for him . . . for roughly eight seconds before he'd buried me under a massive mound of autumn leaves. "Are you worried, princess? Hate for you to break a nail . . ." The mocking grin dropped from his face. "Or your neck," he added quietly.

I didn't fear much, but he made me uncomfortable. It wasn't really the comments, alphas get threats a lot, and I had a big mouth—yeah, I pretty much deserved everything I got. No, it was the look in his eyes. When he caught me in his gaze, the green darkened and I could sense his need for me to be removed from this earth. And the worst part, I had no freaking idea what I had done to him.

I watched him closely but didn't speak. Anything I could say would only make it worse. I'd tried over the years to fix the problem, to no avail.

"And now there's a younger, more pathetic wolf princess." He moved on to Mischa, who was finally starting to pay attention to the bear shifter. Maybe he hadn't noticed her new bodyguard. He was going to get Maximus all riled up. Should be fun. "Maybe one day I'll get the privilege of destroying the entire Lebron line. Bears are not led by wolves."

Curious.

That was the most information he'd revealed in a long time. Maybe this hatred wasn't personal toward me, just that he was ruled by wolf shifters who happened to be in my bloodline. I could see Maximus starting to move closer to me. He'd been fighting a male fey. His shirt was smoking a little from a few fireball accidents.

I shouldn't have shifted my focus. As I turned back, Melly had moved and a fist was coming straight at my face. I threw my head back, twisting to the side, hoping to avoid his massive knuckles. No such luck. The meaty fist clipped me on the side of my chin and cheekbone. I heard the crunch; my screams echoed around the cavernous training room. As I hit the padded mat, I clamped my mouth shut, cutting off the sound of my agony, since opening my mouth seemed to increase the intense stabbing heat. Chaos descended as everyone ran to see what had happened. I was pretty dazed; I wasn't sure exactly how much I missed in the next few moments. The throbbing hum of pain that was pulsing in the side of my face was distracting me from everything else in the room.

"Jessa!" Soft hands gently touched the uninjured side of my face. "Are you okay? Open your eyes." Mischa sounded a tad frantic, and I did not want to know what my face looked like.

I tried to open my mouth, but the ache that stabbed into me again had me closing my lips. Shit. I was going to kill Melly the second my face healed. I was going to cut his arms and legs off and then slice them into little pieces, and after that his eyes—yep, I'd pluck them out one by one and feed them to the closest shifted animal . . .

Maximus interrupted my thoughts. "Jessa, open your eyes, babe." Just when I was getting to the good part. Typical.

I slowly opened the eye on my uninjured side; the other was already sealed shut and wouldn't open. The light was so bright, it took me a moment to fight through the blindness and try to see. I knew my cheek was broken, and I was pretty sure I had a concussion. Everything was blurry and out of focus. Not to mention I had the mother of all headaches and was about ten seconds from barfing everywhere. I was forced to shut that eye again.

"We need a healer in here. Now!" I could hear Braxton's order from close by. His words were so clipped and icy, I was pretty sure a layer of chill had settled over the room.

I lost track of time again. My concentration was firmly on keeping the contents of my stomach where they were, and then I felt hands on me. Warmth spread through my body, and I knew either a witch or a wizard was using healing energy to repair my broken face. All magic users had some healing abilities, but there were a few who were extragifted in that department. If they showed this aptitude, they had an additional year after college learning the art, and then they became healers. I sighed as the warmth turned into an intense heat, and I could feel the actual bone starting to knit together. I'd have healed eventually; this was just ten times quicker.

"She had a fractured jaw and cheekbone, and her skull was cracked in two places," said a soft female voice—my healer was a witch. "I've mostly fixed her up, but she needs bed rest for a few hours or so. Just to give her body time for any additional healing she needs."

My eyes flew open, and I pulled myself up. Maximus was on one side of me and Braxton on the other. They each placed a hand under my arm and lifted me to my feet. I was facing a tall, slender red-haired woman. She had dark eyes that were scanning my face. She looked familiar, but I couldn't remember her name.

"Thank you . . ."

"Grace," she mumbled. "My name is Grace."

Ah, right, now I remembered. When I'd been about fourteen, Grace had declared her everlasting love for Tyson, despite the fact she was a few years older. He'd been a typical immature boy and sent me over to let her down gently. Of course I'd had about as much tact as a troll or a tree, and after my brief stumbling explanation, she'd fled in tears.

"Thank you, Grace," I tried again. "I really appreciate you healing me."

She smiled. It was genuine, and her entire face turned from gamine sweetness to ethereal beauty. She had grown into her lanky looks. "You're welcome. If you ever need any help, Jessa, please don't hesitate to call me."

As she stood, her eyes flicked across to Tyson in a movement almost too fast for me to track. I couldn't read her expression, but she didn't seem to be viewing him in the same romantic light of long ago. She looked a little pissed, actually.

As Grace marched away, Tyson's eyes followed her. The wizard looked a little shell-shocked; some gold was bleeding into his eyes. How strange was it that we hadn't seen Grace for almost ten years? I wondered if she'd left Stratford. I was distracted from my thoughts as the rest of the class moved back into position.

Lincoln was talking to the Compasses. "Take Jessa home and put her to bed and make sure she stays there." Everyone knew they were my pack. "I'll see you all in the next class. I'll inform her father of what happened, and he can decide on the punishment for Melly. He's suffering right now, but I doubt that will be enough for Jonathon."

I'd forgotten about that coward-ass piece of shit—punching me while my back was turned. Scumbag. I pushed through the crowd to find he'd been strung up from one of the huge rafters by a thick, heavy cord. His head was about two feet off the ground as he struggled upside down. Judging from the bruises already forming on his face, and the cut dripping blood onto the floor, he'd been "knocked" a few times during detainment. I pushed a few more supernaturals aside, and bending over I got reasonably close to his face. Despite his predicament, he still sneered at me.

"Always so brave when you've got the quads watching your back." His teeth were a little bloodstained. He spat onto the floor. "You disgust me."

Reaching out, I grabbed his chin, hard, squeezing it slowly between my fingers and palm, letting my shifter strength flow along my arm. His eyes widened, but he didn't make another sound. "You come near me again, Melly, and I will fucking take you apart, piece by piece." I'd already started planning it. "I don't need the Compasses to destroy you; I have every weapon already at my fingertips. You live now only on my generosity. An attack like that, on a council leader's daughter . . . Jonathon is going to want your head." I shoved him hard, he swung out away from me. "And I might just let him have it."

As he swung back, I spun and kicked out. My shin cracked him in the temple, knocking him out cold. "Tell my father to let him go with a warning this time," I said to Lincoln, knowing he'd chat with Jonathon first. If Melly came at me again, I'd be the one to kill him.

Braxton stopped me with a hand on my right biceps. "Jessa, he needs to die." I shook him off. "He fucking hit you while your back was turned. He's a coward, and his weakness is only going to hurt Stratford in the long run."

I could see by the tight jaw, clenched fists, and raging fury in his eyes that Braxton cared nothing for the town. He was pissed that I'd gotten hurt. He was always my sweet protector. But I was a big girl and could look after myself.

"I have a feeling he won't come after me again." I shrugged. "Lesson learned." Okay, I might have been overly optimistic, but I owed the guy one last chance.

Melly groaned as he woke from his little nap.

"If he steps within ten feet of you again, he's dead." Braxton's voice had no inflection at all. He was serious. And scary. "No more chances."

Mischa followed us as we left the room. The six of us were the sole focus of attention from the others, but as the doors slammed shut behind us, I could hear the noise inside start up again. Gossip was already flying around.

Braxton was staring at the ground as we walked, his fists still clenched, and I swear small rumbles were shaking his chest, although I couldn't really hear anything.

Jacob distracted me from his brother. "Don't find yourself alone with that guy, Jess. He has the strength to kill you. If you hadn't pulled your face in the last second, he probably would have."

I shook out my hair, wincing as the slightest tenderness still plagued my head. "I can handle him." I was great at false bravado. "But I don't understand why he would try to kill me."

That would have ended in his death or imprisonment in Vanguard, for a very long time. But my money was on death . . . by one of the Compasses.

Braxton lifted his face then, and I ground to a halt. His blue eyes blazed with an inferno of fury. He was literally vibrating, he was so wound up. "I saw it happening and couldn't get to you fast enough."

"You strung him up?" I asked. Braxton must have been like a step behind Maximus despite the fact he'd been across the room.

"I would have killed him, but I needed to make sure you were okay first. I was heading back to break his neck when Max convinced me that wasn't the best option."

Maximus groaned, rubbing his hand down his left side. "And I'm pretty sure you cracked my rib, asshole. I owe you for that, and despite the fact that killing him was a great option, I figured that wasn't the way you wanted to end up back in the prison."

I noticed then how teary and scared Mischa looked. She had her arms wrapped around herself tightly. "You okay?" I moved closer, standing right in front of her. God, how anyone couldn't tell we were twins, I had no idea. We were identical, everything except for the eyes and a few freckles.

"I don't think I'm cut out for this life of violence. How do you live with it all the time? Watching your backs? I can't sleep; I can't eat. I'm having a breakdown, and I haven't even been here for a month."

She couldn't sleep? It was more serious than I'd thought. I tried to hold back my smile but couldn't. "You're just not used to it. Supernaturals are violent bastards; it's a wolf-eat-wolf world here." I was talking metaphorically because there were so many different races. "And you have us to watch your back also. Trust me, you couldn't have better supes in your corner."

Tyson patted Mischa on the shoulder. "She's not kidding."

Despite the fight between Maximus and Tyson on the day of Markus's staged murder, there had been no more drama in the group. Mischa had been mostly accepted into our inner circle, although I sensed a small sliver of distrust still, mainly from Tyson.

The wizard continued with his wisdom. "It will drive you crazy if you worry too much. Today's worry does not prevent tomorrow's woes. We just have to accept what will come and do our best to protect each other."

Smart, smug bastard. He made good points, though. He still seemed a little out of it as he gazed across the town. I was starting to think that seeing Grace had really knocked him around.

"Come on, Jessa needs to get to bed." Braxton started hurrying us along the path again.

"Jake," I called to the blond fey.

He bounded over to my side. "You called for me, Jessa babe?" He wrapped one of his long arms tightly around my shoulder.

"Can you sing for me?" My head was starting to throb again, and his voice was the most soothing thing in the world.

His voice was uncharacteristically low. "I'd do anything for you." And then he started to sing.

It was my favorite faerie ballad: haunting, hypnotic, and soothing. It was the song of birth or *de la entrée*. The fey would sing it when one of their babies was born, to welcome them into the world. I yawned loudly.

My feet were swept out from under me as Jacob scooped me into his arms.

"You guys are my best friends . . . and I love you," I said sleepily, as I closed my eyes. "I don't tell you that enough." I could have died today. The thought that I should tell my friends and family how much they meant to me had flashed through my mind when that punch landed.

Jacob chuckled again, his chest moving under me. "We love you, too. You're our pack, our family. Don't go almost dying on us again."

I felt hands brush along my face and knew the others were using their warmth to comfort me. With that warmth, and the final humming remnants of Jacob's song, I drifted off to sleep.

Chapter 9

It was time for my date. I'd spent most of the afternoon in bed, but despite Braxton's constant arguing against me leaving, I couldn't lie around any longer. Besides, I'd made a deal, and I was not backing out of it. To be fair, I was a little intrigued to see what this Louis was all about. To see if maybe it was he who had set up the Compasses—to reveal the secrets of the marked in the prison.

An hour before Louis was due to arrive, I kicked the boys out and got ready. Then once I was ready, Mischa came in and redid absolutely everything. Sisters are annoying.

Mischa was sprawled across my bed. "You look amazing. I'm glad I talked you out of shorts and found a dress you'd accept."

Okay, so she had a pretty great eye for fashion. Since I'd never actually been on a date, I did appreciate her input. The casual relationships I usually pursued did not leave much need for dating or fancy clothes. Or clothes of any description really.

I flittered off the bed, the dress swishing around my thighs as I ducked over and gave her a hug.

"Thanks for lending me the clothes." I'd have been hard-pressed to find a dress of any description in my closet. I'd never felt limited having mainly male friends, but, well, I was starting to see that girls had a pretty important place, too, and my sister kind of rocked.

The dress was a dark blue, and I was surprised by the difference it brought to the color of my eyes and the highlights in my very dark hair. It had thin straps and was fitted across the breasts before falling in silky lengths to mid-thigh. I teamed it with my black Converse sneaks because I'd probably kill myself in heels. Mischa had approved, saying it was modern tomboy girlie. Whatever that meant. She'd tackled me into the chair and applied the lightest layer of makeup, lining my eyes with kohl and lengthening my lashes with mascara. Standing before the full-length mirror in the upstairs bathroom, I was surprised by how I looked. Like myself, only . . . sort of more.

Moving back into my room, I shoved Mischa across the bed to sit next to her. We sat in silence for a few minutes. It was nice, though. We'd almost reached the point where we didn't have to fill our moments with chatter.

Finally I straightened. "I should go downstairs; Louis will be here soon." I ran my hands over my silky hair. "I have no idea why, but I'm a little bit nervous." I never had nerves about crap like this.

"You'll be fine," Mischa said, patting me on the shoulder as we descended the stairs. Okay, the girl wasn't the best with reassurances. Another thing we had in common.

Downstairs was empty. Jonathon and Lienda had gone for a run in the forest. My father hadn't said anything about my date, except advising me to proceed with caution. Like I needed the warning. I knew Louis was megapowerful. Anyone with that much oomph was to be treated with wariness. We all knew that power can corrupt.

"What did Jonathon do about Melly?" Mischa asked as we made our way into the living room. I wanted to sprawl out like I usually did, but stupid dresses are not designed for true sprawling.

"He wanted to try him and have a prison term allotted. We might be a little wild here in Stratford, but unprovoked attacks are not allowed.

Especially when it could have killed me." I shrugged. "But in the end it was an A-and-D class, and Melly would simply argue he was attacking within his rights. I told Dad to forget about it."

Which had not gone down well; hence, his need to run off some anger.

"I'm quitting that class," Mischa muttered, her eyebrows drawing together as she picked at her right thumbnail. "I'm not cut out for fighting."

I inhaled deeply, sucking in a lungful of air. "I suggest you think seriously about that decision. You might not feel like it, but you're part of the supernatural world now, and you'll want to be able to defend yourself. Like shifting, sometimes the only way to learn is the hard way." I had no doubt that she was fighting an uphill battle—it would be difficult starting as an adult when we'd been training since kids. But giving up wasn't a great personality trait. I wouldn't encourage that.

"Yeah, we know how awesome I've been at shifting." She moved on to the other thumbnail.

"You'll get it soon, and when it clicks, your wolf side will just fall into place." I was no longer considering that she might be a dragon shifter. It was definitely wolf.

She rested her chin on her shoulder as she stared at me. "Max helped me see some of what I was doing wrong. Because I'm afraid of the unknown and the pain, I'm internally fighting back. It's all in my head; the fears are preventing my shift."

I focused on her. "What's going on with you and Max? You're spending a lot of time with the vampire." *My vampire,* I silently added. Man, I was possessive. I should work on that, right after I deal with selfish, paranoid, and bitchy.

Mischa didn't answer straightaway, and I wondered if she was trying to hold out long enough for my date to arrive. But then as she raised her face and met my pointed stare, her confusion was oh-so apparent.

"I felt something for him the moment I first saw him." Her smile was wobbly. "And he's just . . . perfect—gorgeous, charming, and so sweet."

Well, shit, was she talking about my Maximus? He was a man whore of the worst kind.

"Can a shifter and vampire be true mates?" she asked me.

I scratched the side of my ear in a kind of nervous twitch. I had to remind myself not to continue the twitching. I never wore makeup, and no doubt before this date was over, I'd forget about the eye stuff and smudge it all over my face.

She was still staring at me. I took a deep breath. Why was I always the one to deliver bad news?

"No, your true mate will be within the same race." I hurried on as her face fell. "But that's rare—you can have a mated relationship without being true mates. You can choose who to love." While I adored the thought that somewhere out there fates had chosen the perfect match for me, I also liked thinking I could choose my other half, that my heart could decide.

"I never said anything about love." The slightest pink tinged her cheeks. Her hands trembled a little as she shoved her hair behind her ears. "I barely know him."

"You wouldn't have asked about mates if it wasn't a little more than *I barely know him*," I mimicked her. I wondered then if maybe Mischa was the reason Maximus had had no alibi at the trial.

She gritted her teeth and was just opening her mouth to speak—or yell at me—when there was a knock on the door. I stood in one fluid movement, my questions forgotten as I ran my damp palms along the swishy skirt of my dress. I resisted the urge to check my appearance one more time. Nothing would have changed; I was simply searching for a distraction or something to alleviate my nerves.

"Why am I nervous?" I murmured. "It's a date and I don't even particularly like this magic user."

His voice echoed through the wooden door. "I can hear you, Jessa. You might as well let me in before you convince yourself out of tonight."

Mischa laughed then. "I'll never get used to these extrastrong senses."

"Yeah, well, magic users don't generally have super hearing. Clearly Louis is an overachiever," I said as I stomped across to the door. My cheeks wanted to blush, but I refused to let the blood pool there.

I slammed the wooden barrier open to find his big body crowding the doorway, and his handsome face staring down at me. The slightest grin tipped up the corner of his lips. Frigid air wafted in around the sorcerer. It was cold out tonight.

"Hey," he said, all casual-like, his eyes sparkling at me. He was like a brilliant sunset, spectacular to look at but kind of blinding at the same time.

A smile crossed my own lips, and then the laughter followed. I felt ridiculous all dressed up, but I was looking forward to this date, weirdly enough.

"Are you ready?" he asked, when I didn't say anything.

I nodded and pulled on my long coat, zipping it up. I waved to my sister, stepped out onto the deck, and kicked the door shut behind me. I didn't have a bag or anything; there was no need. Stratford had a few restaurants and the dining hall, but there was no money exchanged. People were expected to contribute to our community, so we had various businesses, but money was only involved for exchange with humans.

Louis was relaxed as we strolled away from my house. He dipped that smile in my direction again. "I'm surprised one of the quads isn't here giving me a lecture and questioning my intentions."

The sun was just setting, and there were still plenty of young supernaturals playing in the street. They paid us no attention, enjoying their variety of games.

I wrinkled my nose at him. "I forced them to leave. As much as I love that they care, it can be awfully awkward having so many protective men in my life. You'd be amazed at how many of my male *friends* have been scared off." In reality, I couldn't think of one sexual partner I'd had who wasn't wary or outright petrified of the Compasses. No wonder I didn't date.

Louis chuckled. "I wouldn't be amazed at all. They have spread the word far and wide that you're off-limits."

Those bastards were going down.

Louis reached out and took my hand. I tensed and almost yanked it free; his power licked along my arm and the sensation was uncomfortable. Gritting my teeth, I stuck it out and soon the sensation subsided. Which was a relief.

Louis didn't comment on my reaction; he was still focused on the Compasses. "I'm not sure you realize how far the quads' reach actually is. I would say the only reason you've had any options for sexual relationships is because you're . . . utterly desirable." I must have made a choking sound because he pulled me to a halt. "I know you can't see how magnetic and fascinating you are. It's not just that you're gorgeous. It's something from inside."

I examined him closely, wondering if he was talking about my dragon mark.

"Men have told me I'm beautiful before," I said, shrugging, "but at the end of the day I'd rather be thought of for more than just looks."

Louis's eyes roamed across my face, and I could see thoughts churning in their unusual purple depths. "Yes, people have told you, but you don't really believe them. Or maybe it's that you don't really seem interested when they say it." He pulled on my hand, and we started walking again. "Why is that, do you think?"

I knew I wasn't ugly, and I had some striking features, like my hair and eyes, but I thought I was much more beautiful in wolf form.

"Beauty is in the eye of the beholder. So my only hope is that when I fall in love, find my one, that he finds me beautiful."

"And there we have a perfect demonstration of the very reason you're desirable," I heard him murmur under his breath.

I changed the subject.

"So where are we eating tonight?" I wasn't sure whether Louis was aware, but I judged harshly on food quality, so it better not be Murphy's. Their restaurant was for the demi-fey and catered to a select clientele. Which, unfortunately, did not include me.

"I thought maybe I'd cook for you." His relaxed demeanor did not change, but I sensed a slight tension filtering into his stance.

I curved my lips upward. "Wow, are you actually taking me to the mystery home of Louis, the great sorcerer?" I didn't really know what to think about that.

He shrugged. "I like my privacy, but there's no mystery. The longer I live, the less I feel the need to socialize with others."

Which felt strange to me. I was a shifter, and a wolf to boot. We loved our packs and, in fact, could get very sick if we were isolated for too long. We needed the touch, the energy of others.

"Probably why shifters and sorcerers don't generally go on dates," I offered, keeping my voice even.

"Probably," he agreed.

Damn, this man was unfazed by my lack of tact. First test passed.

His power whistled over me again. "Besides, I heard there was an incident in class today. I figured you needed quiet and relaxing."

Of course he'd heard about that.

"I can have a word with Melly if you like?" His calm tone wasn't fooling me. I had had too much experience with that false calm men got in their voices right before they killed someone.

I shook my head. "Thanks, but it has been handled already."

"As you wish." And he left it at that, which was a welcome relief.

We crossed the town, moving away from the houses and into the industrial area where most of our manufacturing took place. Anything we couldn't produce was delivered through our networks in the human world. Scattered worldwide were human liaisons who knew about these prison towns. They were pivotal to our being able to exist within a society but not be discovered. We called them the Guild Guides or "Guilds," and it was a family business. They served us for their entire lives and passed the information down to their children; for most it was considered an honor to work for us. Plus, we paid them a crap ton, and mostly they did very little. But it was through them we laundered our money to be used in the human world, procured identification if we had to venture out, and acquired safe housing. Not to mention their valuable knowledge of how to blend. They were becoming more and more important in the age of computers. Humans had a sneaky way of keeping track of everything nowadays.

It was obvious that Louis was not someone who felt the need to fill silence. He just held my hand and walked. Which was driving me a little crazy. I wanted to ask questions, but everything seemed so personal.

As if he'd read my mind, he started talking. "You were so tiny the first time I saw you. Jonathon contacted me; he was frantic. I'd been very good friends with your grandparents before they left for Spain, and I think your dad knew I was the only one who could help him."

I wanted him to continue with this story, so I kept my mouth closed with my many questions.

"I had to touch you to place the protection over your mark, to make sure its energy could not be detected." Using his free hand he rubbed at his chin. "I touched you first, before Mischa, and the power you contained was unlike anything I'd experienced before." Our eyes locked. "For the first time I started to believe some of the stories, that the marked had a strength that would unite across continents and the supernaturals would fall again. I thought I should kill you."

He said it so casually, and I shivered as I scented truth. This man had almost ended my life twenty-two years ago.

"But then you looked at me, your eyes so large and blue, crystal clear with the innocence only a young babe can have." His arm fell to his side again. "I stayed my hand. I let you both live and convinced Jonathon to send Lienda and Mischa away. Together, the marks' energy pulsed off each other. You were stronger around your sister, and I couldn't risk that the hunters would find you. I needed to know you would stay safe."

I was hanging on to every word. Fear and fascination flooded me simultaneously. "Is it safe to be speaking of this here?" My eyes darted around. I could sense no one near, but plenty were strong enough to hide from my senses.

A smile started slowly on his lips, before spreading broadly across his entire face. "Damn, you keep my ego in check without even trying."

I had no idea what he was talking about.

"Our words are disguised. If anyone were listening in, it would sound as if we were discussing the weather. No one hears my words unless I want them to."

I snorted out my laughter. "Right, I forgot you're the big bad sorcerer."

"And there you go again."

We were still walking, past the industrial area and into the forest behind. It was not a place I'd ever ventured into. Which was weird because we had searched all over the forest for the prison.

"Doesn't seem to have affected your confidence too much, so I'm not doing my best job," I said distractedly. "Wait, what is this place? Why have I never seen this part of the forest?"

We were moving closer to a spectacular waterfall, surrounded on all sides by row after row of lush flowers. The scents were washing through me; I had to close my eyes and stop for a moment—tantalizingly sweet and spicy with hints of floral. Finally, I looked up and found a pair of purple eyes regarding me. His expression was guarded. He no longer held my hand, so I tucked them into my back pockets and waited.

"I like my privacy." His low words seemed to drift along the breeze, and there was sadness layering them.

This was getting a little intense for me. I didn't do serious relationships for this very reason. Subject change required immediately.

"Food," I blurted out.

His grin wiped clear some of the sadness, and the heavy emotional tone lightened.

"Well, let's get you some food, then. I've heard stories of what happens if you get too hungry."

I rubbed the bridge of my nose. "Don't believe everything the Compasses say."

"These stories were from your father," he said with a laugh.

Great. Everyone was a comedian. Oh well, I might as well own it; the truth doesn't change, no matter how much I pretend different.

Louis's home was hidden in an alcove behind the spectacular waterfall. It was single level, simple and spacious. He didn't need much, and it showed. Still, there was a feeling of quality and warmth in the dark-gray walls—comfortable furniture and a roaring fireplace. I sat at an island bench in the kitchen while he moved around, gathering, chopping, and cooking. For all of my love of food, I had no clue how to cook. His confidence in the kitchen was eye candy.

He placed a large glass in front of me. It seemed to be filled with something that looked like wine. I was feeling a little overwhelmed, so I didn't question. I clutched the cold vessel and took a huge gulp. It was sweet and bubbly, tickling my throat as it descended. Warmth followed its path. Maybe it was a little stronger than wine.

"Go easy on that. It's fey and can be a shock if you haven't had it before," Louis said before turning back to whatever was sizzling on the stove.

I was surprised. The fey had many amazing things, but most were lost to their dying world. I wondered how the sorcerer had gotten his hands on the drink. It was delicious, though. I took another smaller sip, swirling the flavors on my tongue. Tart but sweet with a strong hint of mint, berry, and . . . something like a spicy herb.

"Why have you waited so long to ask me on a date?" Okay, seemed as if the drink had already loosened my tongue.

"You're young, still far too young for me, but I took the opportunity presented and decided to at least make your acquaintance."

He spoke in an old-fashioned manner, which was not a surprise, considering his age. He continued speaking and also managed to cook, wipe the bench down, and refill my glass. *Wait, when did I finish that?*

"I know you don't do serious relationships, which suits me perfectly fine, and I'd like to have you as a friend."

I twisted the glass in my hands, the sweating condensation on the outside coating my fingers.

"I'd like to be friends also. I'm not exactly sure what I can offer you, besides my scintillating wit and ability to eat the same amount as two grown men. But . . . I've seen stranger friendships."

"You have plenty to offer," he said as he started to dish up. It looked like a stir-fry with thick noodles. The smells were delicious. My stomach started to grumble as the scents of garlic, lime, and chili hit me.

We moved into the dining area, which was a low-slung wooden table with six chairs around it. I hadn't realized, but it was already set, and there was more wine and crusty bread in the center. I placed my glass down, and Louis set the large dish in front of me. It was definitely a chicken stir-fry, mixed with a colorful array of vegetables. I was almost tempted to start without him. He grinned as he left to get his plate. Damn sorcerer was reading my mind.

To distract myself from the food, I drank some more wine, which I really needed to stop doing. The room was starting to get slightly hazy. Usually I could handle my alcohol with no problems—not that I drank a lot, but my fast metabolism burned off any excess. However, this fey wine was potent. Louis was back within moments.

His laughter rang out as he sat across from me.

"What?" I said. Yeah, okay, I might have been sitting there with my fork in my hand, staring at the plate.

"Looks like you're waiting for me to say, 'Ready, steady, eat.'"

Wait, what? Yeah, okay, maybe I was a little.

He waved a hand at me. "Dig in, don't stress manners for me. I usually eat on my own and have no one to impress."

He forked the first lot into his mouth, and with a sigh I stabbed a piece of meat and lifted it. As my lips closed around the fork, I sighed again. The flavors burst across my tongue, and for a moment I might have died and gone to heaven.

"This is amazing, Louis. I'm impressed that you took the time to cook for me," I said around bites. It was taking all of my coordination to stuff my face, breathe, and talk. But I nailed it.

"You're welcome. It has been fun."

I could see he didn't have a lot of that in his life.

"Aren't you lonely out here, isolated all the time? Why don't you move into town?" More tactless questions.

He examined his plate for a few moments, and I wondered if he was going to ignore my questions, but he didn't.

"When you live for a long time, well, there's plenty of tragedy to live through. I made a decision many years ago that I was done with the constant pain, and to prevent any more heartache, I removed myself from the world, stopped caring so much." His voice lowered. "Problem being that to have no love in my world only demonstrated to me how little I was actually living. The pain was gone, but so were the joys."

I swallowed. "Sort of like without the lows, you can't appreciate the highs." I had so much happiness and love in my life, and, in part, it was thanks to Louis. If he hadn't spelled my marks . . .

I spied his face. There was something that had to be said. "I need to thank you. I've had a wonderful life, and I might have been stuck in the prison if my marks had been discovered as a baby." I was pretty impressed with my ability to multitask. I got to express my gratitude and at the same time lay the groundwork to investigate his possible involvement in the Compasses' imprisonment.

He blinked at me a few times. "What makes you think the dragon marked are in the supernatural prison system? Jonathon was sure that you both would be killed."

I shrugged. "The Compasses said that the prison is rife with rumors of breakouts of dragon marked, and that there are some in Vanguard. Brax even met a little boy in there named Nash. He's trying to find the prison again to free him."

My words were kind of muddled and slurring. The wine was going straight to my head, and the food was not helping to get me sober.

"Did you know there were marked in Vanguard?" Ah, crap, did I just say that out loud? "I should stop drinking," I muttered as I stared at my empty glass. *Empty again?* "Hey, who drank my drink?" I was sure I'd had a quarter left.

Louis reached across the table and captured my hands in his.

"Calm down, no one drank your drink. Well, actually, you drank it all not one minute ago." His even voice did help my frazzled nerves and drunk ass. "I had no idea about the marked. I believed, as do most of Stratford, that the marked are killed." He freed his right hand and pushed back blond hair that had fallen across his forehead. "I don't understand how this has been kept a secret."

I didn't understand either. Clearly, council members were not aware. Dad would definitely have told me. Was it just up to the hunters if they killed or captured? Was there another secret council that was higher ranked to make these decisions? I just had so many questions. But for right now there was a more pressing issue. I needed to use the restroom. I pushed back my chair and stood. The room spun, and I reached out and gripped the side of the table.

"Are you okay?" Louis was around by my side in seconds, his arms lifting me and helping me stand.

"Yeah, just drunk," I said. The room was still spinning, and I needed air and to go home before I made a fool of myself. "I need Braxton. Can you get him to carry me home?"

Louis's face hardened then. His purple eyes turned stormy and gray. "I can take you."

I shook my head. "No, I don't want you to see me like this. You were so nice making me dinner and . . . I might spew on your shoes."

He rubbed his eyes and was definitely hiding a grin. "I don't like that you're running straight to the Compasses, but I get it. You don't do intense, and, frankly, I'm not ready for that either." He whipped out his phone and hit a few buttons. Wow, all-powerful sorcerer knew how to text. "This was a nice start," I heard him murmur.

"Do you want my number?" I asked. "You can text me whenever you're lonely. I, like, never have my phone, but I'll check it once a day and reply."

I didn't want him to feel alone anymore.

He kissed my cheek. "I already have your number, and when you get home, mine will be in your contacts."

There was a knock on the door then. "Okay, two things," I said as Louis led me through the house and helped me get my coat back on. "How did Braxton find you here, and how the hell did he get here so fast?" My feet felt funny. I tripped and would have landed face-first if strong arms didn't surround me.

I was lifted, and then I could feel the cool breeze as the door opened.

"You were waiting for her?" Louis said to whoever was on the other side. My eyelids had decided they needed a little rest, so I couldn't see who it was.

"She's my Jessa, and I know nothing of you, sorcerer." Braxton's voice washed over me, and with it came a sense of comfort. "What did you do to her?"

"Stupid faerie wine," I slurred. "Those little shits must have cast-iron stomachs—oh wait, they're allergic to iron." I started laughing. That was hilarious.

"How long has she been like this?" Braxton asked.

Louis chuckled, his chest moving under me. "Long enough to be cute and entertaining. But I don't want her to be sick; she needs fluids and rest. Next time I'll shelve the fey wine for something less potent."

Braxton growled. "You're pretty damn confident to think there will be a next time."

"Be nice," I said, or slurred.

Cold surrounded me as Louis lifted me away from his body, and then I was in the strong, familiar arms of my best friend. His massive chest cradled me, and heat flashed along all parts of my body touching him. I opened my eyes to meet his amused expression.

"You're so hot," I said, patting his shoulder.

"Holy damn, I need to keep her away from the others," Braxton laughed. "They've never seen Jessa drunk. They might be tempted to take advantage of this."

Louis's words were short. "Yes, as I said, very cute." He reached out and grazed my cheek. "Stay safe and I'll text you. Thank you for tonight."

"I'm sorry," I said. A few tears sprinkled my eyes. "I wasn't a very good date and you cooked and everything was so perfect." My babbling trailed off as more tears slipped down my cheeks.

I buried my face in Braxton's chest. "I'm a mess."

"I'm taking her home now," Braxton said, and he started moving before I could thank Louis again. "I've got my eye on you, sorcerer," I heard him murmur.

We crossed out of the secret waterfall alcove and back through the industrial area.

Braxton sounded amused as he strode without effort. "Louis said you requested I carry you home."

"Yeah, it's a pretty long way, and I'd be too heavy for anyone else." I wiggled against his rock-hard body. "Wait, am I too heavy for you?"

He tightened his hold on me. "No, Jess, you're perfect."

I studied the flawlessness of his face. Maybe it was the alcohol, but he looked different tonight. He wasn't clean-shaven, like usual, which seemed to increase the bad-boy façade he wore so effortlessly.

"Why were you so close to Louis's place?" I asked, as he looked down and caught my eye.

He examined me; I could tell he was carefully considering his next words. "Louis is very powerful. There's nothing I could say to make him fear me, and, therefore, I couldn't be sure he didn't mean you harm on this date."

"You were protecting me?" My voice was low. Emotions started bubbling up inside of me, overwhelming emotions.

"Always," he said.

My heart was racing in pitter-pattering beats. I'd never heard Braxton use a tone like that, but before I could think too much on it, his smooth movements sent me off into la-la land.

Chapter 10

"Jessa!"

A shrill voice penetrated the haze in my head . . . my pounding, aching, heavy head. I was not opening my eyes yet; I just knew that would end up with me barfing everywhere. Instead, I attempted to moisten my dry mouth.

"Water," I croaked.

The annoying presence left, and then my nose caught up and I realized it was Mischa.

"Here," she said upon returning. I felt cool condensation coat my hand as I wrapped my fingers around the smooth glass.

"Thank you." I lifted it up. I still couldn't move my head or open my eyes, so I tipped back, aiming for my mouth.

"Argh!" I shrieked as I poured the entire glass onto my face. I spluttered a little, trying not to drown.

I heard the distinct huskiness of Maximus's voice: "Damn." Then strong arms were lifting me, water droplets flying everywhere.

I pried open one eye, and through the pain and light haze, I noticed the room was filled with my grinning pack.

"What the freaking hell are you all doing here?" I slurred. If Maximus hadn't been lifting me, I'd have fallen down.

"I figured out how to shift!" I winced at how enthusiastic Mischa was, her voice rising to a pitch that should have been outlawed in my presence. "And you'll be relieved to know I'm wolf, not dragon."

She had no idea how relieved I actually was to hear that.

"And we think we have found the entrance to the prison," Jacob said, distracting my muddled thoughts. I was thankful that he kept his voice low.

Damn, I had to pull myself together. "Bloody sorcerer and fey wine. Curse them both to hell," I said as I started to struggle in Maximus's arms. "Let me down. I need to shower."

He sounded amused. "I'm not sure that's a great idea." Asshole.

I kicked out, connecting with his side. With a groan, he gently dropped me down to my feet. I still had only one eye opened, but I was in the Compasses' house, and I could have found the bathroom with my eyes closed. I took a single step, and then suddenly the ground was moving closer to me. Weird. My face was about two inches from becoming very acquainted with the carpet when I was scooped up again. Different arms this time—Braxton had me.

"I'll deal with Jessa; you all get everything ready and make sure you okay Mischa joining us with her parents." He shifted me higher. "I don't need to deal with a pissed-off Jonathon."

"Hey!" Mischa's screeching started again, and if I could have moved, I'd have punched her right in the mouth. "I don't need permission, I'm an adult."

Tyson spoke this time. "No, you're not. Technically, anyway. We don't graduate until we are twenty-five, and my calculations have you at twenty."

I remembered they didn't know we were twins, thinking Mischa was even younger than the rest of us. I managed to get both eyes partly open, and they clashed with twin beams of green fury. She was not a happy camper.

"Misch, just go and get permission. Dad knows the deal, and if you can demonstrate your ability to shift and control some aspect of your power, there is no reason he will deny you."

Almost all of my sentence was clear and legible. There was absolutely no need for everyone in the room to burst into laughter.

"Damn, this is almost as entertaining as she was last night. Don't forget to show her that video we took, Brax." Jacob ruffled my hair as he left the room. Everyone else followed suit, leaving just me and Braxton in the bedroom.

"Video?" I narrowed my already squinty eyes and glared up into Braxton's face. "He better be kidding."

"Relax, little wolf, he's kidding. I would never let them take advantage of you in a vulnerable position. I know the best-friend rules. We signed them in blood fifteen years ago."

Braxton and I had made a pact, and so far neither of us had broken any of the rules. Which had included no kissing between friends, no embarrassing videos to be taken, immediate assistance with hiding a dead body—no questions asked—and a few others that may or may not have included naked body parts.

"Right now I need to get you sobered up, hangover free, and able to help me find Nash." The air crackled from his intensity, and I could tell it was eating away at him not to have freed the boy yet. "I need you, Jessa."

If any words were going to act as a shot of adrenalin, it was those. Generally, Braxton was the one giving help, and he never asked for anything. He was too tough to rely on anyone other than himself.

"Shower," I said, patting his arm.

He carried me into the room and hit the lever, turning it all the way to Hard and Cold. I was about to protest when he dumped me straight in, clothes and all. My shaky limbs collapsed under me as the icy water washed away the last of my haze.

"You're an asshat," I groaned, hugging my legs.

He just laughed before reaching above me and shifting the lever to allow warmth to enter the stream.

"Will you be okay while I grab some food, clothes, and herbs?"

I nodded. "Yes, I think I can manage not to drown in the shower."

I wanted to close my eyes—anything to halt the ache pounding away in my skull, but I forced myself to stay awake, shaking out my limbs and kicking my metabolism into gear so it could wipe the last of the fey wine from my system. I managed to stand after ten minutes and stripped off my soaking clothes. I brushed my teeth twice, then succeeded in washing myself, and my hair. The door opened just as I was rinsing the last of the soap from me.

"Everything is sitting on the sink," Braxton said. "Call for me if you think you're going to fall." He closed the door again.

I shut off the water, opened the glass door, and stepped out to grab the towel. Thankfully, my legs barely shook. I wrapped the massive length around myself twice before walking across to the wooden bench. Everything was piled neatly. First thing, I lifted the murky glass of green. Human-made pharmaceuticals do not mix well with supernaturals, but we had plenty of herbal concoctions that helped nature heal our bodies. I downed the liquid and the relief was almost instantaneous. The pounding halted, and the daggers that had been stabbing into the corners of my eyes abated. Feeling much more normal, I pulled on underwear and then my usual form-fitting jeans and a long-sleeved thermal top.

Meanwhile, I was munching on the thick sandwich—bread, large slabs of rare beef, with relish and cheese filling. I groaned as the deliciousness coated my tongue.

"Come on, Jessa, you can finish your sandwich while we get moving."

I had to chuckle. Groaning sounds from the bathroom, well, anyone else would be thinking I was *really* enjoying myself in here, but Braxton knew me too well. Food, how I love thee.

Before leaving, I pulled my long hair back into a ponytail. The mirror was not my friend at this point. I avoided looking too long at my pale, strained features.

"I'm killing that fucking sorcerer," I muttered as I wrenched open the door and left the room, half of the sandwich clenched tightly in my hand. As if I'd summoned him with my angry words, there was a knock on the door and Louis entered the room.

"Not my worst welcome," he said. His white smile hurt my eyes. He was so goddamn cheery, which was making me feel a little more murderous.

"What do you want?" I snarled. I was not my best in the morning, and hungover made it a lot worse.

His grin did not waver. "I thought you might need a bit of relief this morning," he said.

Braxton was on his feet, and between the sorcerer and me, faster than I could blink.

"I'm hoping you mean of the magical-hangover-cure variety," I said, moving around the mound of muscled dragon shifter. "Because my sense of humor seems to have temporarily fled the building."

And so apparently had Braxton's.

Louis showed not one ounce of concern. "Relax, guard lizard. I know the strength of the fey wine. I should have realized Jessa would not be accustomed to it. I don't like that due to my oversight, she suffers this morning."

Stepping closer to me, he lifted both hands to hover on either side of my head. "May I?" His eyes bore into mine. I swallowed loudly before nodding.

He cradled my head. I closed my eyes to escape the probing intensity of his gaze. An immediate warmth flooded me, hot enough to be unnatural but not quite burning. This warmth washed away any lingering effect of the wine, and I felt myself again. In fact, as he finished and removed his hands, I realized I felt fantastic. My eyelids lifted, and there was no more pain or stabbing. I threw my arms around him.

"Thank you. That was like coffee, only a million times better."

His expression was unreadable when I pulled back. "You're welcome, Jessa. I'll see you around." He left just as silently as he'd arrived.

I schooled my features as I faced the grim Braxton. "Let's go find the others," I managed to murmur as I shoved the rest of the sandwich into my mouth.

Braxton examined me, his face kind of blank, but his eyes were alive. Then he exhaled in a visible motion and strode out the door. I followed along, having no idea what was pissing him off. We walked in silence through the quiet, cool morning forest. It was tranquil, and yet at the same time a plethora of noises flooded through the shrubbery. Braxton was marching along, his face still sort of expressionless, but . . . that light in his eyes: that happened when he was seriously contemplating something.

I broke the quiet. I never could stand that uncomfortable silence between friends. "You worried? About Nash?"

His head flicked around, and the slight widening of his eyes surprised me. My question seemed to have jolted him into remembering Nash. He clearly had not been thinking of the little boy. And just like that, he was back on point and focused on the mission.

His pace increased. "Come on, Jess. Let's move it."

I had to jog to keep up with him. We found the rest of our group in a small clearing at the western end of the forest. Mischa was there, so I guessed Jonathon had caved. Braxton, Mischa, and I were dressed in simple, warm, and easy-to-shed clothes. The other Compasses were in army-style fatigues, formfitted so as not to catch on anything, and in dark colors to blend in.

Jacob grinned at me. "Nice. You look like my Jessa again, and not like moldy old ass." The fey's white-blond hair was glistening in the slivers of sunlight penetrating the gloom.

I flipped him off as a reply.

"Harsh, man," Tyson piped up. "It was more like drunken-chicken ass."

I refrained from kicking him in the ribs, which is what I wanted to do. "Ha-ha-*hardy har*. You're all freakin' comedians. Let's get this show on the road."

Braxton pulled us in close. "We have one shot to do this; the entrance moves in twelve hours. I don't want any heroes. Follow my lead. I'm in command here."

He pointed a finger at Tyson. "For once you're just going to have to suck it up and listen to someone else."

The wizard middle-finger-saluted him in reply, but I knew in the end, he'd have his brother's back. Maximus stepped up to Braxton's side. As always, those two were extraclose. They had the same sort of badass personality—you knew if they wanted to, they could destroy you. Not that Jacob and Tyson weren't badasses, they were. It was just that they joked around more, so you thought they were more easygoing. It was a great cloaking ability they'd developed. Braxton and Maximus had no cloak. What you saw was what you got.

"Mischa, stay close to me or Jessa," I heard Maximus whisper. "If things get out of control, I expect you to bail. Don't you worry about the rest of us; save your own ass." With a sigh, he flicked his head in my direction. "I won't even bother to give you the same orders, Jess. I know you won't listen."

I shrugged. Damn right I wouldn't listen. I'd never bail on the Compasses. Never. Death would take me first.

Braxton encased me in strong, warm arms. It was a brief hug but . . . unexpected.

"What was that for?" I asked as he pulled back. I blinked a few times, trying to get my heartbeat under control again.

"Because you're . . . damned amazing. And my life is better with you in it," he said. "But if you sacrifice yourself for any of us, I'll be pissed off, and you don't want to see me pissed off."

I snorted. "I've seen you pissed off more times than I've seen myself naked."

He blinked a few times, those beautiful blue eyes glinting as he stepped closer. "Nope, you've only seen me . . . annoyed. I repeat. You don't want to see me pissed off."

What the hell was he talking about?

"I've seen it once, and it was not something I'd forget in a hurry," Maximus said.

I looked at all four of them, unsure whether they were kidding. Was there actually something scarier than Braxton's dragon? Since no more information was forthcoming, I guessed only time would tell.

Braxton started to move then, and I recognized that expression: he was focused; nothing would blow him off his current path. In so many ways he was as unmovable as his dragon. The personality of our animal definitely bled into the human, and in turn, we tamed the beast inside. It was a beautiful symbiotic relationship. I always felt as if one could not survive without the other. I certainly would not want to exist without my wolf.

We continued through the forest. It was colder today, but no snow. I would guess we were due for another storm very soon. Even with my shifter metabolism at peak, I still had chills racking my arms and legs. It was dark under the canopy. Keen eyesight took care of that; I simply let my wolf out a little and she lent me her senses. From our many years of roaming this massive landscape, I had a pretty good idea where we were heading—toward the back left pocket, where the largest of the old redwoods were.

Mischa was close to my right side. I reached out and grabbed her hand, our frozen fingers tangled together. She looked scared, but managed a smile. No one spoke, knowing on instinct to stay quiet. The boys surrounded us like the four points on a compass. Pun intended. I knew when we had reached the spot. Braxton's back was one mass of rigid muscle as he held a silent hand aloft to halt our progress. I flicked my eyes left and right trying to determine what he had noticed. But nothing looked amiss. We stood at the junction of two large trees; their trunks had grown into each other, swirling around and around in a crazy manner. Branches, leaves, and twigs intertwined. There was no order to their growth and structure, only chaos. There was a small gap at the base of the trunks. Was that the entrance?

Jacob stepped out of our formation and placed both hands on the closest and largest tree trunk. His blond hair was barely visible in the low light, but I could sense his fey energy working. The very forest around us responded. The fey were earthy like that. Jacob spun his head back and gave us one sharp nod. Braxton and Tyson strode forward, and before I could order my feet to follow, the two of them dropped down to their knees, like bookends, heads bowed in submission.

Okay, so I would be a liar if I didn't admit to one or two fantasies of mine that had started just like this, but come on, guys, it really wasn't the time for role play.

Just as I stemmed my inappropriate thoughts, I noticed the swirls of energy they were releasing between the two of them. Tyson was working some magic, and Braxton was helping. It started to form something dark, a misty hole, and as they raised their heads and hands upward, I could clearly see a large hole had shaped between them. It was weird, shadowy, and shifting as I tried to focus on it. I heard Mischa's sharp intake of breath and barely stifled my own gasp as the two of them plunged forward and entered the misty door headfirst. They disappeared.

Jacob and Maximus came in behind us, and staying at our backs, they ushered Mischa and me toward the space. I so didn't want to enter that door, but I would die before admitting to being a coward. My wolf rose to the surface, allowing me to share her courage and strength.

Mischa's soft voice broke the silence. "I can feel my wolf." She sounded strangled. "She wants to be free."

I reached out and grabbed her hand. "No, she's reacting to your fear. Trying to help you. When you are more experienced, you'll be able to bring her close but not shift, sort of existing in an in-between state. But right now is not the time."

Thankfully, she was distracted by Jacob's nudging us into the portal. Just as the boys had done, we entered headfirst. I dropped in a slow motion sort of twirl. I knew magic was at work here; I could scent a high-level magic user all over this. I landed smoothly, in a crouch position, almost as if I'd been guided the entire way down. I stood, relieved to see Mischa next to me. Her wide green eyes were just visible in the very low light. We were underground in a dirt-lined cave entrance, small lichen mosses up high on the walls giving off a soft, ambient glow. Shadows moved toward us, but I was glad to see that it was only Braxton and Tyson. Jacob and Maximus appeared behind us, and we were all ready to go.

Braxton took the lead and started to step cautiously through the tunnel. My eyes were darting left and right as I followed along, but so far there was nothing but dirt and rock surrounding us. We were moving toward a light or an area that was brighter; it shone as we stepped closer. Finally, as we moved from that small dark tunnel and hovered near the edge of the light, I raised my hands to cover the series of gasps and curses that wanted to fall from my mouth.

The space before us was massive. From what I could see, the underground area was almost the size of Stratford. Beyond the cleared space stood an immense circumference of spotlights, suspended on tall poles. The bulbs shifted around on a rotation, keeping the area well lit. The prison walls towered into the sky. I had no idea how high the ceiling was—I couldn't see any end from where I stood. The prison looked a little like the human-made ones I'd seen on television: solid gray walls, styled like stone, but I could sense the other elements weaved into the structure. Iron, which was a weakness for many; salt, for its purity; varying bloods, which were strong enough to spell for protection and strength; not to mention the standard silver, copper, and gold— elements of vulnerability for all five of the supernatural groups.

Which made sense considering who they were containing. But how were we going to traverse this area without being affected by these built-in defenses?

Braxton answered me by stepping forward and slipping a leather chain over my head. It had a turquoise stone, around the size of a quarter, tied on to the base. As it touched my skin—resting between my breasts—I felt a sort of buzz.

He leaned down and murmured in my ear: "The stone is spelled to shield us against the protections of the prison." I noticed Maximus place the same thing over Mischa's head. And all the boys had one, too.

I raised my eyebrows at him. "Where did you get these necklaces?" I whispered back.

"The guard."

I silently snorted. I should have figured that.

Jacob was close enough to add to our very low conversation. "We skillfully persuaded him."

Most likely scenario: they beat him until he promised the stones. Typical Compass persuasion.

There were lots of different supernaturals milling around the outer zone of the prison. Some were in dark-gray uniforms, carrying what looked like weapons, so I was going with guards. Others were more official, their uniform black, with decorative stars and decals lining the shoulders and lapel area. Managers or specialists.

"I don't suppose you have uniforms for us to blend in," Mischa asked.

Maximus shook his head. "No, but we know that there's a guard shift change very shortly. They all meet around the front for a brief rundown. They seem to be more relaxed on the outside than the guards inside. Most of the time, they expect prisoners to break out."

I was reminded of the breakouts that had been happening around the world, the dragon marked. This was probably the worst time to attempt a prison break. Surely security was going to be beefed up. Not that I could see anything specific. Maybe there was stronger magic at work or something, aspects of which I could not detect with the naked eye.

"On my signal," Braxton breathed. All of us lowered ourselves and prepared to move.

His flat palm came up, which meant wait. He held it there for about thirty seconds, and as we watched, the various prison workers started to move like clockwork, converging on a central point right at the main entrance of the huge structure. As soon as they were focused on their meeting, Braxton's hand straightened and pointed to the right. Time to move. We hugged the rock wall of the cave surrounding the prison as we slunk along, low to the ground and still out of the spotlights. As we headed around the left side of the building, there was no cover anywhere; we would have to expose ourselves long enough to make it to the prison wall.

My heartbeat was reasonably steady, but I could feel a fine line of sweat forming on my brow. I was nervous, although hiding it reasonably well, I thought. I wasn't sure what would happen if we were caught. I guessed my father would be brought in, and there would definitely be a punishment. Who knows? Maybe they'd just shoot us on the spot; they were pretty protective of their secrets. Braxton paused for two heartbeats at the edge of the darkness, waiting for something I couldn't see. Then when he moved, he was swift, like a shadow, as he dashed across to the side of the wall. We were right behind him. The entire time I held my breath, waiting for the call of detection, but there was nothing.

We plastered ourselves to the side of the massive stone wall. The true size of this prison was becoming apparent. It was freaking huge. And despite the amulet I wore, I could feel my wolf reacting to the silver, iron, and other elements in the walls. It didn't burn me, as it normally would, but it was uncomfortable, like the sensation of my skin cells attacking one another. I shivered. I did not like it. I heard a stifled sob from Mischa and knew she was struggling harder than the rest of us, but thankfully, after that first hitch of breath, there was no more. She was a Lebron. We were tough, and she'd already pulled herself together.

We moved swiftly along the lines of the wall, but came to a sudden halt about halfway along. I forced my breathing to a shallower pace, silencing even the smallest noise, as my eyes flicked left and right. Were we made? I couldn't see anything, so what was Brax—

My thoughts were cut off as all four of the Compasses leaned down again and, just like in the forest, were performing an incantation.

"This is the weakness. See how all the lines join and form this gap?" Braxton's voice was almost too low to hear, but I was pretty close to them. I could see what he was talking about. It was as if joins from all the stone pieces on this side of the wall converged into one central point.

This point looked a lot like a mini-inlet, and I remembered Braxton saying it was something to do with the water or sewage release. But it was far too tiny for any of us to fit through; the Compasses especially did not have a shot in hell. I had no idea what they thought was going to happen, but I trusted them enough to wait patiently. I scanned the zone so as not to miss the guards' return. For the moment, this side was still minus any uniformed security.

Maximus reached out a hand and took Mischa's arm. "The magical protections are weakened here to allow for the tunnels below. We're going to create an entrance. Ty and Jake have been working on this since we got out." His tone was soothing, probably to stop Mischa from running out in a screaming mess. She looked like she was about to lose her shit.

"Let's hope it works," I heard Tyson mutter.

Braxton was stone-faced. I couldn't tell if he was worried; he was the master at concealing his emotions. While the women of Stratford loved Braxton, they also feared him. Men, too. The hard-ass was the main side that he showed the world, but I knew him well enough to call him on his bullshit, so he tended to keep it to a minimum around me.

The boys stood, and all I could see was the same stone and small drain space. Had it not worked?

Jacob grinned. "Time to head inside," he said as he shoved Tyson straight in. "Good of you to volunteer, Ty," he murmured as the wizard disappeared into the prison wall.

Okay, so there was definitely an entrance. I grinned. Jacob was a dead man when Tyson got his hands on him. One by one we entered. I was second to last, Braxton coming in behind me. With a deep breath—you have no idea how hard it was to throw myself into what looked like solid stone—I ducked my head and closed my eyes . . . before diving forward.

Chapter 11

The smell was almost unbearable. My nose was twitching as I fought against the urge to throw up or growl. The six of us stood silent, waiting to see if our entrance had been detected. It was really dark under here, hard to see our surroundings even with help from my wolf. The sewage area we were in was small and narrow. The boys had to crouch to keep from hitting their heads. Maximus had said that this was just an offshoot, not the main thoroughfare.

Before we'd started this mission, the Compasses had explained the general layout of the prison. There was a large circular room in the center, which acted as a mingling zone. Every day for a few hours, the five different supernatural races were allowed out to have shared lunch, to interact, and to exercise. Spanning off this area were five thin tendril-like zones. They formed the prison cells for each group. There was no mingling between different races in the cells; this was strictly enforced—vampires were only with vamps, and so on. There were very specific protections on these areas. They catered to the weaknesses of each supernatural race. If I had to guess, judging by the wolfsbane, silver, and blood-sacrifice power that I could see threaded through the stone structures above our heads, the spot we had entered seemed to be underneath the shifter zone.

After a few minutes of silence, everyone let out the breath they'd been holding. We seemed to be in the clear. Well, no one had followed us through the wall, which indicated we had not been seen.

Braxton started to creep his way along the tunnel, bent almost in half to fit. "Follow me," he said. It took about ten minutes for us to emerge into what I would say looked like the central sewage line. Braxton stayed in the lead, giving us a quick rundown: "Nash told me how to find the area he slept in. It's in between the shifter and vampire sections of the prison. These are the sewage systems he uses to get around."

"So this area is not really accessible from the main prison?" Mischa asked.

Braxton nodded. "I don't think so. I did a reasonable amount of exploring but never could quite figure out how to get into this eastern section of Vanguard. Nash sort of clued me in on how to do it."

We started walking again, sticking close to the wall. On the other side of us was a semicircle dip in the stone that contained whatever disgusting muck ran through a sewage system, and I was very grateful not only to be wearing shoes but also to not have to go into that shit.

After about ten minutes, Braxton stopped. "We'll go up here." He reached out and rested his hand on a metal ladder that hugged the rock walls. I hadn't even noticed it until right then. "Let me go first and make sure the area is clear."

Just like that he was gone, scaling the heights in seconds. The others stood around chatting, but I stayed right near the bottom rung, staring up, waiting for him to return. I was about eight seconds from saying "Screw this" and following his path, when his voice echoed down to us.

"All clear."

I was four rungs up when Maximus plucked me off the ladder and set me back on my feet.

"I'll go first, just in case it's a trap."

I managed not to roll my eyes. I knew they protected because they loved, but still . . . give the Superman shit a rest, boys. It must be itchy under all that spandex.

I ended up following Maximus, Mischa right behind me, and the other two bringing up the rear. It was a lot higher than it had looked from the ground, and unlike Braxton, it took me quite a few minutes to make it to the ceiling. There was a small dark opening; I slithered up through the gap into the next space. The room was narrow with no natural light at all, just a few wizard stones embedded high in the wall. They cast the blue tones of fake illumination, and I hated trying to see into it. It messed with my eyes.

We had to walk single file. The Compasses were almost brushing the walls with their broad shoulders. Braxton and Maximus, in front of me, had the tunnel pretty thoroughly blocked, and I hated that I couldn't see anything. But I wasn't afraid, despite the dark and eeriness of our surroundings. No one spoke, and I took this as a sign to keep my mouth shut. Although, as we continued our trek, I was starting to wish I'd asked for more information before we got in here. Like, how big was this freaking prison?

I was just about at the end of my limited patience when Maximus came to a halt. Of course I ran straight into his back, and Mischa smashed into me. Which did not move him even one inch.

I heard the grating of what sounded like a rusty door, and we were moving again, pivoting to the left and through a metal opening. The rusty door was apparent now, shoved back against the wall, showing signs of pockmarking and corrosion. At last we entered a larger room. The quads spread out to the side and I could finally see around their broad shoulders.

My heart stopped beating. Or the world stood still.

Holy fucking hell!

Instead of the one small boy I'd expected, there were so many faces turned toward us . . . so many faces. Both young and old. My breath caught in my throat as I frantically scanned from one side of the room to the other.

They were all dirty as they crouched low to the floor. I swallowed loudly, my hand lifting to press against my rapidly beating heart. I was still trying desperately to take in the entire room. How was this possible? There were children of all ages . . . even a few infants mixed in with the adults. In the semidarkness I noticed the large cuffs that secured them to bolts embedded in the floor.

I was suddenly angry enough to scream. I didn't care what these supernaturals had done, this was the cruelest form of punishment I could ever imagine. My demon snarled at me, along with the wolf, both of them straining to break free of the restrictions I had placed on them, both of them wanting blood for this.

Maximus sounded as pissed off as I felt. "What the fuck is this, Braxton? You said there was one boy. There are . . . at least fifty here."

Braxton's already rigid features tightened. "I never came into this room," he bit out. "Nash just gave me directions to the place he slept; otherwise, we only interacted when he found me."

Mischa's low voice sounded close to my ear. "Do you think they're dragon marked?"

I couldn't answer; I was trying not to cry. There were babies here. I wasn't the biggest fan of rug rats with their whining and sticky fingers, but this was torture.

"Braxie." A tiny voice echoed through the room, and a boy moved toward us. He appeared to be the only one not shackled down. "You came back."

As he moved closer, I noted the ragged, shoulder-length brown hair; pale, unhealthy skin that should be olive in tone but was sickly white; and huge brown eyes that dominated his face.

"Why did he not just escape himself?" I had to ask, unable to tear my eyes from him. He'd obviously known there was a way out. He'd directed Braxton on how to get in here.

Braxton had something feral moving behind his eyes. His voice came out harshly. "Firstly, he couldn't have fit through the exit point without the help of magic, and he has none. And he was afraid. This place is all he has ever known." He strode forward and swept the boy into his arms. "I promised you I'd return," he murmured to Nash.

"We can't leave the rest here," I said, managing to keep my voice at a low shriek. "We have to save them all."

The Compasses exchanged glances.

Jacob spoke first. "We can't, Jessa. For more than one reason. First, their chains look to be carved with runes, and I can feel the magic infused. We can't bust them out of those without the key or some serious power. And second, I think this many trying to escape would be noticed by the guards."

Maximus swept his arm around. "And we don't know what they're in here for. We might be freeing very dangerous criminals."

I exchanged a quick glance with Mischa. We knew what they were, and deep down the Compasses did, too. What Maximus was really saying was they wouldn't risk freeing the dragon marked.

Damn them. Babies . . . fuck that. I would die before I'd leave them here. But I knew the boys wouldn't let me stay or put myself in jeopardy. I'd have to be smart about it. My eyes were trained on two little girls, no more than three or four, clinging to each other, just managing to stretch their chains far enough to huddle together. They reeked of fear and desperation. And desolation . . . as if there wasn't one ounce of hope in them.

I suddenly swung my head around to the boy who was close to Braxton's side. "How did you get your chains off, Nash?"

He regarded me solemnly, with eyes too large and weary for a little boy. "I broke my thumb, and now it's always out of its socket. It fits through the shackles."

I flinched at the thought of his pain. Although, depending which supernatural race he was from, his pain might have been hidden by his other side. He waved his hand at me and the angle of his thumb was definitely off.

"Do they ever remove everyone else's shackles?" I managed to ask.

He nodded. "Once a day, guards take us to the bathroom."

That was my chance.

"Get that look off your face, Jessa." Maximus was all business, and he was standing too much in my personal space for my liking. "We cannot save them. There are lots of hard decisions in life. This is one of them. You have to accept that we have your best interests at heart."

I widened my eyes and blinked a few times at him, my impression of a brain-dead bimbo. I don't take orders from anyone, especially not a man who thinks he can demand my obedience simply because he was born with a penis and I was not. I mean, I'm not a complete moron; I can take advice and ask for help. But blindly following orders—that isn't me and is never going to be.

Braxton's deep tones jarred me from my crusade. "I will help you, Jess." His words eased some of my anger. He had a way about him, that man. "But for now we're not prepared to rescue this many people. We'll find the doorway again, and the next time we *will* save everyone."

Truth.

I stared up into the stunning blue of his eyes, a color that was one of my favorites in the world. I trusted his word. He meant what he was saying. But I could not sleep one more night knowing there were children suffering here. I could see by the set of Braxton's jaw that he was struggling with it also; that was the soft heart that had brought him back into the prison to save a little boy. But he was also very practical, his logical brain telling him that the odds of succeeding at this mission were slim. So he was going to find another way, at a later date.

I understood the logic; I simply chose to ignore it.

"Okay, Brax." I wasn't really lying. I did see his point. "Let's go, then."

Relief crossed all four of the Compasses' faces. If they weren't so caught up in the danger here and the need to get to safety, they would be questioning my compliance. But, stupid boys, they were happy to take my word at face value. The only one who even cast a suspicious glance in my direction was Mischa. It had to be because we were twins, or she was thinking the same thing as me, because she did not know me well enough to know my "tells" yet.

As we moved back toward the doorway, I forced myself to keep walking, closing my eyes so I couldn't see the desperate supernaturals we were leaving behind in the cells. I mentally promised them that I would be back very soon.

Braxton caught my arm just as I was about to step back into the narrow tunnel. "Don't pull any bullshit stunts, Jessa," he whispered.

Innocence poured off me in droves. I hadn't lied to him; he wouldn't have scented the mistruths I hid in my heart. But clearly he had paid closer attention to my actions than the others had. Damn Braxton, always so observant.

He kept a close eye on me, staying at the rear, although Nash was between us. The little boy wouldn't get very far from Braxton's side. It took us no time at all to make it down the ladder and through the sewage system.

"Okay, we're going to have to wait it out," Maximus said when we reached the spot that would expel us back out of the prison. "The next guard change is not for another ten hours."

Mischa leaned forward. "Won't that be cutting it awfully close to the twelve-hour time frame?"

Maximus pushed his hair back. "There's no time frame on exiting the underground area. But if we try to come back in again, the doorway will have shifted."

He leveled a gaze on me, warning in his dark eyes. I tried to cover up the emotions flooding through me. He had no idea the gift he'd just given me. If I could time it perfectly, I'd be able to "fall behind" or something equally lame, and, I hoped, by the time they noticed, it would be too late for them to get back through the doorway.

I was kind of nervous about being in here without their support and protection. But I reminded myself that this prison was legitimately run, the council was always here, and my father would not let me rot if I was captured. I owed it to those poor people, whether dragon marked or not, to at least attempt to free them.

The hours passed slowly. Nash fell asleep curled up next to Braxton. It was obvious he was very used to sleeping on a hard stone floor. He never shifted to get comfortable. The conditions those people lived in . . . if they weren't supernaturals, they would have most certainly died from the cold or disease.

Mischa used the time to chat with Maximus and Tyson, learning about our people, history, rules. All the little things she'd missed out on by not growing up here.

"So you find your mates through kissing?" She sounded intrigued.

Tyson snorted. "Not exactly . . . it can happen in any sexually charged situation. Which for some might be kissing. For others it won't be until sex."

"It's been known to happen from a single glance," Maximus added, his tone dry.

I leaned back harder, wiggling until I found a groove in the rocks. It still wasn't comfortable, but I didn't mind. "There were these two shifters who were sleeping together, and they kept saying it was just a casual thing. But strange enough, they were mates . . . for them the bond didn't form until they moved past their denial and acknowledged their true feelings for each other."

Mischa raised her eyebrows at me. "Was that our parents?"

I laughed. "I guess Mom shared that little story with you also."

She was rolling a small stone between her fingers. "Yes, but obviously not the mate and wolf part, because she never told me about that. But the story she gave me was pretty similar." She lifted her chin and looked at Maximus. "So how many supernaturals are there in the world?"

He answered straightaway; this was all textbook information for us. "Around half a million worldwide. There are six thousand living in Stratford, another twenty thousand scattered throughout the US."

Mischa's eyes widened. "Are you saying there are lots living on their own in the human world?"

Braxton answered this time. He'd been speaking quietly to Nash, who was going in and out of sleep but clearly still listening. "We don't make anyone stay in the communities. Our towns are there as a safe haven and as a gateway to protect the prison. Many supernaturals choose to live as human. They even have human partners and children."

"The children are half-breeds, and besides a few extrasensory gifts, are pretty much human," I added.

"Amazing," Mischa breathed. "This is both fascinating and incredibly unbelievable for me. If I hadn't seen some of these things with my own eyes . . ."

I couldn't help but grin at her. "There is so much more for you to learn."

"I'm just really glad I finally have a chance to live as I was meant to. I can't imagine why any supernatural wants to live among humans, denying their true family." She shook back her dark hair. "I'll never go back."

I could see the shudders running through her body.

"That we don't age is leading to some problems in the human world," Jacob said. "Supernaturals live over eight hundred years. In the human world they have to move constantly, change their identities. And the ones with families have to do the same, even if it means leaving their loved ones behind."

Her mouth dropped open, heaves of breath coming in and out. "Even more reason to stay in the communities."

More questions were forthcoming.

"So there are no female dragon shifters?" she asked, her green eyes wide.

Braxton shook his head. "Female dragons are the rarest of creatures. There have been none born in the last few hundred years. Before that, the rest were killed off."

"Why?" Mischa was working her lip between her teeth. "What is everyone's problem with dragons and dragon marked?"

I crushed some pebbles in my right hand. "Fear. The supernatural world is afraid of dragons. They're the strongest and most powerful of any of us, and when the ancient dragon king almost took over the five races, they decided to never allow that chance again."

Jacob nodded. "No one knows what the dragon marked even are. The guess is that it's some way for the dragon king to claim members of all five races. Supposedly after he died and made his declaration, the marks just started showing up on babies." His eyes turned stormy. "Of course those infants did not live to tell their tales."

"But clearly they didn't kill them all." Tyson sighed. "Which leads me to ask the question: Why are there imprisoned marked? And who are the two women freeing them from the other prisons?"

We had too many unanswered questions, and I wasn't sure where I fit in with all of this. I didn't feel dragon marked, having spent my entire life ignorant of the fact. Now I wondered what the future held for me and Mischa.

"Just so I have this straight," Mischa said, distracting me. "Most supernaturals only breed within their own race, producing purebloods. If they crossbreed between races, they produce hybrids, like the Compass parents. And if they breed with a human, it's a half-breed, who has no real power."

She looked at each of us, and everyone nodded at once.

"Pretty much," I said with a shrug. It wasn't that complicated, but it could get messy. Sometimes from all that genetic chaos came anomalies, like the quads.

After this, the conversations died off for a bit, everyone lost in their own thoughts. Braxton went back to silently staring at me. I swear the dragon had not taken his eyes off me for more than a few minutes since we'd sat there. He so knew I was up to something. If it hadn't been for Nash taking some of his concentration, he would definitely have confronted me by now.

I closed my eyes, listening to Jacob. He was communing with nature or whatever he did when he zoned out and started softly singing in his beautiful fey voice.

I squinted one eye open. Braxton was still watching me. The damn man had a stratospheric IQ; nothing slipped past him. If this plan had a hope in hell of working, I'd have to be really convincing to lift his distrust.

Time to act normal.

I gestured to the trusting little cherub. "So what are you going to do with Nash? They'll notice a new child running around Stratford, especially if he's bunking at your place."

He straightened, careful not to disturb the boy curled up on his side. "I'm hoping Jonathon and Torag can smooth things over with the council, pretend he's an orphan or a relative. Mom would love another boy to look after."

Braxton wasn't kidding. Jo would be thrilled. And Jack wouldn't be far behind her. Something in their hybrid natures had given them pure souls with so much love to give. Yeah, they could be brutal if required, but mostly they were all about love.

"Do you ever think about having kids?" Braxton asked me.

I raised my brows as I stared at him for a few extended moments. "Uh, no, not really. Mostly I find they are pains in the ass. All those questions and getting into shit."

He grinned. "Typical answer, Jessa, but I see the way you look at babies."

"I just can't stand when children are treated badly. They're innocent and deserve a chance to grow up strong and healthy. Adults can fend for themselves. But children . . . well, that's an entirely different story."

His voice was lower than before. "I admire a strong heart. Your father should be very proud of you, Jessa. The shifter you have grown into is to be admired."

I wasn't sure how to react, there were so many layers to his voice. So many unsaid things in that simple yet touching statement. I blinked rapidly a few times. Most people only saw my smart-ass exterior. I wasn't sure I liked the way he was staring into my soul, seeing things I'd rather the world did not.

"Luckily, I have many years before I start worrying about having a rug rat running around my feet." I lightened my tone, ready to move past the serious conversation.

Braxton just smiled at me. Smug bastard.

Eventually we whiled away the hours. I snuck in a few naps, knowing I'd need my energy later. I was starving, though, despite the few snacks Tyson provided from his jacket pocket. I was missing my meals. Another thing I'd have to get used to for a bit.

Finally, Braxton, who'd been keeping an eye on the time, got to his feet. He had Nash's hand firmly clasped in his own; it was time to go.

"Stay quiet and follow my lead," he said. And we were off through the weird portal again. I hoped it would still be open when I came back; otherwise, I'd be in trouble.

The side of the stone wall was deserted. The timing had been perfect. We dashed as one toward the shadowy sides. Braxton picked up Nash and tucked him under his arm, the muscles standing out as they flexed beneath their load. We made it to the edge, blending into the darkness. I slowly let myself fall back a little. In his rush to get everyone to safety, Braxton had moved forward, taking his eyes from me. Never a great idea. Although the boys still surrounded us, they'd fanned out and let me continue to drift backward. Mischa seemed to be keeping pace with me, but I wasn't worried about that, she wouldn't be hard to lose. Her senses were not fully functional yet. And more important, she didn't know how to call on her wolf.

We were in the low tunnel again, and as luck would have it, I found myself at the back of the pack.

Braxton's voice drifted to me. "All clear now. Let's move into the forest." I watched them exit one by one through the doorway. Braxton and Nash first—he was solely focused on getting the little boy to safety.

I slowed my footsteps but didn't stop them. I would follow all the way, right until the end so there would be no time for them to notice me pausing. Despite their mild suspicions, I don't think any of them, including Braxton, thought for one second I would stay in the prison by myself. If they'd had even a small inkling of what I was planning, I'd be over someone's shoulder, with no chance for rebellion.

They were going to be so pissed at me.

Jacob was second from the end, about to dive through the mist. I couldn't see Mischa. I assumed she'd gone in somewhere through the middle.

"Hurry," Jacob called. He had that glow about him, like at this very moment he was connected to the forest. His head was already on the other side.

My heart was pounding in my chest. I could still halt my plans now; it wasn't too late. And I knew Braxton would keep his word and help me search again. But, in reality, what could we do to better prepare ourselves to rescue all of the supernaturals? I didn't want to give myself a chance to chicken out. Something told me, deep in my gut, that if I didn't do this now, I never would. I was being urged on this mission, which should have freaked me out, but I was just going with it.

As the last of Jacob's blond hair disappeared, I stopped and pressed myself solidly against the wall. The sudden silence was almost deafening. I huffed in and out, gathering my strength, searching for a speck of bravery. Damn, I was not cut out for these cloak-and-dagger, save-the-world missions.

Before I either cried or freaked out, I turned and sprinted back the way I had just come. I needed to get back inside that building before shift change started again and the portal was closed. I didn't stop or hesitate, tracing the same steps right back to the water inlet, and, thankfully, the side was still clear. I could hear voices coming closer, and I knew it was time for them to start their circumnavigation of the perimeter again. I crossed the wide space, staying low to the ground to blend into whatever shadow I could find, sprinting at full force.

I reached the convergence spot and sighed in relief as my hand entered to the other side. The portal still existed. I licked my dry lips, and without pause leaned forward to dive in headfirst. My hands had just entered when something gripped my ankles and yanked me backward.

Chapter 12

I was dragged for about five meters before the grip loosened on my legs. I flipped over immediately. I couldn't fight what I couldn't see.

I froze. Well, I was in some big-ass trouble.

Four guards stood above me, the gray of their uniform indicating they were part of the perimeter patrol. I swear to freaking God I had not even heard them approach, and even this close I could not scent any of them. They were cloaked somehow and deathly quiet as they stared down at me. Two of them clutched whips in their hands; the others had batons. I could see guns on their hips, but at least they didn't have them drawn yet.

The stare-off continued, and I wondered what they were waiting for. Then a fifth came into view, holding a struggling Mischa in his arms.

"Let me go," she snarled.

Wow, little kitty had some wolf claws after all. I wanted to tell her that struggling was useless. These were highly trained guards, and we were outnumbered. Plus, they'd seen us, and everyone knew who we were.

One of the vampires lifted his head in my direction. "On your feet; hands behind your back." His thick, bushy eyebrows narrowed under the brim of his gray cap. "And don't try anything stupid. I don't want to hurt you, but I will if you push me."

Mischa had stopped struggling at this point. She was breathing deep, her eyes wide and shocked as she stared at me. I placed my hands flat on the ground and pushed myself up to stand. I winced as some of the grazes on my legs protested; that drag across the ground had knocked me around a bit. I placed my hands behind my back.

One of the guards crossed behind me, and I felt the straps clip across my wrists. Immediately a buzzing sensation flowed down my body, like a veil had fallen along my skin, and I couldn't touch my energy inside. My wolf and demon were still there, but they were muted. There was a barrier between us now, and I knew I wouldn't be able to shift.

The sensation had me wanting to cry my eyes out. But I didn't. This was not the time to fall apart. Mischa put up no more resistance as they cuffed her also, as if she had stopped fighting the moment she saw me. Or maybe it was my own lack of fight that had paused hers. The five guards surrounded us, and we were marched at a rapid pace back across the space and through the tunnel.

Weird. They were taking us into the forest.

We emerged in a different section from where we had entered. The forest was thinner, less dense here. And there was a man waiting for us in a small clearing. Kristoff.

Awesome.

The guards marched us across, and the entire way I stared at the smirking features of the sorcerer. Evil bastard.

His hands were clasped across his chest. He lifted one of them and halted us about four feet from him. "I couldn't quite believe it when the guards contacted the council to let us know they'd detained you two. It seems as if this might be my lucky day. The Lebrons are going to prison."

I didn't say anything. My mood was somewhere between depressed and effed off. I did not manage to save those prisoners and I was now in a truckload of shit. And so was Mischa.

"How I wish I could just throw you in there and let everyone think you'd disappeared. But I swore an oath from the council, and you will get your trial. Of course, I can resign myself to the fact that you'll be spending at least a week in Vanguard. Knowing how popular your father is, well, someone will probably take care of my little problem."

Jonathon had spent many years capturing supernatural crims and throwing them into the prison. Fear flooded me; there was every chance that if I went into Vanguard, I would never come out again. Adrenaline replaced the fear. The urge, either to fight or take flight, was strong. But with my hands cuffed, there wasn't much I could do.

Kristoff continued to stare, this intense sort of energy vibrating from him. With a head tilt, he leaned in close to my ear, away from Mischa so she wouldn't hear.

"You were my next intended victim as a frame for the Compasses, killing two birds with one stone. Literally. But now, well, I won't have to get my hands dirty again."

Hold up a freaking minute. Was creepster here actually admitting that he'd killed Markus and framed the Compasses?

I was distracted then, my head spinning to the side as intense thrashing could be heard through this section of the forest. The thundering and tearing indicated something large was heading in our direction. Mischa and I both jumped as more noises exploded. Something really large. Then they burst into the clearing.

The Compasses.

Mischa's voice shook as she turned her head to find my gaze. "I'm thinking we might be seeing the angry Braxton."

The guards tightened up around Kristoff, their first duty to protect the council leader.

I couldn't answer Mischa: I was pinned to the spot, unable to move or pull my eyes from the dragon coming my way. A very familiar dragon. And yet Braxton was also very different. A flame coated his scaly body—blue, intense. Even from the distance between us I could feel the heat billowing off. It was spectacular, lighting up the darkness beneath the canopy. But it also gave him an otherworldly look I'd never experienced before.

Something uncoiled inside my chest. The demon was starting to wake. But it couldn't do more than bash at its invisible cage, the magical cuffs keeping it contained. I was almost grateful to have the chains. I wasn't sure in that moment if I could have stopped it from bursting through my skin and doing whatever it had been trying to do for twenty-two years.

As they marched closer, Braxton continued to call the dark energy inside of me. I worried it would no longer be contained.

Mischa stuttered out her words: "S-something is happening inside . . . feels like my wolf fighting. Only it's not her."

I couldn't tear my gaze from Braxton. His dragon had never called the demon before; it must have something to do with the blue flames. And it sounded as if my twin had a demon inside, too, which was most probably about our marks. We needed more information on what was going to happen. Clearly, dragon marks responded to dragon shifters.

"Jessa!" Maximus's bellow was loud, roar-like. He looked to be pretty vamped out, his eyes black, hair blonder, fangs fully extended. The pissed-off aura he was throwing around could be felt even across the distance. "Don't say anything to . . . annoy . . . Braxton. He's not himself."

Thank you, very helpful. I could see that for my freaking self.

Okay, I would heed his warning and tread carefully with the dragon shifter. Only problem, my demon was dragging me closer, my feet starting to move of their own accord. Mischa was right beside me. I could see that Jacob, Tyson, and Maximus were trying to get around their brother and reach us first, but Braxton snarled and shot flames every time they moved out from behind him.

As the quads moved closer, Kristoff and the guards dived off the path, hightailing it for safety, leaving Mischa and me in a very vulnerable position, still cuffed with our energy contained.

Just when I wasn't sure I could stand Braxton's pull any longer, the flaming dragon paused. As he stilled, the dead foliage around him started to burn. Jacob was keeping it under control with some water energy. Then with a glow and flash of light, Braxton started to shift back.

No longer dragon, he was now all magnificent man. A very naked man. I ran my eyes over him. Damn . . . maybe *magnificent* was an understatement. I forced my gaze upward, thankful that the pull inside of me had lessened, the heat that had been racing through my limbs and into my veins abating.

Mischa leaned forward, visibly shaken, her breathing ragged. "What the hell was that?"

"I don't know," I murmured.

The men were almost to us now, and I was glad to see that Braxton had put on some shorts—although the rest of his heavily muscled body was free to be devoured by my greedy eyes. Holy shitballs, I was acting like I'd never seen him shirtless before. I guess it had been a while. But it looked as if the man had muscles on muscles. There was so much of his delicious, creamy expanse of dark-tanned skin on display. It was safe to say I'd never been quite as aware of him as a man as I was right then. Meanwhile, the look on his face had me wanting to run as fast as I could in the opposite direction.

The four of them surrounded us. Points of a compass, like their name.

Braxton's voice was low, smooth, but not like his usual tone. "Tell us everything."

I attempted to swallow the lump in my throat. It was going to be impossible to talk around it, but I couldn't seem to find enough moisture in my mouth.

No one moved, and finally Mischa spoke.

"We went back; we were going to rescue the rest of the prisoners." She lowered her eyes. "They caught us before we even made it inside."

Three sets of narrowed eyes zoomed in on her, but Braxton's remained on me, and I was still frozen.

Mischa had both hands in front of her, pleading with them to understand. "They had babies. We had to at least try."

Jacob groaned. I noted that his hair looked disheveled, green eyes wide and a little wild. Usually the fey was very smooth and together. But not right now. In fact, all of the boys looked out of sorts. Tyson's eyes were gold, which was never a good sign.

Finally I found my voice. "I'm sorry, I should have told you. I just couldn't leave them there." It was killing me right now to think that those poor souls were still in that disgusting room. I tightly squeezed my eyes closed. I was a freaking failure. I'd failed those babies.

Braxton reacted then, as if my voice had cracked the anger he'd been projecting hard enough to break something. He moved faster than I could see, and I was in his arms. He was everywhere, his expanse of silky skin pressing into mine and his heat encompassing me whole. The hug was hard, almost to the point of pain, but still there was a tenderness to the embrace. He could have crushed me in an instant if he had wanted to. Instead, he held me as if I were precious. I wanted to wrap my arms around him, offer some comfort, but of course the cuffed hands made that difficult.

"If you ever do something like this again," he murmured, "I will fucking kill you, Jessa."

I pulled back, unsure if he was kidding. His expression wasn't giving much away.

Tyson's head flew up then, golden eyes gleaming in the half-light, although they were starting to bleed back to their honeysuckle color. Jacob's head followed.

"The rest of the council members are coming," they both said together.

Kristoff must have run off and gathered the others. He would have needed their power to even have a hope of stopping the Compasses.

Speaking of, I needed to tell them something. "Listen, I don't know if he was talking shit or not, but Kristoff just pretty much admitted to me that he framed you four, sending you into Vanguard. I don't think his plan is over yet. You have to watch your backs." I needed them to be extracareful. They were so confident; they thought they could never be taken down.

Tyson nudged me gently. "Two steps in front of you, babe. Jonathon told us they're gathering evidence against Kristoff. Have been since the trial. Apparently he used the fey to kill the vampire. They had the sucker stored until they could set up the scene, but then the fey had second thoughts, so Kristoff had him killed also. It's all starting to unravel for him—we're going to nail his ass soon."

I took a step back to see them all better. "Dad . . . and you all have been investigating him? Why didn't you tell me? And why did he do such a bad job with the crime scene?"

Maximus narrowed his eyes, his fangs had retracted enough for him to speak clearly again. "We do not want you involved in this. It's dangerous and Kristoff is desperate to keep his role as council leader. In reality, the frame job was not too bad. If we hadn't had Louis step in and gather that magical evidence, well, it probably wouldn't have gone our way."

I blinked a few times. "It doesn't make sense, though, if it's not you as leaders, they'll just bring in someone else."

"Apparently there's an old law: if they can usurp three of the five council members, then a vote can be taken to extend out the current rule another term," Maximus said. "He'd have an even better chance if he got rid of four of the five."

I'd never heard of that law. But if it was correct, then if Kristoff imprisoned or killed the Compasses, he'd have removed the majority and could rule for another twenty-five years. Our conversations were cut off as the power of the leaders washed over us.

Braxton moved close enough for me to feel the heat of his skin. "What do you want to do now?" he asked. "If you want to run, hide, or fight. We have your back."

The other Compasses nodded. My heart filled and overflowed in the form of a few tears. Which, I'm glad to say, I got under control immediately. Jonathon was wrong. I'd never believe my boys would hunt me one day, dragon marked or not. Never.

"I don't want to run or fight. Not yet at least. If I'm found guilty at trial, well, that's a different story."

Mischa nodded, scooting closer to me. "Yes, we'll face the punishment."

Power was scooting through the forest now. I could feel the five races mingling, which was the mark of the leaders. The group stepped into view. There were at least ten of them now, with the council and the guards who had detained us. The Compasses moved in front of us, leaving only small gaps between each of them, effectively blocking us from the group.

"How did you all find out so fast that we had returned?" I asked their broad backs.

Maximus swung his head and found my gaze. "Ty had an alert set up for you."

"The council did the same, but mine's bigger . . . I mean faster." Tyson definitely had a grin on his face; I could hear it in his voice. Cocky mage.

"Why did you come in dragon mode?" I asked Braxton. "And what was with the flame?"

He didn't answer me, his gaze firmly locked on the council. I peered around his side and was relieved to see Jonathon front and center, Lienda at his side.

Tyson distracted me. "Braxton's been in his flaming-dragon form since the doorway shut without you and Mischa."

The last part was muttered, his voice low and strained. I had caused them a lot of stress with my little stunt. No doubt they'd try to exact some form of punishment at a later date.

Kristoff edged his way forward to speak. "Jessa and Mischa of the Lebron wolf shifters."

My mom and my twin had dropped the last name Jackson and went by Lebron now. They were officially part of the family.

"You are charged with infiltrating Vanguard, the American supernatural prison. You will be escorted to the prison now, and there will be a trial in seven days."

I stepped forward, nudging my way through the Compasses. Braxton reached out and caught my arm, preventing me from moving forward. Actually, he was trying to shift me behind his back, but I wasn't budging.

"Mischa only came in to stop me," I said. No reason we both had to go down. "She is innocent of this charge."

"Jessa!" my father's bellow was loud and filled with power. "Do not say one more thing."

I shut my mouth because I knew when he meant business.

Jonathon faced his fellow council members. "Lienda and I need a minute with our daughters before anything is decided. You've outvoted me on their imprisonment, but I would like to ask a few questions before they're taken."

No one but Kristoff objected to this, so our parents crossed the space between us. When he reached my side, Jonathon enclosed me in a hug. We stepped back behind the Compass line of men. He then pulled Lienda and Mischa in with his other arm. We were a Lebron puppy pile.

"What happened?" Jonathon's voice was so low I could barely hear him.

I swallowed my angry tears. "There's a secret room in Vanguard filled with . . . babies . . . kids, every age and race. It was disgusting." I spat the last part. "We were going back in to save them."

"Are they dragon marked?" he asked, close to my face.

I shook out my hair. "I don't know. I didn't see any marks, but we were only in there for a moment."

Lienda had her face clenched so hard; her nails were cutting into her cheeks. "We can't let them go into the prison, Jon. They will be targeted."

Mischa paled. "Kristoff said the same thing . . . Why are we going to be targeted?"

Our parents seemed to be doing some loud, rapid breathing exercise, so I answered for her. "Dad was the wolf-pack alpha long before he became council leader. He's been instrumental in imprisoning a lot of criminals who are in Vanguard. It won't take long before the shifters scent us and know we are Lebrons. Then they're going to find us and exact their revenge."

I'd already resigned myself to this fate, but poor Mischa looked as if I'd punched her in the face.

"We're dead," she murmured.

"I won't let that happen," Jonathon said. "I have some pull with the guards. I'll make sure they look after you."

We all knew they couldn't stay on our asses all day and night. Eventually they'd have to step away or lose concentration for a few minutes, and that's when we'd be hit. We might only be in there for seven days—I had no doubts they'd make the charges disappear at the trial—but seven full days could be an awfully long time.

Braxton got right into my personal space then. "I won't let this happen. I will be dead and buried before you end up in that prison."

I reached out and rested my head against his right biceps. I could feel the strength beneath my cheek and the vibration of his anger as it trilled through him.

"I have no choice, Brax. I don't want to run like a criminal for the rest of my life. I need you all to focus on the trial, and bring Louis in to help. Make sure these charges disappear; figure out a way so the book can't convict us. Pretend we accidentally stumbled into Vanguard and got lost or something."

That is if we were alive long enough to make it to trial.

Braxton's blue eyes blazed with light, a beam that would cut through anything that ended up in his path. I could sense his struggle to hold his form, to not let the dragon free, to not plunder and pillage as the old cliché goes. But his strength as a man was unsurpassed. No one controlled Braxton, not even his dragon.

"A compromise, then," he finally said, his words hard through his locked jaw. "I'll take Mischa's place in the prison, a life for a life. The old rules still exist, even though most don't remember them."

I furrowed my brow as I attempted to recollect this information from our supernatural history class. I couldn't remember hearing of such a law.

"Yes," Maximus said. "You step in for Mischa, and I will for Jessa. Neither of the girls will have to go in there."

Jonathon shook his head. "I wish I could take you up on this, but Kristoff wants Lebron blood and you know the council has right of refusal." He tented his hands on either side of his face, as if massaging a migraine. "But I could possibly swing it for Mischa alone. They mostly associate Jessa with me, and I would be a little less homicidal to know that you were in there watching her back," he said to Braxton.

Lienda stepped in then. "I don't want either of my girls in there, Jon. There must be something else we can do?"

He shook his head. "I'm sorry, my sweet, but Braxton's idea is better than anything I can think of. Jessa is trained to fight, unlike Mischa. It is the best option."

There were nods all around. No one looked happy, but they were a little more resigned.

"We will make sure the trial never has a chance for success." Tyson kissed me on the cheek. "You just have to make sure you survive." His voice got a little louder. "Do you hear me, Jessa babe? Your only job in there is to survive."

Jacob dropped a kiss onto my other cheek. "Forget about the prisoners in that room. Now you have to be selfish and only think of Jessa."

A blast of energy had all of us turning back to the large group waiting across the clearing. Their patience had ended. It was time to go quietly.

Jonathon's face went dark and stormy. "Give me a moment." The fact that his voice was low and growly was a pretty big indicator that he wasn't calm.

Lienda reached out and looped one arm around Mischa's shoulders. The other went around me. My arms were starting to ache from being held behind my back, and I was missing my wolf like crazy. But I knew this sensation was something I was going to have to get used to, at least for the next week. We watched as Jonathon started to argue with the council, putting forth the proposal for the Braxton and Mischa switch. He only needed a majority vote, and I knew Torag would be on his side.

Three hands went into the air, which left Kristoff and Galiani, the fey, on the opposing side. That was victory enough for us.

Mischa was breathing rather rapidly for someone who'd just been given a reprieve.

"What?" I said.

She swallowed audibly. "I'm not okay with you going back in there without me. I don't think I will survive the worry."

I left our mother's side and nudged into her. "Don't be afraid for me. Braxton will never let anything happen to me, and more importantly . . . I can take care of myself." I let the smallest of smiles grace my lips.

"We will make sure you don't go back after the trial," Lienda said. They all seemed to feel the need to repeat this. "Your father and Louis will figure out how to make whatever evidence disappear, including the guards' memories." Her voice dropped even further. "But if you're convicted, we will run. I have done it once. I sure as hell will do it again to keep you safe."

It wasn't hard to see where she'd gotten the strength to run with Mischa, to leave behind her mate and other child, to keep her family safe. She might be a wolf, but the mama bear was there in spades.

Jonathon turned to us and, with a wave of a hand, indicated it was safe to walk across. I knew, as the quads closed ranks around us, that it went against their instincts to let this happen. They wanted to fight. The set of their jaws, the fire in their eyes, the power that rode all of them, they wanted to fight so badly. But there was a time for fighting and a time to wait, and now was the waiting part.

The trip to Vanguard was pretty uneventful. Braxton had been cuffed, and we were both blindfolded. The leather necklace had been removed from my neck, so I knew I was going to feel every single one of the security measures. But there was comfort in the warmth of Braxton close by. I was attempting not to think of the hard faces and tight hugs of my friends and family as they were forced to watch us leave. I hadn't said good-bye. I refused to acknowledge that I might not see them again. Despite the odds against us, I was determined to survive, and I was hardening myself to the experiences on the inside.

By the time the mask and cuffs were removed, we were in some sort of front entrance waiting room. I rubbed at my aching wrists and swung my arms a few times to move the blood through them again. The scent of this part of Vanguard was very different from that of the sewer area I'd been in; this place was clean and sterile.

The first thing they did was separate me and Braxton. His expression and low growls indicated he wasn't very happy about this move, but he didn't say anything. He knew when to fight his battles. I assumed he'd already been through this and knew what was about to happen. I took comfort from that.

The next part wasn't too bad, just goddamned degrading. I was stripped, searched, and clothed in a simple tank and shorts. All cotton, gray and drab. Nothing on any garment could be used as a weapon; there wasn't even a button or stud. I was allowed a hair tie for my hair, but that was the only accessory. Even my bra was minus underwire. I guess I needed to wrap my head around the knowledge that most of the supernaturals in this prison were hard-core criminals. Murderers, drug runners, human and supernatural smugglers, black market magic users, terrorists . . . we had them all.

The woman, who'd just had her hands all over my body, led me out of the small room and into a hallway.

"When did they change the policy of placing those awaiting trial into the main prison?" I knew she probably wouldn't answer me, but it never hurts to try. Something told me the change had simply been for the Compasses benefit or detriment. But it looked like I was going to get the same *special* treatment.

The woman glared at me, tugging me along roughly. I clenched my fists tighter but forced myself to calm. It was going to get much worse than this. The hardest part of being an alpha was the way my wolf needed to be the strongest, always in control. It made situations like this near impossible to stay calm in. The restrictions, lack of freedom, fear, control . . . all antithesis to my wolf.

Plus, I was freaking hungry. No doubt the food was going to suck ass in here. No chocolate cake, no pie . . . they might as well have signed me up for torture.

I was led back into that first room, and relief flooded me to find Braxton seated, his extralong legs spread out in front of him. He looked relaxed. And the boy could fill out some prison cottons. Who knew gray could actually look sexy on a person? *Go figure.* His eyes landed on my face well after they had taken a leisurely look, starting from my bare feet and moving over my own gray ensemble.

"You okay?" he rumbled.

I nodded, falling down into the seat next to him.

There was one man in the room with us now, although I could hear heartbeats of the others stationed outside the door. This robust man, who was not tall, but had thick, strong muscles, dropped down in a chair across from us. There was a desk between us. He leaned forward, resting his elbows on it. His eyes were dark brown, his hair turning salt-and-pepper a little around the temples, so he was pretty old for a supernatural. I was getting a magic vibe from him, thinking he was a wizard or sorcerer.

"Welcome to Vanguard," he started, his words faintly accented, as if it had been a long time ago that he'd come to America. "My name is Jeremy. I'm the head of the guard and magical protections. When we leave here, you will be escorted to your cell first." His eyes narrowed. "I don't agree with this, but it has been dictated that you two will share a cell, for safety. Then you'll be led out into the center zone. It's mingling, lunch, and activity time, and we need to get you two out there and try to nip any threats in the bud."

I shivered a little. I had no idea how bad it was going to be. I kept hoping they were exaggerating, but something told me they weren't. I turned my head to the side and met Braxton's eyes. He nodded. At least we both agreed that our bunking together was a bonus. Thank you, Dad.

We turned back to Jeremy.

"I know what you've been accused of doing." His eyes narrowed slightly. "I have no idea why you would have been trying to infiltrate the prison, and to my knowledge there is no doorway where you were found. I think this is all a misunderstanding, and I have no doubt that these charges will be dropped. The fact that you are forced to be in the main jail is not ideal, however. Powers above me have dictated."

Truth. I could hear the frustration in his voice. Seems as if, no matter how high you were in the pecking order, there was always some douche canoe with his hand up your ass, controlling your actions.

He stood then. "Follow me," he said as he turned and moved toward the door. I wondered if they were just going to let us wander freely behind.

Yeah, not happening. Our hands were magically cuffed at the doorway by the two guards waiting there. I liked to think it was me they were so afraid of, but I knew better.

The guards stayed around us as we were led out of the office section and toward the large barred gate that seemed to mark the beginning of the actual prison. Upon Jeremy's command, there was the distinct whoosh of magic, followed by locks clicking across. The metal double doors swung open. The moment I stepped across the threshold, I almost fell to my knees. I paused and had to close my eyes. My breathing was deep and even as I fought to regain equilibrium.

"You okay?" Braxton's low voice had my lids shooting open. "Keep breathing; it can be hard to adjust to the loss of power. Especially when you're strong."

He wasn't kidding. I used the familiar and piercing blue of his eyes to ground myself. It felt as if there was a dampened cloth pressed onto my energy. This was like the magical cuffs, only a thousand times stronger, pushing my power down, suppressing my natural urges, and limiting my strength.

I attempted to call on my wolf, but I couldn't reach her. She was there but hidden, out of touch.

I howled then, in one long, unbroken note. Where was she? I'd never been away from my wolf before. I was dying.

Braxton stepped into me then; he couldn't hug me, his arms were secured behind his back, but his warmth still surrounded me, his scent washing over me, his comfort enough to halt my hysteria. I rested my face against the hard planes of his chest as I gulped down the emotions, my breathing rapid and shallow. He continued with the comforting touch until, finally, I was able to stand on my own.

"I'm okay . . . I'm okay," I repeated a few times. "I just . . . can't touch her, my wolf. She's locked away from me."

He nodded. "I know, but she's still there. Don't let your brain convince you that she's dead or you'll go insane . . . well, more insane."

"Thank you," I murmured into his hard chest. "I love when you point out the obvious to me." I tilted my head back to glare at him. He returned my look with a lazy grin.

Jeremy jarred us out of our little bubble. "Move it."

I shifted my glare to him, but couldn't summon up enough anger to bother with words. Then we were moving again. Apparently, it was time to dive into the jungle.

Chapter 13

The clinging pressure of suppressed energy was worse in the long channel of the shifter wing. There were more woven securities there. Silver bars lined the rows of cells, which were about twenty-six by twenty-six feet. We walked along the length. There were hundreds of cells, one after the other along both sides of a center stone path, each sparse room empty. Finally, Jeremy led us into a cell that was close to the end of the corridor. Inside were two small beds with thin mattresses. Other than that, there were a sink and toilet, which, I was glad to see, had a curtain that could be pulled across for a semblance of privacy, and a small desk that held a few books and pens and paper.

Jeremy freed our wrists. "You are entitled to literature, art supplies, and, once a day, outside of mealtimes, you can request a beverage and snack. This is on top of the lunchtime, which happens in the main circle." I rubbed at my arms again. "Keep your heads down, don't cause trouble, and this week will be over before you know it." He made his way back to the door. "Showers are in the morning. You receive new prison cottons then. Mack and Sam will take you to the circle now." He waved at the two beefy guards before turning and leaving our cell.

The larger of the guards moved closer. "Don't try any bullshit moves, Braxton." He looked like a Mack, so I was going with that. "You know I have my whip, and I will not hesitate to use it."

I'd seen those whips when we were captured.

Braxton didn't move his eyes from Mack. "Their whips have silver imbedded into the leather. It hurts like a bitch, and the healing is really slow."

I pulled my eyes away and narrowed them on the men. Those fuckers hit my boys? People needed to die, seriously.

"Move it, bitch." I was shoved out the door by Sam. I stumbled but stayed on my feet, although my arm brushed the silver and I could feel the burn. It was only the slightest graze, so like a mild sunburn, but it would take a while to heal.

"Don't touch her." Braxton's voice barely changed tone, he sounded so matter-of-fact. But whatever it was, both men backed off a little.

We traced our path back along the shifter wing, one guard in front of us and one behind. Braxton made me go first so he was at my back and had Mack at his. As we threaded our way through, I was starting to really understand what the quads had tried to explain to me yesterday. Vanguard was designed like an octopus: the large "main" circular body for mingling and food, and then the tentacle-like legs formed the different cell wings for each of the supernatural races. Long and winding was the shifter wing. I could only assume the others were the same.

We had to pass through many silver-coated doors, each locked with multiple-key dead bolts and hand-sensor recognition. When you thought about it, they were using pretty bad judgment having the dragon marked in such an insecure location. I guess they never expected anyone would know they were even there. If it weren't for Nash, we never would have known. I really hoped the little boy was okay. I'd have to ask Braxton if they'd had time to get him set up.

Finally, we seemed to reach the main exit. It was a much larger doorway than had been down the stone path. It took both guards to simultaneously press their hands to the sensors to activate the unlocking mechanisms on this one. I could hear the loud shouts and raucous uproar beyond, before the door had moved even a sliver. There was some serious intermingling going on out there. I was relieved to find that, despite the suppressing of my wolf, my senses were still functioning, almost normally. The security measures seemed to target just our supernatural animal—the predator that lived inside of a shifter—except for those bloody rabbits. They weren't predators, they were just bitey little shits.

The door swung open. I expected it to be slow and loud on its hinges. It was massive, but it opened silently. Although the noise beyond was anything but. The shouting hit me like a slam of water in the face. Not to mention the scents and the pull of thousands of supernaturals. It wasn't exactly pleasant, yet at the same time it brought forth memories of home. Of pack. Of the spice and bite that made up the supernatural community.

"It's lunchtime. Try not to get eaten." Mack grinned his asshole grin and left us there. The doors slammed shut again.

Braxton spun so fast I almost missed it, although I was pretty distracted by everything beyond our position. He gripped both sides of my body, almost lifting me up to face him.

"Do not leave my side. Do not let them separate us. They will try; you need to be aware." His voice was low and close to my ear. I could feel his breath caressing my cheek. "Use your training, Jessa. One-on-one you have it over all of them, but we are vastly outnumbered."

"Do you have any friends in here from last time?" My eyes were still trying to dart around and take in the entire room.

He nodded. "Maybe, but none that I trust. You don't really have friends in here; you form alliances. There are vast differences. Alliances can be shifted easily. Many here gravitate to whomever they think is the most powerful. In their eyes, I'll have lost much strength without my brothers."

Jaymin Eve

I swallowed. It was a visible movement. Then I schooled my face. It was time to act tough. Well, tougher than I was currently feeling.

We strode into the middle, and unlike in the movies, everything didn't stop so people could stare at us. Hardly anyone even glanced our way. They gave zero craps about us, and that was fine with me. My guess was that it would be in a day or so, when someone either scented me or word got around, that we'd have our trouble.

Braxton reached out and gripped my hand. His touch was nice, and then he threaded our fingers together. "First thing, we walk the perimeter, learn the layout, and then we eat."

I nodded. My tension had me gripping his hand tighter.

The round room was massive, and I mean gi-freaking-gantic massive. It had high stone walls, glittering with strands of mineral and stone embedded throughout. There was this weird half roof on sections, which allowed sunlight to flood the area. We were still underground, so this was a sun of a magical nature, but it at least gave the illusion that we were outside. I swear, a breeze even ruffled my ponytail. Dead center were three huge rows of bench-seat tables and chairs, clearly used for eating. They were a lot like the cafeteria ones in Stratford College. These tables were half-filled with supernaturals: some in large groups, others solitary as they focused on the food in front of them.

"There are a lot of demi-fey in here," I noted.

From my limited view, I could see two ogres seated at an especially large table, their bulbous noses the first giveaway; the second was the cobalt blue of their stone-like skin. A hairy cousin of theirs was the source for the Bigfoot legend. As far as I knew, he was locked up in one of the Asian prison systems. Celebrities are whisked away from their home countries. Too much exposure if they are ever seen or manage to escape.

Just down from them was a table of tiny pixies, each about the size of a hundred-dollar bill and shaped like Barbie dolls, but sort of pointier. They fluttered around, sipping their nectar. Imps could be seen playing some sort of game across the way. Those mischievous creatures were not to be trusted. Devious and sneaky. But funny.

Braxton had followed my line of sight. "Yes, the demi-fey are the least like humans. They don't blend well and get into trouble a lot."

There were even a few that I'd never seen up close before. Satyrs and centaurs seemed to have their own yarded-off section. Neither were a demi-fey breed that we'd ever had permanently in Stratford. They were actually pretty rare nowadays. Fearmongering humans had hunted them to near extinction. There were four centaurs, their silky coats on the bottom half, ranging from black, brown, and even a pinto with white spots. The male upper halves were humanlike, but with more animal infused into the features and long manes of hair.

The satyrs were much smaller, their cloven hooves pattering across the stone floor. I loved their tiny ears and little horns that peaked above their curled hair.

My focus shifted as we halted near a glassed-off section. I couldn't see what the area was used for until we moved closer and I noticed the water filling it. It was a tank, with water so clear it was hard to detect. My eyes bugged a little as three mermaids raced past the glass. Supernatural mermaids are nothing like the ones in movies. Instead of beautiful, flowing red hair, they had green seaweed-like tendrils, jagged teeth, clawed hands, and long scaled tails. The colors of their tails ranged from black to murky brown, and every shade of green in between. Not pretty. Ugly. Very, very ugly. And they were mean and vicious. Killing many an unsuspecting human. I was pretty sure the legend of the beautiful mermaid was from some of the fey sirens who used to sit out on the rocks and lure sailors into the deep. Yeah, we had a few skeletons in our closet.

I was glad when we continued to move. Mermaids gave me the creeps. The next tank was filled with selkies, their smooth, seal-like bodies gliding through the murky water. They liked it a little dirtier and brinier than their cousins next door, and unlike mermaids, they could exist on land, transforming back into a female. Although the sea always called them back. Also, unlike the mermaids, they were mostly gentle and kind. Just don't piss them off; they could be very animalistic in their temperament.

I expected water-loving sirens in the third tank, but it looked empty. Which didn't always mean anything. We continued to walk around the room.

Braxton lifted my hand, drawing my attention. "Why did you really break back into the prison?" He was still pissed off, but he also seemed a little hurt that I hadn't waited for him. "I told you I'd help. You should have waited for me."

I wasn't sure how to explain the drive I'd felt to save the children. From the moment all of those dirty, desperate faces had turned to me, I'd been single-minded. I had to save them. The more I thought on it, the more I truly believed they were dragon marked. There was just no other explanation for that secret room. But Braxton still didn't know I was dragon marked, so it was hard to explain my reasoning.

"What happened with Nash?" My segue distracted him.

Sort of.

He dropped his hooded eyes. "I'm not sure. I only had enough time to get him to Louis. He assured me he could do some spelling and paperwork to pass him off as an orphaned cousin. I left Nash and came looking for you." Braxton's voice was smooth. Damn, that poor kid was probably freaking out without his Braxie.

I sucked down my guilt. "How did you get to Louis so quickly?" It couldn't have been more than twenty minutes from when the boys exited the door till Mischa and I were brought back to the forest.

Braxton tilted his head at me. "He was waiting in the forest when we emerged. I think the sorcerer has some sort of tracker on you." His smile was feral. "He's going to be pissed when he realizes you're in here."

I rubbed my nose. "As long as Nash is okay, I can live with being in here."

One of those poor victims was safe. Not great, but better than nothing.

Braxton snorted. "Louis, at least, has some uses. He will be instrumental in trying to make the evidence disappear."

I had no doubt he would be; he'd worked magic on the quads' case and would do the same for mine.

As I continued to observe the multitudes of demi-fey breeds scattered around, I was struck by a thought.

"Have any demi-fey ever been dragon marked?"

Braxton met my gaze, and there was something fluttering in his eyes, something that read deeper into the question. He finally answered, "I've never heard of demi-fey being marked. Most of the accused are shifters, and then the rest scattered among vamps, mages, and a very limited number are fey."

That was interesting. I wondered if the majority were shifters because the original dragon king had been a shifter. Although he'd also been a sorcerer. Maybe shifter was the side he had most related to.

"Why are you not marked?" I asked him.

He was one of the few existing dragon shifters. It made absolutely no sense that he wouldn't be marked.

He shrugged. "I don't need the extra powers connected to the marked. I'm already dragon."

"What do you mean extra powers?" I knew so little about the mark. I'd wanted to ask the victims from that room, but we'd never made it back.

Braxton's eyes darted around, keeping a close watch on the other inmates as we continued our circumvention of the mingling zone. "It's only rumor, but allegedly any that are marked possess an ability to partially shift into a mist . . . like a dragon spirit. And they mimic many of the abilities I already possess. In a manner, the dragon king created an army of dragons who also possess the souls of our other races."

No way! That was both scary and freaking awesome. I wondered whether I'd have that power if Louis released my mark. I'd sort of be like Braxton then, not a real dragon but close. My heart ached for a moment, and I had no idea why I was feeling like that. Seriously. Maybe it was a heart attack—nah, highly unlikely for a shifter who was only twenty-two.

I inhaled through my nose in one long movement. I think I had, well, a major case of the feels. Something had hit me hard in the heart, and my emotions were overflowing.

"You okay, Jessa?" Braxton brought his face close to mine, tantalizing me with those masculine looks that had every woman in Stratford panting. As we locked eyes, my hurting heart thumped extrahard and I had the strangest urge to kiss him.

What the hell?

I'd never felt like that before; he was my best friend. I would not ruin that with romance. It could never work, especially with any of the Compasses. They weren't made for the long term. They were the first to admit that. I needed to pull myself together and get laid. It had been way too long for a shifter.

"Jessa?" he asked again, and I realized I hadn't answered his question.

"Yes, I'm okay, just tired and hungry."

He tilted his head to the side, calling me on my bullshit. But I was glad he let it go without more of a confrontation. We continued on our journey. It would take us at least thirty minutes to walk around the entire area.

"How long do we have out here?" I questioned, while squinting at a strange sight across the way. "And are we back in our cells after that?"

Braxton followed my eyes. "The schedule allows an hour in the morning for the shower area, four hours of mingle time out here, and then back to our cells."

"Are they having sex?" I blurted out.

We were both staring at the couple across from us. It was a fey female with long golden-red hair and a lanky, black-haired vampire male. He had his fangs deep in her neck and the movements under his coat were pretty clear.

"That would be an affirmative." Braxton turned away.

I stared for only a beat longer. "Do they not care what happens inside here?"

He laughed, harsh and grating. "As long as no one escapes, they don't give a damn what goes on inside these walls. That's why we have to be careful. If we are attacked, no one is going to come to our rescue."

I wondered if that was true. I'd seen a few of the guards watching me closely. I knew Jonathon would have someone on the inside to keep an extra eye on our safety. Anyway, I hoped so. I would die if anything happened to Braxton; it was my fault we were in here. As we rounded off the end of the tour, we passed what looked like a stable, a round yard, and a jousting arena. Like I said, it was a large area. Finally, we arrived in front of the buffet.

There was a line, so we stood on the end and waited patiently. No one lingered too close to anyone else, except for a few who were clearly friends. But I was starting to see Braxton's definition of a *friend* versus an *ally*.

The man in front of me was quiet as he waited, but I could sense something very strong inside of him. And his profile was strangely familiar. He shifted his head in a slow-motion movement. There was nothing remotely normal about that creepy head spin.

Braxton nodded at him. "Vlad."

Holy shut my face in the door! Vlad? As in Vlad the Impaler. I had no idea he'd been taken from Romania and placed in our prison. It did make sense; they always removed the celebrities from their local zone. Since his inability to keep himself under control—many years ago— had majorly outed the vampire legend, well, he was set to be locked up for a long time. His list of crimes was massive.

"Dragon." He returned the greeting.

His bloodred eyes flicked across to me. I fought the urge to shiver; he was like the mayor of creepy town, right down to the clichéd pale skin, black stringy hair, and razor-sharp pointed nails. But the part that cemented his status as Creepy McCreep was the eyes for sure.

"And who is this delicious little morsel?"

I fought the urge to barf in my mouth. It was either that or punch him in the skeletal protrusion that he was working as a nose.

"None of your fucking business," I said, curling my lips. The movement was involuntary.

Braxton tightened his grip on my hand, but otherwise didn't show any signs of concern.

"Everything in here is my business, little girl. I run Vanguard."

I flicked my ponytail behind me and let out a sigh. "I'm pretty hungry. Can we just move this interrogation along?"

The smallest of smiles lifted the corner of his mouth. "I like you. I think I won't kill you for a while. Although . . ." He breathed deeply. "The scent of your blood . . . very tempting."

His hard features lighted on Braxton. "Keep her under control. Muzzle the bitch if you have to."

Braxton moved then, in his usual move that was faster than the eye could track. His hand hovered over the vampire's neck, but he didn't touch him.

"Don't threaten me or Jessa. I don't want to take you on, but if it comes down to it, I will. And you will not best me."

Something slid across the red depths of Vlad's eyes, and without another word, he turned away. My worried eyes followed him. He was very old and powerful; I did not want Braxton anywhere near him. We were at the food table now, so it was a convenient distraction for him to turn away. But it also spoke of his hesitation with the Compasses. I wouldn't have guessed their reputation ran deep enough to have penetrated the prison system. Maybe they'd left an impression when they'd been in here for their short time.

Silence reigned as we traversed the length of the buffet. For once I couldn't even find enough food to fill my plate. For the first time since we entered the prison, I was depressed.

I dropped my tray with a huff and slowly sank onto a bench seat. Braxton grinned as he sat down right next to me. "All that we've gone through in the last few days, and finally you're upset because of shitty food." He flashed me a double row of blindingly white teeth.

I picked up a bread roll that could actually be used as a weapon. It was like a rock.

"Shitty?" I almost screeched, throwing my rock down. "This food is so bad it should be used to feed the criminals who are on death row in the human prisons. It would actually kill them."

We didn't have death row in our prisons. When supernatural criminals were hunted down, many of them received immediate death sentences in the field, mainly because it's in our nature to fight back. But our laws state that if you come in quietly and accept imprisonment, you get to keep your head. Which was the reason Vlad, who wore the blood of millions of humans, was still kicking. It wasn't exactly a law I always agreed with, but that's what we had.

I picked at the lumps of crap masquerading as food on my plate. Tension filtered through my body as a large figure dropped into the bench seat across from us. I lifted my head, wishing I could call on my wolf. I was really lost without her.

The new arrival was a massive vampire male, bald-headed with scars riddling his visible skin. He had one particularly nasty gash: red, raised, and ropy, which ran from the corner of his right eye and down to his chin. He didn't say anything at first. I think he was hoping his appearance alone would work as intimidation. Braxton and I just stared back, although I did have my bread rock in my hand again. A girl needs to be prepared. Just sayin'.

"I've heard a few rumors of your reappearance, Braxton." His voice was low and sent chills down my spine. He was dead inside—you can always tell by the voice, nothing good left there anymore. "And of the little wolf that's been glued to your side."

"Last time you started trouble, it ended badly," Braxton drawled. "For you."

He grinned; his teeth were a little pointed. "Ah, but this time you are minus your brothers. With the addition of a pretty large vulnerability."

His eyes settled on my face, and I wanted to turn away. I felt dirty just having his gaze on me. But I'd played this game before—not with a crazy criminal, of course, but I knew that the first to break eye contact lost. I might be a little separated from my wolf, but being alpha never went away, and I was all alpha.

"Jessa is more than enough backup," Braxton said. My limbs warmed at his compliment. The Compasses spent so much time protecting me that I often wondered whether they knew how well I could fight. I was trained; I could be a weapon. I just never needed to, because of my four guardsmen.

Scarface stared at me for an extra beat before giving a nod. "Jessa, now I realize why your scent is so familiar. You remind me of my jailer . . . and I have such fond memories of Jonathon Lebron."

Ah, shit. Our flying under the radar had not lasted long.

"Your father is on more than one list in here, wolf princess," he said as he stood. "I'll be seeing you."

He walked away. I wasn't sure if he realized that he'd just lost our staring-dominance contest. Being a vampire, he probably didn't care.

His threats had my heart beating a little rapidly, but panic didn't fully settle into my limbs. No point inviting worry yet. If things were going to go to shit, I'd deal with them at that time.

"Worried?" I tilted my head to see Braxton.

He grimaced before throwing down the last of the assfood that had been on his plate. I couldn't believe he'd managed to eat any of it.

"We'll see," he muttered as we dumped our trays and left the eating area.

He led me to the section that we'd walked past but I hadn't explored, a gym and pool combo filled with many muscle-bound inmates.

"I need to work off some steam," Braxton said.

I could see that he did.

I had a sudden thought. "Can you touch your dragon?" He didn't seem to be suffering as badly as me.

He cocked one brow in my direction, before winking. Holy effing eff. Was he for real? I might have to beat the information out of him later when he couldn't escape me.

"Can I swim?" I asked, sure he would say no, since he wanted me glued to his side. But he wasn't the only one who needed to work off some steam.

"Sure. I'll keep an eye on you from over here."

That's what I really loved about Braxton: he understood when to hover and when I needed space. It was hard for dominant men to ever give up their control, and Braxton rarely did. But on occasion, he did with me. I left him on one of the weight machines and strolled the thirty feet to the pool.

There weren't many swimming in the crystal clear water. I decided to just go for the gold, clothes and all. It was hot enough that the thin cotton would dry in no time. I dived in and powered down one of the lanes. I could hold my breath for a long time, so it was many minutes before I emerged and started to slice through the water. My limbs welcomed the strain. Exercise was a daily part of my life, and I needed the release to calm the wolf and demon inside.

I almost swallowed half the pool when a sudden realization smashed into me. My demon. Was it still in there or did the security measures limit it also? I sent my energy down, passing my caged wolf—who I knew was unhappy, even though I couldn't feel her—and into that little dark space I kept locked. The demon rose and, well, rubbed against me like a kitty, although there was no way any feline could feel this dark.

I'm here, it seemed to whisper to me. For the first time I was relieved about this. Although I couldn't shake the fear that if I freed the energy, I'd never be able to keep it hidden again. But if it came down to Braxton's life, I would not hesitate. Not for one fucking second.

I continued to swim, only breaking off as a dark shadow emerged beneath me. My heart skipped a few beats, then I recognized the massive shape. It was Braxton. I'd swum with him enough times to know what was about to hit me. I stopped swimming, throwing myself backward and scooting in backstroke the way I'd just come. I had to get out of the water or he was going to . . . a hand grabbed my ankle, halting my frantic kicking motions.

Damn. Too slow.

Braxton's arms came around me, and then he lifted me into the air. I went high, crashing back down and sinking close to the base of the pool. I was in fighting mode as I dived for him, my momentum enough to dunk him beneath the water. His face was close to mine, and it felt as if his lips brushed my hairline. But before I could kick out to free myself, an alarm started to sound. It was loud, long, and easily able to penetrate the water.

I gasped in a few deep breaths when my head broke the surface. I narrowed my eyes on Braxton as he rose next to me. He looked sexy as sin, all wet, clothes clinging to his hard muscles. Damn him, the dimples flashing in my direction. It was enough to undo any woman. Luckily, I was immune to the Compass charms. Swear.

"Time to head back to our cell," he said to me, his hand finding mine in the water.

Oh well, at least the alarm wasn't anything serious. Although I'd had a faint hope that someone was coming to break us out.

Chapter 14

Braxton and I lay on our bunks. They were just a tad softer than the stone floor, but smelled worse. I'd almost ended up crashing on the ground. It had been lights out for a few hours, but I couldn't sleep. The howls and screams that echoed along the shifter wing were part of the problem—shifters go crazy locked behind stone walls, and some had been here for many years—but the other problem was my head. It just wouldn't stop thinking. I was worrying about the dragon marked, Mischa, my family, and the Compasses. I knew Kristoff was evil, and there was no way he would stop at enacting revenge, because his plans kept going awry. Louis flittered across my mind on occasion, too, but he was a little farther back than the rest.

The noise of Braxton's bulk moving on his bunk had me turning my head to the side. In the semidarkness I could see him watching me. "What's going on in that pretty head of yours, Jessa?" His voice was low, gentle. Kind of unlike his normal tone.

I made a decision right then to share some of my burden. I had a secret that I'd been keeping and I hated that. It was eating away at me like a poison, and I needed to get it out before it did permanent damage. I rolled off my bed and padded silently across the small room—four steps and I was right beside his bunk. His ancient eyes, so out of place on his twenty-two-year-old face, caressed my features.

I dropped to my knees right beside his head. "I need to tell you something." I leaned in close to whisper. There were too many ears in this place.

He shifted himself over then, pressing his back against the wall and I crawled in next to him. It was a tight fit; he had to drape his arm around me, and we lay facing each other, our mouths close.

"You can tell me anything, Jess." I could feel his breath hitting my face. I almost had to close my eyes so I didn't press my lips to his. Damn, my urge to kiss him was strong and annoyingly inconvenient. Now was not the time to have a sexual meltdown.

"There was another reason I was so determined to free those prisoners," I said slowly. "I believe they're dragon marked. And . . ." I took a deep breath. "I'm marked also."

Blue flashed darker in his eyes; they looked indigo in this low light. "What do you mean?"

I snuggled my face into the crook of his neck, and in whispers told him the entire story, from my birth as a twin, to the lengths Jonathon and Lienda had gone to keep Mischa and me safe. The way Louis had spelled the energy to help us hide.

When I finished, I lay still, my body tensed as I waited for his reaction. He didn't move for a long time . . . and hot tears were building up behind my eyes. I willed them not to fall, but if Braxton decided he didn't know who I was anymore and that he didn't want to know me, I'd probably fall apart.

Then his arms moved tighter around me, and he crushed me into his chest. "Why didn't you tell me when you found out? Please, for the love of all things, please tell me it wasn't because you were fucking afraid of my reaction?"

I shook my head against his chest. "Dad said that the last quads born, the Four, are infamous dragon-marked hunters. He seems to think that's to be you and your brothers' fates also. He didn't want me to make myself vulnerable to you."

Braxton cursed. "There's no way we would become dragon-marked hunters. I don't care about the call."

"The call?" I asked, stilling. I'd never heard of that.

He was very calm as he spoke. "On the day we join our powers together, we will feel the call. The original four, their calling was to hunt dragon marked—they can track the energy and are lethal at their jobs. No one knows what our call will be, although many guess it is going to be the same thing." His fierce eyes locked on me. "But we would never hurt you. It wouldn't matter; I would kill myself first. And I know that Ty, Jake, and Max feel the exact same way."

"You're my best friend," I whispered to him. "I'm thankful every day for you Compasses."

His lips pressed against my forehead, one of those firm, lingering kisses that sent thrills from the tip of my head down to my toes. "Do you need to tell me anything else?"

Strange that he'd used the word *need* and not *want.*

I swallowed, trying to get myself under control. "Do you know any more of the stories of the dragon marked? What exactly is it everyone is so afraid of?"

He settled back against the stone, bringing me with him. "The time of the king of the dragons was filled with war and bloodshed. So many supernaturals lost their lives. When the king made his proclamation, they were in Drago, which is a cave that rests in a mountain range in Romania. We're right on the cusp of the thousand years since his fall. Legend says the best chance for him to rise will be at the end of this year."

That was less than a month away.

"How is that supposed to happen?"

Braxton shrugged. I could feel the movement along the mattress. "I don't know; no one seems to. Something to do with the dragon marked and a sacrifice."

During our history lessons, I remembered the teacher explaining that there were words—or an incantation—supposedly inscribed on the walls of his tomb. Of course this was hard to prove because no one had been able to enter the Drago tomb since the king was interred.

"So, from the original four quads, is the shifter a dragon?" I asked.

Braxton's hands were gently running along my arm now, the movement soothing. "No, they're old enough that if he'd been a dragon, he'd have been killed."

We lay together in companionable silence for a while before eventually I went back to my own bed. I needed to get some sleep if I was going to make it through the next day.

The dream hit me hard and fast that night. It was the same one I'd had all those weeks earlier, with Mischa and the dragons. I fought against the pull again, and again with the attack—death, fire, heat, and pain filled the world. I found myself jarring awake. I managed not to scream, but my whimpers were pretty damn loud.

Braxton was crouched beside my bunk, one hand resting on that space between my breasts and throat, his warmth filling my heart and offering comfort.

"Wh-what time is it?" I croaked out. I couldn't orientate myself without the sun, and there were no interior lights on yet.

"Still early, you were thrashing around for a while. I was waiting for you to wake."

In that moment, I was vulnerable, half-asleep, half in the dream world. I couldn't suppress the emotion like I normally would.

"I'm afraid, Brax." I let the words slip through my bared teeth.

His hand flexed on my chest. I could see it was an involuntary movement; he didn't even seem to notice he'd done it. "I won't let anything happen to you in here. I promise."

I closed my eyes, sucking in a deep breath before meeting his unwavering gaze again. "Not just about being in here, more about the future. The mark—even though it's spelled, it's going to come back and find me. Secrets don't stay hidden forever. I don't want to fight. I don't want to be hunted."

I didn't want to ever find myself on the opposite side of a war with someone I loved. My dreams continued to indicate that it was going to reach a point where I had to choose between my twin sister and something else.

He was opening his mouth to answer when the dangling yellowed lightbulb above us flickered to life. The fake illumination spread around the dark spaces, and suddenly the world felt a little more exposed. I knew today was not going to go as well as yesterday. Everyone who had ever gunned for my father was going to be gunning for me today.

"Twenty minutes until shower time," Braxton said as he gritted his teeth. "They don't separate us, even in the bathroom. But unless you want me in the same stall as you, well, you'll be out of my sight for a bit."

I found myself having to work very hard to hide my thoughts right then. Holy fuck me. Braxton in the shower, water running over those deliciously hardened muscles. Too much for a sexually deprived wolf shifter . . . way too much. I could not be trusted with naked male parts right now.

"I'm sure it won't have to come to that," I kind of blurted.

His lazy grin was enough for me to want to throat-punch myself. Clearly, I had not hidden my emotions very well.

"I don't think I can remember the last time you blushed, Jessa." His dimples assaulted me as he stood stretching out his giant frame.

I swung my legs over the side, flipping him off at the same time. Yeah, I totally nailed that comeback. Stupid dragon, throwing me off my game.

It felt like an hour—while I was pacing the cell in an agitated manner—for the silver-threaded barred gates to slide open. They were on some sort of automatic-locking system that opened every door at the same time. Braxton and I waited until the majority had left and were heading down the long corridor. We joined the back of the crowd, and again he had my hand clenched tightly in his own. Just before we reached that large double-barred door leading out into the circular area, the group veered off to the right through a smaller door I hadn't noticed yesterday.

Another corridor: The walls were rock near the start, but as we walked along, they slowly morphed into tiles. The walkway opened up and I realized it was one large shower room, massive and square, with rows of showers down one side, hundreds of them, each with a curtain that could be pulled between them for separation.

"Screw it," Braxton growled. "I'm coming in with you. We can just turn our backs on each other."

I knew what had gotten him so upset again. A lot of stares were being leveled in our direction, and there was a distinctive dark nature to most of them. Surprisingly enough, the majority of venom was coming from the women. Which I was used to, especially since I was always with the Compasses. The female supernaturals wanted the biggest, baddest boy in their race. It was a sign of our own female strength, power, and attractiveness to snag an alpha. Pathetic, I know. But Braxton, Maximus, Jacob, and Tyson were the best of the best. I was the number one reason to blame for them not settling down with anyone. Which was bullshit. No one controlled those men, and that was mainly why they were forever single. That, and they believed in finding their mates, which they had yet to do.

Whips in hand, the guards spread out around the room. I wanted to flinch at the silver glinting in the leather, but I forced myself to stay calm.

"You have forty minutes to clean yourselves up," a stocky mage yelled out into the room. "Move it now."

Forty minutes was longer than I'd expected.

Braxton and I strode to the shower right on the very end. I knew why he would want this stall. If we were attacked, there were only two sides from which they could come at us, instead of three. We stepped into the tight space, the curtain sliding across to block out the world. I reached down to lift off my shirt.

"You know what, I'll go in the one next to you." Braxton's voice went low. "No one can attack you from the side and I'll see them pass mine to get to your stall."

Just like that he was gone. I stood there for a moment, staring at my bare feet that rested on the tiled floor. Thankfully this place looked to be cleaned with magic, so it was sparkling. No foot fungus here. Okay, what was Braxton's deal? It had better be that my body turned him on and not that he found me repulsive, because I was totally not cool with that. Best friend or not, I thought he was the yummiest thing since chocolate cake, and it hurt somewhere deep in my chest that maybe . . . maybe he didn't see me the same way.

Did this mean I wanted to date him? Hell no. It just meant I wasn't blind or stupid.

Shit, I was acting like a silly girl. We had more important things to worry about. I quickly stripped off my clothes and hung them on one of the pegs. The water was automatically running in each stall, so I stepped under it. I expected it to be cold, some sort of prison torture, but instead it was deliciously warm. Since it had been pretty cool outside in the stone-and-tile room, my limbs relaxed under the warmth. There were soap dispensers attached to the tiles. The entire time I kept my back to the wall and my eyes locked on the thin curtain. No one was getting the drop on me, and I was so not thinking about Braxton's naked body just inches from my own. No freaking way.

"Don't drop the soap, Brax," I teased through the thin layer. We needed to get back to our usual selves. Something was changing, and I wasn't sure I was okay with it.

I heard his groan. "Jessa, you're going to be the death of me."

I snorted, no idea what that even meant.

When I was finished, I reluctantly stepped back from the water. There was a towel hanging on a hook, and I knew the clothes were out on the shelves that lined the walls.

I slipped past the curtain, the white cotton towel wrapped tightly around me. Braxton was already there, waiting, dressed and watching for me to emerge.

"I got you some cottons," he said, holding out a lump of gray material.

"Thanks." I took them and slipped behind the curtains to throw them on.

Gah, I was already sick of this color. Even the underwear matched. Oh well, guess I should be grateful to even have clothes. I'd heard that one of the prisons in Europe had to mandate a full-nudity policy. They were having incidents with concealed weapons and smuggling of goods. There was no screwing around in these prisons. If things needed to be done, they happened . . . immediately. Although one would have thought that the nudity thing would lead to problems of another nature. It would have been a full-on disaster in human prisons. Luckily, supes were naked a lot so it didn't end up being a huge deal, and it worked. The incidents of concealed goods and weapons dropped dramatically.

Stepping out of the stall again, I moved to my guard dragon's side. The shifters were congregating now, forming a line to get back out of the shower area. We were a little in front, our hands linked.

"Don't come to the mingling room at lunchtime." The voice was female, low, and whispered directly into my ear. I spun around to find a small red-haired woman ducking back down through the line.

I started to follow her, but the guards walking the line stopped me with a hand on my arm.

"Forward! Shower time is over" was the gruff order.

Braxton didn't look worried, which meant he hadn't heard her. She'd definitely been warning me, but I couldn't tell if her position was that of friend or enemy.

"Do we have to go into the mingling room, or can we stay in our cell?" I asked Braxton, standing on tiptoes to move closer to his ear.

"We have to go." He glanced at me. "Why?"

I shook my head. "No reason, just worried about being attacked."

He didn't say anything, but I could sense his unease. Most wouldn't have noticed, but I knew him.

We were back in our cells for a few hours. I spent most of the time curled up, pretending to read a book. Braxton did weird stuff, like push-ups and crap. I don't think I'll ever be bored or stressed enough to do a push-up. But we'll see. My head flew up from the shifter romance I was reading at the ominous sound of our barred gate opening. Uniformed guards lined the hall and started ushering all of us along. I recognized a few of them; they gave me a head nod as I passed. No matter what they personally thought, I was still their alpha and council leader's daughter, and respect was given.

I hated to admit it, but I was surprised as I observed many of the prisoners around us. Most of them I would never have picked as criminal. Yeah, I'd fallen into the bad habit of thinking they'd be like their stereotype. The scarfaced guy from yesterday, he'd been my idea of most supe crims. But in reality, most looked just like Braxton and me: young, clean-cut, innocent—well, kind of innocent. Until you saw their eyes. Lots of dead eyes in this place. Fair bit of crazy going on, too.

Braxton and I didn't waste any time that day. We went straight to the food, although I didn't hold out much hope that it would be any more edible. Carting my pathetic selection, Braxton behind me, I stopped at one of the empty tables. I dumped my tray down and was about to climb over the bench when someone slammed their tray down right next to me. A glance over my shoulder had Braxton a couple of steps behind me. Shit, he was too far away to help me.

I dodged the first attack, a small man throwing punches, which were simple enough to block. I even managed to connect with his face, resulting in an instant fat lip and bleeding nose. Unfortunately, the small man had a partner: a big man. A very big man. Freaking bear shifter. The hairy beast reached out and slammed his hand around my throat. I choked and brought my hands up to fight against his grip. But before I could struggle, he lifted me up off the floor and I was dangling above the ground. I couldn't breathe, and he was squeezing hard enough that dark spots were already dancing in front of my eyes. Since he hadn't crushed my throat immediately, he was wanting to draw it out. But why?

Between the deafening echo of my own frantic heartbeats, I could hear Braxton roaring, and I could see from the corner of my eye that he had at least ten men on him. He wasn't going to reach me in time. If I wanted to be saved, I was going to have to do it myself.

"I'm very sorry about this," said the dark-haired bear politely. His wide eyes were hard and cold, black as night. "You are just collateral damage in a war that you have no idea about. An innocent victim, punished for crimes you did not commit."

I'd recovered my equilibrium, and even though this man was exceedingly strong, I had to fight back. I lifted my body and slammed my feet into him. At the same time I used my fingers to dig into a pressure point in his hand, weakening his grip just enough for me to punch him straight in the nose. Cartilage cracked under my hand, but he didn't drop me until I chopped his wrist. I hit him hard enough that

I heard another crack and could add two broken bones to my tally. I dropped to the ground, landing in a tangle of limbs. I gasped for breath. I couldn't seem to get the air in there fast enough. I knew I needed to move. Sure enough, bear man recovered quickly. I rolled away as his feet came down at me. He was barefoot, but the strength of his stomp could definitely crush bones.

I got to my feet. I was fast and strong. I would not let him get his hands on me again. Braxton seemed to be holding his own; there were plenty of bodies littered around him.

"Do not fight me. I don't want you to suffer unduly," the bear said. His nose had already stopped bleeding. He held both hands in front of him with no indication he had any pain. Fucker. "If you submit, I'll make it quick."

And yet he hadn't made it quick, he'd wanted me to understand why he was killing me.

What a freakin' gentleman.

I laughed, harsh from my painful and swollen throat. "I don't submit to anyone," I rasped.

He swung at me, which I saw coming from a mile away. It was easy to duck. Bears were strong but lacked speed. I spun around backward, jumping so I could crack him in the head with my shin. I connected right at his temple area.

He shook himself out a little before tilting his head to the side and observing me closer. I'd surprised him. He charged at me, and just as I was bracing myself to dodge again, something hit the bear from the side. Braxton. Without pause, the dragon shifter started to lay into him relentlessly without any kindness. He beat the other shifter until he was nothing but a bloody lump of supernatural on the floor.

The guards stepped in then and broke up the fight. Or more like wrestled Braxton off the unconscious bear. If we didn't heal so quickly, there was no way the bear would have survived that beating. But he would live another day if he received medical attention. Although, as they carted him off, I had my doubts that that was where they were taking him.

Braxton, whose blue eyes were turbulent, was huffing in loud and long breaths. There were so many broken and battered bodies around us, I wasn't even sure what to think or where to look. So I focused on him. He noticed my gaze and took the two steps to my side. Reaching out, he hesitated before gently tracing a finger down my throat.

"Are you okay?" His voice was filled with death. Hard. Angry. And scary as hell.

I could only nod.

He spun away then, and taking one step, hopped up onto the bench seat and then onto the table.

"Listen up, and listen good." His voice was powerful, and still scary. "If anyone lays a finger on Jessa, one fucking finger, I will end them. Do you understand?"

He seemed to look around the entire room, slowly, allowing everyone to meet his eyes. Power was bleeding off him, along with the commanding presence he was born with.

"I know you think you can best us with numbers. But I promise you, anything you deliver I will return, and it will be a thousand times worse. I will never stop. I will come at you for the rest of your days."

I could feel the winds of death in his voice. In that moment I didn't even recognize Braxton. If I didn't know him as well as I knew myself, well, I would be afraid. Very afraid. And judging by the lowering of the eyes, I wasn't the only one.

Braxton scooped me up in his arms and strode from the room. I hadn't even noticed him leave the table; clearly my attention was still a little scattered. I wasn't sure what signal he gave, but when I looked up again, we were back in our cell and the door was secured behind us.

"I thought . . ." I had to clear my throat again to get the rest out. "I thought we couldn't stay in here during mingling time."

He sat me on the bed, his hands more gentle than the fierce expression he still wore. "Let's call this exceptional circumstances and a friend who owed me a favor."

It must have been a pretty big favor—food was delivered to our room and everything. And it was freaking edible food.

"Almost worth dying for," I said around my sandwich, my chicken-bacon-ranch-dressing-deliciousness sandwich. My throat had healed just enough that there was not too much discomfort in swallowing.

"I just can't find the will to laugh at you right now, Jessa." Braxton wasn't eating, his tray untouched in front of him. "You have no idea what it was like to see you in trouble and not be able to reach you." He stood as if his anger needed an outlet. "Twice in the past week you have taken ten years off my life, and I'm thinking of a way to collect."

I narrowed my eyebrows at him. "Not my fault, and you better get used to it. I'm sure to get worse with age."

"I don't think I'll survive it." His voice was honest, no joke in his tone.

I licked a bit of sauce off my index finger. "Are you going to eat that?" I was on my feet and halfway across the room when he snatched the tray up and held it above his head.

"Yes!" he growled.

My face fell, and he shook his head a few times before staring at the ceiling. With a sigh he reached up and grabbed something off the tray. The smallest smile finally graced his face as he handed me a paper plate. Nestled in the center was a slice of lemon cake.

I stared at it for a moment before a tear escaped the corner of my eye.

Braxton laughed. "You are still the only supe I know to cry about cake."

I sucked down my sob. "There are very few things in this world that can move me to tears." I hugged the plate close to my chest. "This is just beautiful."

I stared at it for a few extra beats, but finally I couldn't resist any longer. I lifted the sugary goodness up and placed a corner to my lips. Moans fell from my mouth as the smooth, buttery lemon taste coated my tongue. When I finally finished the cake, I noticed Braxton was just staring at me, his sandwich halfway to his mouth.

"What?" I mumbled.

"You almost died and this . . . this is what moves you to tears and moans."

I widened my eyes and bit my lip. What was he saying? I was shallow? How dare he, asshole . . . Okay, maybe I was a little.

But then he exhaled, and a flicker of his dimple appeared. He seemed to wrench his eyes away from me. "Don't ever change," he said in a low tone. "Ever."

Hmmm, maybe *shallow* was not the word he was thinking, then.

The rest of the afternoon was peaceful, which is strange considering I had almost died that day. The bruises on my neck came out in spectacular fashion by the time dinner trays were delivered. Shifter healing was extraslow with all of the silver around. The trays held no cake this time, but that was okay. I'd already had my fill for the day. The next few days followed in the same routine, and like good supernaturals, most of the prisoners were taking Braxton's warning very seriously. But for some reason I felt as if something big was coming my way.

Two days until the trial, we were sitting in the gym area. Braxton was lifting like a thousand-ton weight or something ridiculous. I was doing sit-ups.

His voice startled me. "Jessa, I haven't heard any more numbers after eight." Shit . . . I'd fallen asleep on the blue mat.

I struggled into another sit-up. "I did like fifty—I just didn't count them all." I smoothed back a few tendrils that had escaped my ponytail and wiped off the trail of drool from my mouth.

I flicked my head around at an increase in the already impressive noise level. I stood to try to find the source. The multitude of guards that were usually camped out around the perimeter started going crazy, sprinting from their stations toward the front gate. As an alarm began to wail, Braxton pulled me closer to him. This siren was really different from the short burst that announced the end of mingling time.

"What's going on?" I wondered if Braxton had a better view.

He shook his head, using a towel to mop up sweat. "No idea, but something is definitely up. Let's move closer." He was all business as he dropped the white cloth and gripped my hand, pulling me through the masses.

As we moved through the crowd, I recognized one of the guards dashing past us. I reached out and grabbed his arm. He glared down at me, before shaking himself free.

"You might be my council leader's daughter," the wolf shifter growled at me. "But in here you're a prisoner and you don't get to touch me."

I ignored his words. "What's going on? What's the alarm for?"

The siren was loud enough to make talking difficult, but I knew he heard my questions. He hesitated. I didn't think he would answer, but then with a sigh he said, "I'm not totally sure. We haven't been briefed yet, but that alarm generally means there's been a breakout."

He took off then, leaving Braxton and me staring around the room.

"I heard it was more dragon marked," a female said from close by.

My head spun to find a witch, with very short pixie hair, watching the room. She continued to speak. "It was from a secret room. Two women, alone, staged the breakout."

Braxton and I exchanged a glance. Could they have freed them from that room we got Nash from? How the hell were these women doing this? Just two of them? It would be impossible if they didn't have inside information. I tried to contain my excitement that those poor imprisoned supernaturals might be freed now, especially the children. They had not been far from my mind, even with all the prison drama.

The chaos continued for hours, quieting down only when we were finally back in our cells. The information spreading around was exactly what the witch had said. Prisoners freed from a separate section of the prison. What the hell was going on?

The day before we were due to stand trial, I'd just finished in the shower and was stepping out to get dressed. For the first time all week, Braxton wasn't waiting there with clothes. That was odd. He was so diligent in his protection of me that even in our cell he seemed to always be on my ass. And not in a good way. I scrunched my towel a little tighter, tucking in the lip to stop it from falling down. Looking left and right, I saw there were lots of shifters around, but no massive dragon man to be seen.

I was worried, but knew I needed to get dressed before I started searching. With my eyes darting around, paying attention to my surroundings, I crossed the freezing tiled floor in the direction of the shelves. I reached the women's section and moved down to find something in my size. I'd just turned my face to see what was in the next row when something hit me hard on the side of the head.

I know I let out a strangled yelp, but darkness descended across my mind before I even had a chance to see my attackers. I fought the pull. If I let the fuzziness win, I was as good as dead. If I knew anything, it was that an unconscious person can't fight back. And I wasn't going down without a fight. I dropped to my knees; my head wanted to pitch forward, but I held on to consciousness. As my attacker wedged their hands under my armpits, I swung out with all my strength. A male curse sounded as I hit something solid, and I took the opportunity to struggle as hard as I could, yelling and hollering. Of course, all of that came to a stunning conclusion with a second blow to the temple.

Chapter 15

Consciousness returned slowly, the ache in my head almost as bad as the fey wine hangover. Except this time I didn't have that moment of disorientation where I couldn't remember what had happened. I recalled the events perfectly. I'd been attacked in the showers.

I didn't open my eyes straightaway. I tried to get my bearings. I was flat on my back, hard cold stone beneath me. Judging by the chill, I was naked still and my hands were tied above my head. Icy metal was biting into my wrists; my feet felt the same.

Great! Could I be in a more vulnerable position? Naked and chained spread-eagled across the floor.

I had to know what I was up against, so I opened my eyes. The room was dark, stone walls embedded with earth elements and magic. Still inside the prison. From the small area I could see, there was no one close by. Although I sensed someone there, just out of my line of sight. I fought against the bindings on my wrists. The metal cuffs held no silver, which was a bonus, but I wasn't strong enough to break them, especially without full connection to my wolf. I could feel her howling, but couldn't reach out and touch her.

Where was Braxton? What had they done to him? Icy tendrils of fear were churning in my gut. I was afraid for myself, but more important, I needed to know my friend was okay. It had to be something big for them to be able to take him out.

"Awake I see." A shadow crossed over my face and a male stood over me. Scarface.

I snarled at him. I was in such a submissive position, and I hated it. If my wolf hadn't been chained down, she would be going nuts.

Scarface grinned as he continued to stare at me, his stone-like eyes eerie. "Sorry if my boys were a little rough. We only had moments before your guard awoke."

I schooled my features to hide my relief. Did that mean Braxton was alive?

"Simple tranq took care of him . . . for five minutes," he muttered. "We left him be. Our issue is not with him, but with Jonathon Lebron."

He stepped a little closer, and I started growling. I wished I could attack him. He tilted his head to the side, watching me closely.

"Sins of the father are the sins of the daughter. So you must die."

Well, damn. That was harsh.

"Although, my friend wants to have a little fun with you first." He looked away from me, and as if he'd sent a silent signal, another shadow peeled itself off the dark walls.

Vlad. Great, he'd be looking to punish me for my attitude the other day, and Braxton for his threat.

With nothing to lose, I decided it was time to speak up. "Little pathetic, don't you think? You didn't even give me a chance to fight. There is no victory in winning like this." I spat each and every word at them.

The two men exchanged a glance, and once again an unspoken conversation passed between them. Scarface gave me one last smile before he left the room . . . left me with one of the most insane, violent supernaturals alive.

Vlad knelt next to me. "You're mistaken if you think this is about me proving my dominance. I don't need to best you in combat. I don't care for that accolade. This is purely about punishment and my own personal enjoyment." He leaned even closer and his foul breath washed over me. "And you couldn't be in a better position for what I have in mind."

I froze then, my entire body and mind shutting down, as if it couldn't process what was about to happen. I had no doubts of what his words meant, and fear blasted me like a snowstorm. Sure, I was a tough wolf shifter, but the thought of rape is enough to bring anyone to their knees. There's nothing quite as debilitating as having your humanity stripped away.

I refused to show fear to this creature, though. He would never know that he had brought me to a place no one else ever had. A place of being a victim. He hadn't even touched me yet, but my imagination needed no help. I knew what was to come next.

I went with false bravado. "Someone is going to find me. I have friends on the inside here."

He grinned, the pointed teeth reflecting the small fragments of light in the room. They must have a lantern or something lit. "I have a lot of power inside these walls, and I spent the entire week working out the exact logistics of capturing you. Trust me, by the time they find you, well, actually, there will be nothing left to find. This is not the first time we've done this; people disappear inside here all the time. They're used to it."

I calmed my voice. "Not the shifter alpha and council leader's daughter. I'm thinking they might investigate a little further into my disappearance. And the Compasses . . ." I grinned for the first time since my capture. "Oh, the Compasses are going to have fun with you."

At least I knew that much. Even if I did die in this shithole today, my revenge would be exacted. It made facing the next few hours of my life almost bearable.

His confidence faltered so minutely that if I hadn't been boring holes into his face with my eyes, I would not have noticed it. But he'd let it slip.

"If you let me go, I will forget this happened. We both walk away and never speak of it again."

Lie. I was going to fucking kill him. But he was a vampire, and they couldn't scent truth in someone's words as easily as a shifter. I'd always been an excellent liar. I'd steadied my heart rate and controlled my fear.

For a second there I thought I'd gotten through to him. Then he straightened, resolve crossing his features again, and I knew that he'd moved past the fear. He was back in a position of crazy sociopath vampire. No thoughts, no worries.

He reached behind him and grabbed something dark. I struggled, throwing my head from side to side when I realized what it was. He gripped my face tightly, holding it in place as he shoved the entirety of the strip of material into my mouth.

"Stop talking, wolf. I'd like to enjoy myself, and this incessant chatter is making me angry. Angry enough to kill you. And I promised I wouldn't do that. That's someone else's joy."

As he released my face, I started struggling again, spitting and swearing behind my gag. I could feel myself morphing into something a little feral, animalistic. My caged wolf howled and screamed with me, and I was still thankful to have her, suppressed bond and all. I fought and bucked more as he leaned into me, and then with no hesitation he sank his fangs into my throat.

I'd never let any vampire drink from me, not even Maximus. Although he'd healed a few of my cuts and said my blood was delicious. So I had no idea of the sensation of being fed on, and now that I knew, well, I didn't like it. It hurt. Badly.

Vlad wasn't trying to make it nice for me. He was rough and mean and did not send even an ounce of calming energy toward me. He wanted my fear and anger; strong emotions made the blood change. See, I'd paid attention in vampire studies.

I knew I was starting to lose a lot of blood. I could feel that crazy, light-headed haze that preluded a blackout. I wanted to fight, but my strength was disappearing.

He pulled away from me then. There was a loud crack. It took me a few moments to realize he'd slapped me. The pain was a dull register.

"Don't pass out on me yet. I want you conscious for this. It's no fun if you don't know what's happening."

He was going to die a thousand deaths, in this life and every single one after this. The right side of my face was numb, which meant he'd hit me hard enough to do a bit of damage. In fact, my eye was starting to swell and close already.

"Your blood is incredible. I'm tempted to steal you away and keep you as my personal sex and blood slave." He sighed. "But alas, other important people need some of you, so I'll just have to enjoy my fill today."

He started to touch me then, running his finger from my lips down my chin to my breasts. Despite my lethargy, this sent a shot of adrenaline through me and I started to fight and scream around the gag. I would not let this happen. I could not let this happen. I tried to reach my wolf, fighting the bars that caged her. But it was like trying to dig through stone with my fingertips. Useless. We both started to howl together. And then a third voice joined in.

My demon.

The vampire's fingers were moving lower again, circling around my belly button. The piece of shit was prolonging this, driving the fear, the anticipation for himself, so full and flushed with my blood.

I flung free the cage on the demon. After twenty-two years I was damning all consequences and releasing the bonds. An unearthly whistling started to ring through my body, so loud I couldn't tell if the noise was inside or if the vampire could hear it, too. Then power flooded me, strong, thick, and all-encompassing. The cage around my wolf was blown away, but in that moment I was too overwhelmed to latch on to her. In fact, she seemed to be cowering away a little, letting the demon power free. It continued to fill me. I could see the tide flowing, and I wondered what would happen when it reached the top of my head.

As the swell reached its peak, I knew I was about to find out. I closed my eyes, as if somehow that was going to make this easier. It didn't.

A thousand knives stabbed through me, filleting my skin, breaking my bones, destroying everything that I was and remaking me as something new. I'd felt a similar pain the first time I'd shifted to wolf, but such a minute piss-poor version of this that it was barely worth comparing. I huffed in and out, my breath limited behind the cloth. I needed more air. I needed to be free. There was nothing worse than this sort of pain and the inability to move around on the ground. My eyes were still closed. I couldn't seem to open them. I burst free from my chains, and in the same heartbeat I shifted.

It took longer than usual, and afterward I was disoriented. Getting to all fours, I expected to feel like my wolf. But something was wrong, off about the shift. Why the hell was the floor so far away? My eyesight was strange as well. Generally I saw things in a black, white, and grayscale landscape, but now I had superintense vision. Even in the darkness, the room was so bright, colors streaming at me in long waves. Was I seeing the freaking light spectrum?

I was hungry, so hungry. I wanted to eat, and there was only one thing in this room even remotely edible. I stumbled, unsure of these new longer limbs. It felt as if I were heavier at the back; something dragged along and tripped me up. It took two steps to reach the vampire cowering in the corner.

Enemy.

Must be destroyed. Instinct driving me, I opened my mouth.

"Jessa!"

A shout halted my movement. I spun around; my head seemed to be able to swivel at least ninety degrees farther than it could as a wolf. Braxton stood on the other side of the room, his hands held aloft. I'd reacted to the noise of his yell, but the name meant nothing to me.

I was not a Jessa. I was a nightmare brought to life. I could kill, destroy, and hunt with ease. I was never going to be weakened again. I was a dragon.

It had taken my mind a few minutes to piece it together. Not a shadow spirit, I was the real deal.

Braxton didn't move, but his voice lowered and started to caress my senses. "It's okay, sweetheart. Nothing will hurt you now. You need to shift back, find Jessa inside."

I stepped closer, more sure on the clawed feet. Then his scent hit me; it was that of family, kin. He was me, and I was him. We were not enemies, but friends. I opened my jaw and a loud, echoing roar emerged. In that moment I found myself again. If I hadn't had so much experience controlling my wolf, I think the dragon would have taken me over forever. But I could fight it and I did. My demon was a dragon. I was a dragon *and* a wolf, somehow.

Dual shifter? I'd never heard of anything like that in my life. I knew the demon, uh, dragon, would not go back into its cage. So now it was about learning how to live with her. Already the wolf had accepted the third part of me. Human, wolf, and dragon. It was not natural, and I wasn't sure how to control it. The only thing I had working for me was that I'd been dealing with the wolf and demon energy my entire life. It was this strength I drew on, pulling the dragon energy back far enough to trigger the shift to my human form.

After my change I lay on the freezing floor, unable to lift my head. Shudders continued to flow over me. The dragon settled back inside, almost voluntarily moving into her cage. It was as if now that she'd been free once, she was more confident in her place within me, no longer fighting me but coexisting, like my wolf.

Warmth draped over me, and I was gathered into strong arms. "You're safe, Jessa." The deep voice wrapped around me as warm as the shirt he'd laid over me. I could scent Braxton all over the material, so it was probably his own shirt he'd removed. "We're getting out of the prison."

I wasn't in pain any longer, but a deep-seated exhaustion had taken hold and didn't seem to be letting go. It was strange. The first time I'd shifted to wolf I'd been energized, but now I felt drained.

"What color was I?" My slurred question was unexpected. Of everything I could have asked—like, where had he been? Was he okay? Or even, how were we getting out of the prison?—I'd asked about my color. But I was trying to picture the dragon in my head.

"Blue and silver," he said. "Like an iridescent wash of rainbow but in those hues." He hesitated. I felt his chest heave.

"What?" I mumbled.

"I've never seen this on a dragon before, and there's no reference in the history books, but, well, you had fur."

I squinted one eye, trying to figure out if I'd understood him correctly.

"Fur?"

He pulled me closer into his chest. "Yes, in most ways you looked like my dragon self, only smaller and more delicate. But then, sort of in the same places as a horse's mane, you had this strip of black hair or fur, and the rest of your body looked like it was . . . furry. It was almost as if some of your wolf had bled into the dragon."

"How is this possible, Brax?" My shivers had subsided a little as we continued our journey through the prison. "Dual shifter."

For the first time since he'd found me, some of the confidence fled his voice. "I don't know, Jessa. But for now I think we should keep this discovery to ourselves."

I nodded into his chest. That sounded like a good idea to me.

"Where were you, and how are we getting out of the prison?"

I also wondered what had happened to Vlad. I really hoped I hadn't eaten him; I'd be picking vamp from my teeth for weeks.

His chest rumbled. "Someone hit me with a dart when I was climbing out of the shower. It didn't last long in my system, but it was still enough time for them to disappear with you. When I woke, there was a shifter in the room. She helped me get word to Jeremy, the head guard. Jeremy ferried my call for help to your father. Word came back almost immediately: we're free to leave; Jonathon pushed for an early trial. We're on our way there now."

Clearly, it was easier getting information out of the prison than in.

Braxton lowered his head; his fierce blue eyes met mine. "They know you're most probably injured. It should—if Louis has done his job—be dismissed immediately."

I hoped so. I needed this nightmare to be over so I could move on to the next problem. Dragon marked and dual shifting. I was one special cupcake. Special enough to be dead real fast.

"Vlad was not in the best state when you finished with him. You smashed him with your tail when you turned around."

I totally did not remember that.

Braxton's voice was hard when he spoke again. "I couldn't find you, Jessa. I was going crazy, trying not to panic, but thinking I wasn't going to make it in time. Then . . . it must have been when you called the dragon energy." Reverence crept in. "I could feel you . . . like we were connected. There was almost this string that emerged from my chest and I followed it straight to you. I made my way into that room just as you started to shift. I wouldn't have believed it if I hadn't seen it myself."

"I'm still not sure I believe it." I had a sudden thought. "Which shifter helped you and got in touch with Jeremy?"

"I don't know her name," he said. "She was standing over me when I came around after the tranq. I almost killed her."

I knew it was going to be the same lady. "Red hair?"

He narrowed his eyes as he glared down again. "Yes, how did you know? She did tell me that long ago she was friends with your mother. She recognized you when you arrived, and as an owed favor to Lienda, she tried to look out for you."

"That first morning in the shower room, she warned me about the impending attack."

I waited for his reprimand. We both knew I should have told him, but he took pity on me and left it for now. I was starting to fade out. My mind was going to force me to rest and recover. Finally, the motion of being carried was too much and my eyes closed. I drifted off into a semiconscious sleep.

Screams left my throat as I started to thrash around. I was captured, naked, vulnerable. I wouldn't let them have me; I'd rather be dead than submit to these men. When hands touched me, I fought harder.

Voices started to penetrate my subconscious. A symphony of male and female. All of them familiar to me.

"Stop her; she's going to hurt herself."

The sound of my twin sister's voice was what got through to me first. A door slammed open somewhere.

"Get your hands off her; she doesn't know who's touching her." Braxton's voice was icy as he barked out his order.

The warm hands left me, and my body started to calm. Even though a part of me had been aware that I was safe with friends and family, I couldn't halt the racing panic until everyone removed their hands from me. Braxton understood. My wolf and dragon flexed their energy, each asking if I needed them. I sent reassurance their way before lifting my heavy eyelids and taking in the scene around me.

Jonathon, Lienda, and Mischa were along one side of my bed, and the Compasses on the other. I was in my room. Standing farther back, in the doorway, was Louis. I sat up. I couldn't stand to be beneath everyone at that moment. In fact . . . I got to my feet and stood on my bed. The tension that had been gripping my chest eased a little as I positioned myself as the most dominant in the room. No one challenged my place right then. Glancing down, I was thankful someone had found the time to put Braxton's shirt on me. It hung almost to my knees and hid everything important. Right now I wanted none of my body on display.

"What happened?" My eyes sought my dad, and as he tilted his head in my direction, I knew he was asking if he could approach.

I sucked in a ragged breath before nodding. I could use some pack energy right now, some strength to draw on. He slowly stepped to the side of the bed, and his strong arms enveloped me as they had done so many times throughout my life. I collapsed into him, letting his energy soothe me, and despite the fact that being touched wigged me out right now, touch also helped heal some of the hurt.

"Vlad has been taken care of, Jess," he whispered into my hair. "He'll never bother you again."

Good. The only thing that would have made that better was if I'd been the one to kill him.

"At this stage they've temporarily halted the trial. But you will have to be present at a future trial. Formality, really. Louis has been 'disappearing' the evidence, but it needs to be officially dismissed with you there."

Let's hope Jonathon was right. One never knew what the *Book of Guidance* would decide.

"I have some news." Louis was still slouched in the doorway, his broad shoulder nudged against the frame. "Something we need to deal with immediately. The Four are on their way to Stratford. Something set off their hunting instinct. They're going to be looking for marked."

"Shit," I said, pulling away from my dad. "That was probably me. I think I broke the cage you had on me."

Louis nodded. "Yes, you did. The energy sent a blast wave through Stratford, and obviously out into the universe. Most wouldn't have known what it was, but I recognized the mark." His eyes flashed. "I knew you were in trouble. I was coming to the prison when I intercepted the guard heading for Jonathon."

Ah, that was how word got to my father so fast. Louis. I should have known.

"What?" This word from Maximus was slow, drawn out. There was a hint of anger but more of disbelief.

Jacob and Tyson also straightened and moved closer to me. "What are you saying, Jessa?" Jacob's fey features were unreadable, but the green of his eyes shone in the half-light.

I sucked in deeply. I had forgotten they didn't know of my mark. Only Braxton knew.

I held both hands in front of me. It was time to tell the truth. I should have trusted them with this secret long ago. My voice barely wavered as I started to speak.

"I owe you all the biggest apology. There's something about me that you don't know, something I only just recently found out myself."

Braxton moved closer, and I could tell that he wanted to jump in and smooth this over with his brothers. To protect me from their anger and pain. But this was my thing, and I needed to alpha up and take the punishment.

"Mischa and I are twins, and we are dragon marked," I blurted. My sister straightened and crossed her arms over her chest. She was waiting for the fallout, too.

Silence descended over the room, a heavy silence that was filled with angry thoughts and three thunderous expressions.

I hurried on: about how Louis had spelled us and Lienda had fled to save our lives. That I'd only found out that morning in the forest, and how Jonathon thought it was best to keep it secret. The entire time I was babbling, I continued to hope they would interrupt and give me a break from the guilt.

Maximus did finally speak, but it wasn't what I thought he was going to say. "You told Braxton?" Hurt poured off him. "Why did you trust him but not the rest of us?" *Why not me?* was his unspoken question.

Tears were burning my throat again. My wolf and dragon both wanted to howl.

Braxton interrupted him. "It wasn't like that. We were in Vanguard, and she needed me to know so I could protect her. Pull your heads from your asses and stop and think about the situation she was in. This is a topic so controversial our own father thought all dragon marked should be imprisoned or dead."

I could see just the slightest relaxation in Jacob's and Tyson's rigid features. But Maximus shook his head and stormed from the room.

I pressed my hand to my chest, my body trembling slightly. Somehow, this moment felt worse than when I'd been held captive by Vlad. As if I were being stabbed repeatedly in the chest. Jacob and Tyson stepped right up to me.

Jacob's voice was low. "It's okay, Jessa babe. We understand. Just know there is nothing you could ever tell me that would change the love I have for you."

"Ditto," Tyson said as he kissed me on the cheek. "Max will come around. He just needs a few moments to think about it."

I squeezed my eyes shut then and howled like a baby, hot gushes of tears. Arms encased me and I let free all the emotions that had been building for days. After a while I managed to pull myself together; the quads had moved back and I was standing next to my bed. I decided that now the secrets were out, it was time to ask a few questions.

"Did you hear about the prison breakout?" I asked my dad. "Was it dragon marked?" I'd been needing an answer to this for days.

Jonathon moved over and brushed my hair off my cheek, his warm hand lingering for a moment. "We've received bits and pieces of information. Two women were seen outside the perimeter, and then the next thing anyone knew, they'd disappeared. And the account is that some prisoners are missing also." He brushed a hand over my hair. "Strange thing is, everyone in the main area was accounted for." His growl was low. "Which leaves me to guess that it had to be your secret area."

Louis, who'd had an unreadable expression on his face during my little breakdown, stepped farther into the room. "I have contacts around the world. It is the same in all the prisons. Prisoners escaped, but none from the main prison."

"So the most logical conclusion," I mused: "they're freeing dragon marked." I was strangely relieved about this. No more babies in chains.

Tyson spoke up. "We've had some other drama here also. Kristoff has been arrested. The council's a bit of a mess at the moment."

I turned to my father. "Kristoff was arrested?"

He nodded. "Yes, caught trying to plant a spell on Jacob."

I searched for the blond fey. He was against the wall, looking perfect. Not a hair out of place. "What was the spell?" I asked him.

"An influence spell. He wanted me to attack Tyson and Maximus. He had some sort of dark fey crystal, which we all thought had been destroyed. It made me very susceptible to influence."

Jonathon cleared his throat. "Of course he didn't know we were watching him. Caught him in the act."

Tyson straightened. "Which was lucky, since this crystal would have hidden all of his magical essence. There would have been no way to trace the spell back to the sorcerer."

"But it's over now?" I asked.

Lienda and Jonathon exchanged a glance. "He still has to be tried, but he's off to Vanguard right now." My father grinned. "I'll bet now he wishes that he hadn't pushed for that quick little law change about holding those awaiting trial in the main prison."

A grin also crossed my face. Nice to see karma was still doing its job.

Well, that was one asshole out of the way, but there were four now heading directly for me, and I was no longer safe from the hunters. "Can you block my energy again?" I asked Louis.

He shoved both of his hands in his back pockets, leaning back all sexy and confident. "I can try, Jess, but if my senses are correct, you're probably too strong now." He turned then and started to make his way out of the room. "We have a little time. Find me tomorrow. You know where I'll be." Then he was gone.

Damn, I was hoping he could help me, or I'd have to run. Or fight. Shifting my head, I clashed eyes with Mischa. She had both of her hands covering her mouth. She seemed to be sobbing into them. Before I could stop her, she ran straight up to me and threw her arms around my waist. Her hold was tight, her face buried in my chest. She didn't seem to care or probably even know that she'd put herself in a submissive position to me.

"I was so scared for you. I haven't slept for days." She let the sobbing words trail off, and it was clear she'd thought I was going to die in there. "And Maximus . . . he's so angry."

I held her tightly. "The boys are right. Max is hotheaded, but he's also incredibly smart. He'll understand." I sucked in deeply. "And I'm okay. Nothing too insane happened in Vanguard."

Maybe if I repeated it enough, I'd even believe it.

Although, in the end, it was true. Nothing too crazy had happened. I knew it wouldn't take me long to get past my time in Vanguard. And Vlad was no longer kicking, so that made it much easier to bear. Lienda came in from the side and Jonathon followed. The four of us hugged, one big family group.

"I know you weren't aware, but I owe you thanks for whatever you did to help your redhead friend long ago," I told my mother. "She was a huge help."

Lienda's blue-green eyes flashed in my direction. "Cherise," she breathed. "It had to be. She was my brother's mate. She got herself thrown in Vanguard to be with him. Seems I owe her big-time." Her grip on me tightened. "I was so worried for you. Your dad and I tried to get into the prison, but security is a hell of a lot stronger than it used to be. Lucky that Jon was able to cover up our actions."

"You tried to get in to find me?" I blinked a few times.

A soft smile graced her lips. "We will do anything . . . anything to keep our daughters safe."

My heart swelled at her words, and I sent out a small beam of hope then. Hope that my family would find the time to become the strong unit we should have always been.

Chapter 16

I slept like the dead that night and was thankful that no nightmares woke me from my slumber. Opening my eyes in the morning, I wasn't really surprised to find Braxton slouched in a chair across from me.

I rubbed my eyes a few times, smothering a yawn.

"You know stalking is illegal, right?" I pushed my black hair off my face; it went everywhere when I slept.

He grinned, lazy and smooth. "I'm not leaving you alone while the Four hunt you."

His words reminded me that I needed to visit Louis today. I jumped out of bed. "I haven't missed breakfast, have I?" I'd never been so excited in my life to get to the dining hall.

Braxton straightened. He didn't even bother to hide his grin. "You haven't missed it. I'm going to head home now to change and shower. I'll be back in forty minutes. Ty and Max are downstairs, so you won't be alone."

"Max?" I breathed, hope shooting through me.

Braxton flashed his dimple at me. "As you said, he is hotheaded, but he's never been able to stay mad with you."

Thank God.

The dragon shifter dropped a kiss on my forehead before opening the window. With one leg out of the frame, he suddenly paused, looking back.

"I thought you should know—Nash is marked. Mom told me they discovered the branding on him. Louis spelled him, so he should be safe from the Four."

We exchanged long, intense glances for a few moments, and I knew he had told me so that I'd know my theory of the marked being locked in the secret room was true, that my urge to rescue those poor souls had come from somewhere, most probably the link I shared with them.

With an inclination of his head, he launched out the open window and dropped two stories to the ground. I leaned out after him.

"Five seconds to walk downstairs. Seriously, Brax. Five freaking seconds."

But he was already gone, missing my ladylike cursing. I spun as my door swung open. I was still a little jumpy about having anyone come in at my back. Mischa stepped inside; her hair was damp from a shower and she was dressed in dark denim jeans and a white top.

"Hey, you're awake." She flashed me her blindingly white grin. Way too chipper for this time of the morning. "Just checking on you."

I stifled another yawn, not fully recovered from yesterday's ordeal. "Yep, just about to jump in the shower and then . . . breakfast." I pretty much rubbed my hands together in anticipation.

She wrapped a strand of her hair around and around her fingers. "I'll go with you; I can't wait."

I snorted. "Oh, yeah, I'll bet you're dying for your bowl of cardboard and piece of fruit."

She flipped me off. I wrinkled my nose and stuck my tongue out at her. Very sisterly-like.

"So what happened with you and Brax in the prison?"

Her question caught me by surprise.

"What do you mean?" I hedged as I shuffled through my drawers, grabbing some clothes for the day. I went for the warmer items. The open window had let in some icy winds. It was freezing outside.

I could feel Mischa's eyes on me. "Let's just say he always had that too-gorgeous brooding thing going on, but now he's so intense. Like something happened."

I slammed the drawer shut, clothes clutched in my trembling hands. "You mean besides the fact I was kidnapped by a crazy scar guy and an ancient homicidal vampire, then almost raped and killed right under his nose?"

Yeah, I was unnecessarily harsh, but I didn't want to think about Braxton's intensity right now. It gave me thoughts I didn't know what to do with; and I didn't know which box I could put those feelings in. I liked my life; I didn't want to lose anything. My heart was just too fragile to risk.

Mischa's face fell, the smile wiping itself off like magic. "God, Jess, I am so sorry. That was really insensitive of me."

I shook my head, waving my free hand at her. "No problem. I know you didn't mean anything."

And she hadn't. My sister had an innocence about her, an innocence most of us in Stratford had lost long ago, despite our being pretty much imprisoned in the town. She had an innocence that could only have come from . . . no freaking way—she couldn't really be. I'd likened her to it when she first arrived, but there was no way.

"Are you a virgin?" I blurted.

Okay, tact was definitely not my middle name. I probably could have asked that a million different ways.

Mischa blushed, red as freaking lava. She opened and closed her mouth a few times before lowering her eyes to stare at what must have been the sudden appearance of a sixth toe on her left foot. That's how hard she was concentrating.

Holy effing hell! How was this even possible? No, not the toe part. The virgin thing was much crazier.

"How is that possible?" I repeated aloud. "We're shifters; we *need* sex. It keeps our animals from ripping some asshat's face off."

A need that I'd been ignoring for too long now—it was going to make itself known soon. I mean, we aren't like nymphos or anything, we could go a long time without sex, but at some point after coming into our powers—it was seventeen for me—we started to get the hot flushes, the urges to touch and be touched. I'd never heard of a twenty-two-year-old virgin shifter.

Mischa lifted her face, which was back to a ripe-tomato color. "Now you sound like every man I've ever known. *Babe . . . I like neeeed sex. I'll die without it.*" Her male mimicking was spot-on.

I couldn't halt the peals of laughter. Who would have thought that not even twenty-four hours since . . . Vlad . . . that I could be doubled over, holding my aching stomach? Safe, with my sister. It was a gift.

When we'd finished losing it, she perched on the edge of my bed.

"So now that you know I'm yet to cash in my V card, do you think I'm a loser?"

Her face, the mirror of my own, was blank. But the green eyes were depthless, and in them I could see her pain and fear. I'm guessing she'd been called a loser on more than one occasion.

I dropped down next to her and put my arm around her shoulders. "No freaking way. I think you're awesome and clearly a strong woman who knows her own mind. I'm sure the fact that your wolf was suppressed allowed you some reprieve from the hormones."

She clunked her head onto my shoulder. "Yeah, but now I think I'm feeling them twofold." Her voice was an embarrassed whisper.

I snorted. "Well, it looks as if you and I both need to get some action. But I need to warn you . . ."

She lifted her face and met my gaze, interrupting me. The pause between us was extended.

"Still takes me by surprise," she finally said. "Like looking in a mirror."

It was eerie.

I nodded. "Yes, it takes me by surprise, too, but back to the point. Remember that we can find our mates through sex, and once you find your mate, you will be bonded to that shifter for life. So just be aware."

"You're making that sound really negative. Mom and Dad are so happy and in love. Why don't you want that for yourself?"

I sat there for a few moments, then shrugged it off and waved her question away with a grin. I knew the reason, deep down in my heart, why I was afraid of a mating. But now wasn't the time for this confession.

"I'm gonna grab a shower. I'll meet you downstairs." I kissed her cheek and took my chance to escape her probing expression.

In the quiet bathroom I shed all of my clothes and stared at my reflection for more than ten minutes. Not because I was vain, but because, finally, I could see the dragon mark. It was black with slivers of red threading through it. At first glance, it looked tribal, but that was only if you couldn't see the entire picture. The image was a weird, shadowy specter of a dragon, larger than I expected, wrapping around from my lower back and up the left side of my stomach. I continued to turn and spin, trying to see it as clearly as I could. But it seemed an impossible task, especially as it continued to shift and move. Finally, I couldn't stare any longer. I needed to finish my shower and get downstairs to find Louis. I couldn't let the Four find me.

By the time I'd made it downstairs, the living area was filled with massive individuals. I was scooped up by Tyson. "Hey, Jessa babe, you look like yourself again," he said as he kissed my cheek and handed me off to Jacob.

The fey squeezed me tightly, before singing a few bars of my favorite song into my ear. He knew that calmed me like nothing else. Then it was Maximus's turn. The massive vampire crushed me to his chest, and I knew—because it was his personality—that after Braxton, he'd been the most worried when I'd gone missing. This was also the reason he'd taken the secret so hard.

"I'm so sorry." I was babbling again. He just held me tighter.

His low growls started in my ear. "I told the boys we shouldn't be friends with girls," he muttered. "I told them that they're mean and will do things like break our hearts and scare the shit out of us." His deep words washed over the room. I heard a few chuckles.

When he pulled back, I examined his tense features. "When did you tell them that?" I asked.

Jacob snorted. "Remember when we were five, and you stole Max's piece of cake? Right around then."

"And when we were eight and you ran him over with your bike," Tyson added.

"Not to mention when you kicked him in the b—"

"Okay, okay. Apparently Max has spent much of our childhood lamenting that I was an annoying girl."

Braxton stepped in the front door, his dark hair damp, stylishly tousled. "Don't let them fool you. Max loved you from the first second you came into our lives. Twenty years."

Maximus eyed his brother. "I'm not the only one, bro."

Their intense exchange continued for a few long beats. I didn't even want to know what the hell that was all about. I was only grateful to feel that things were repaired between Maximus and me. The small rift that had appeared last night seemed to be gone. Everything felt right and normal.

Lienda broke the moment. "Okay, then, maybe it's time to head over for breakfast?" She was all snuggly with Dad on the couch. Which no longer seemed to piss me off. I'd gone from hating the woman to respecting her strength and thinking of her as a mother. Mind you, it would be a long time before I would call her that.

"Wait!"

I spun to find Louis in the doorway, his cheeks with the slightest flush to them, as if he'd run the entire way here. Still, I knew he could magic himself from one place to another, so I doubted he had run.

"The Four are here. They just requested permission to enter the perimeter. I need to spell Jessa now."

I let out a large sigh. "Those assholes could not wait until after breakfast, seriously?" My parents' horror-filled eyes locked on me. "What? A girl's got to eat. It's just rude."

I huffed my way across the room to stand before the sexy mage. "Come on, let's get this over with."

Jacob snorted. "That's what all the girls say to Louis."

With a grin, the sorcerer waved his hand and Jacob seemed to freeze to the spot. The fey opened and closed his mouth but couldn't speak again. I stepped even closer into Louis's personal space. We were mere inches from each other.

"First time I've ever seen someone shut Jake up."

Tyson laughed. "I need to learn that nifty trick."

Louis chuckled before sweeping me into his arms and striding out the door.

"Fucking sorcerer," I heard Jacob curse as we stepped into some sort of blurry wormhole thing and out the other side. We were at Louis's home. He dropped me to my feet.

"My wards here will protect us while I try to contain your massive energy." He leveled all of his intensity in my direction. "Tell me what happened when your mark was released."

His purple eyes regarded me, and I felt as if he already knew I'd shifted into a dragon.

But I trusted Braxton's judgment. If he thought I should keep my dual nature to myself for a while, well, that's what I would do. Even if Louis suspected, I wasn't going to confirm it for him.

"Just a burst of power that released my wolf. I was no longer restricted by the securities of the prison." I stayed as close to the truth as I could. "I sort of got some dragon features, but I locked the power back inside before anything too big happened."

He nodded. "Your power is immense. I'm guessing that you're so used to keeping it all contained that you haven't even noticed the massive increase."

That wasn't exactly true. I could feel the curled sleeping power of my dragon. She was happy, content. It was strange—I had expected a snarling beast, and I knew that part of her could emerge at any time, but for right now. . . it was almost as if she were part wolf.

"I'm going to have to place my hands on your chest." He had both of his arms aloft in front of him but hesitated to drop them on me. I knew he was waiting to see if I was okay with such intimate contact . . . especially after yesterday.

I bit my lip before nodding. "Thanks for checking in on my mental state, but I'm fine. Touch away."

Dark streaks of blue flashed across his eyes. "I imagined you saying those words, just in slightly different circumstances." He raised his eyebrows at me a few times. "But I'll take it."

We were still standing close to his hidden home and the waterfall that concealed it. Soft strands of green grass curled around my bare feet, and small slivers of sunshine broke through the canopy. It was cold today, but somehow Louis kept his area nice and temperate. My toes were thanking him for this. In one smooth movement he placed both hands on my chest, in the space just above the swell of my breasts. I flinched minutely, unable to stop my thoughts from returning to yesterday—my disgust and fear as that creature ran his hands over my body. I could still taste the bile and smell the fear that had permeated the air. My fear.

"Jessa." Louis's voice was commanding. I raised my eyes to meet his. "Look at me." His voice softened. "Focus on me."

I did as he said, focusing on his face and forcing myself to take long, deep breaths. I would not let this beat me; so many women had had it far worse. They hadn't been saved. I needed to remember that.

"Time will get rid of those memories, Jessa. Don't be so hard on yourself. You don't have to be strong all the time."

"There you go reading my mind again." How did he do that?

He dropped his forehead against mine. "I can see it written across your face. You keep beating yourself up for what you consider your weakness. I know how hard it is to be strong all the time and not know what to do when that falls away." Lifting his face, he dropped a kiss to my forehead, in the same place his head had just rested. "What happened yesterday in no way diminishes your strength."

"Thank you," I whispered.

We were quiet for the next few minutes, and in that time the strain across Louis's features increased.

"I can't lock your energy away. It's strong and has taken root, moving through your body, into your cells. It's part of you in a way I can no longer separate. Our one chance is for me to cloak you. It will hide the energy from anyone searching for the dragon mark, but it's not locked away. You can access the power, and if you do, they'll be able to find you."

"Why didn't you just do that originally?"

He laughed. "We worried about a child having that much power, and you wouldn't have had the restraint to stop yourself from accessing it. Now, hopefully, your control is good enough for this. Remember, the Four will find you if you use your mark power."

I nodded. Warning duly noted. There was a sharp jab, followed by what felt like tingles caressing their way up and down my body. Then

Louis stepped back. I shook myself out. It was the strangest sensation, as if he'd poured a second skin over my body.

"Going to take some getting used to," I said, forcing myself not to scratch at my arms.

"The itchiness will die down shortly, and the sensations will be much easier to deal with."

I freaking hoped so. I was like thirty seconds from dropping to the ground and rolling around in the grass.

Our heads spun toward Stratford as the town siren started to blare. The alarm wasn't used much. It was a signal for the townspeople to gather in the city center.

"Is that because of the Four?" I asked.

Louis nodded. "Yep, they're infamous in the supernatural world. Their presence alone demands some fanfare. They'll be wanting to search out the source of the mark energy."

He linked his hand through mine and started to lead me into town. The itching sensation was subsiding, but still a little irritating.

"How powerful are they?" I was having trouble imagining what they were like. The fear their mere names created just didn't ring true.

Louis turned his head, scanning the area. "Individually, they are no more powerful than your average alpha or race leader—less powerful than some, I'd say. But their real strength lies in their ability to join together and elevate the power of one another."

I remembered Braxton saying the same thing. I rubbed my free hand over the smooth, worn denim of my jeans. The chill was increasing the farther we got from Louis's place. Luckily, my metabolism was in fine form, or I would probably be on my way to frostbitten feet.

"So this ability to connect and increase their power is the same that the Compasses are supposed to possess?"

Louis nodded. "Yes, quadruplets are so rare that everyone pretty much expects your boys will turn into carbon copies of the Four."

I snorted. He regarded me silently for a moment. "Not going to happen," I felt compelled to add.

The Four were coldhearted dicks. You'd have to be to lock away babies. The Compasses would never be that. I'd kick the shit out of them if they even started looking in that power-crazy-dictator direction.

"Do you know the exact location of the mountain of Drago?" As soon as the question left my mouth, I wondered why I'd asked him that. I let loose way too many of my thoughts around him.

"It's in Romania. The Krakov supernatural prison and Drago are both in the Carpathian Mountains." He didn't ask me why I wanted to know, so of course I felt the need to babble out my reasons.

"Braxton said that the king is supposed to rise at the end of this month and that he rests at Drago." Again, Louis was quiet, not giving anything away, so I continued: "Have you heard this before?"

He exhaled lightly, but still more forcefully than he usually breathed. "I've lived a long time and heard many stories about the rise of the king, but there is some truth to the thousand years. It was said that all dragon marked need to be in the mountain at the time of the rising. If they aren't, there is a trigger inside the mark energy that will bring about their destruction."

Great! That was just great.

"The dragon king was pretty big on his 'You're either with me or against me' motto, and he must have figured that any not at Drago when he rises, well, they would be against him."

Of course they were. No wonder they had cut his head off, he was crazier than the Four.

"Is he supposed to just rise on his own?"

Louis stared off for a few moments, his face blank. "No," he finally murmured. "There has to be a sacrifice, and there's a ritual, but I don't know what it entails."

If Louis didn't know, I wondered if anyone did.

"Why are these two women freeing the dragon marked?" I asked him, needing to understand.

His features hardened. "I have my suspicions, but in reality my guess is as good as yours."

I was thinking that maybe there were some out there who knew the ritual, and I couldn't figure out if they were freeing the marked for that reason or if they were looking for someone.

Entering the outer zone of town, we started to move with the masses of people. When that siren rang, everyone responded, no matter what they were doing.

Which probably explained some of the states of undress I was seeing. There were naked shifters, who'd clearly been out for a run, and then a few couples who were clad only in their underwear. Of course they'd had time to grab clothes—and, not to mention, clothing bins were scattered everywhere—but we really didn't sweat nudity the same way the human population seemed to. Besides a few shy exceptions, most of them wouldn't have thought anything of their appearance. Certainly not enough to stop and look for clothes.

The city center was already half-full. There were too many of us to fit into the town hall, so we would congregate outside around the fountain. Louis and I started to move closer to the front. Not that I thought being near the Four was a great idea, but I wanted to find my family, and I knew the council leaders would be at the forefront. We didn't have to push; people moved aside for us—okay, mostly for Louis, but a girl could dream.

Power, glorious power.

At least the tingles of his cloaking had died right down to almost nothing. After a few minutes of dodging the crowds, my nose crinkled at all the scents assailing me. I noticed my father standing off to the right. That was where we needed to go. I lowered my head, ready to plow my way through the last few yards. I was almost there when Louis grabbed my arm and halted me.

"I'm not sure what is going to happen right now," he said, keeping his voice low. "If it goes down the way I hope, then everything will be fine, and you won't have to worry. But if things skew offtrack, you need to listen to my instructions and follow each one, without question. You will just have to trust me." He dropped a kiss on my cheek. "I've got to go and check on something now, but I'll find you again."

I was opening my mouth to ask him what the hell he was talking about, when he disappeared. Like literally, into thin air. The scent of ash coated the inside of my nostrils. He'd used some pretty powerful magic just then.

Pushing down the tendrils of icy fear and worry, I stomped the rest of the way. I was just about at my family when a figure caught my eye. He was tall, casting a shadow as he stood off to the side of the fountain. Despite there being supernaturals everywhere, he stood in his own space. Melly. He held both arms by his side, fists tightly clenched. He was staring at me through the crowd, and his expression was hard. This wasn't exactly anything new, but in that extended moment the huge shifter reminded me of something . . . or more important, someone—the bear who had attacked me inside Vanguard. He'd worn the same expression and said I was collateral damage in a war I knew nothing about. I'd just assumed that was to do with Jonathon. But what if it hadn't been, what if there was more to Melly's hatred of me?

I was distracted from my thoughts by Mischa grabbing my hand and dragging me across to the edge of our group. When I turned my head back to the spot again, the bear shifter was gone. So freaky.

Jonathon leaned in close to me.

"Are we all good?" he asked. I could see by the serious expression and hard blue eyes that he was stressed.

I bit at my lip. "Well, the power is too strong for Louis to lock away again, so he put like a cloaking around me. Hopefully it's enough." As long as the dragon didn't decide to burst free.

Jonathon ran his eyes over me, and then reached out and touched me. "I can't sense anything unusual about you, but then I don't have the tracking skills of the Four. I hope Louis knows what he is doing."

Lienda gripped his forearm tight enough that every knuckle stood out on her hand. "I don't want to risk it. We need to run."

Jonathon pulled her closer. "If we run, they will ask questions, and then the Four will come for us. And they always find those they hunt. We need to play the game and stay calm."

I wondered where the Compasses were. Usually they would be front and center during something like this.

"Are they bringing in someone to replace Kristoff?" I asked Dad.

He was staring out over the crowd, trying to keep an eye on what was happening.

"Not until after the trial. He can't be stripped of his position unless he is found guilty."

Slimy bastard would probably find a way to get out of this one, too.

The noise started to die down around us, and even craning my neck gave me no better view of what was happening. I was tense, my hands clenched into fists, my nails biting into the soft pads. Where were the Compasses? And what had Louis taken off to do? I felt as if I was getting bits and pieces of a story, and the ending was going to shock the shit out of me when it came. Silence was descending across the thousands of Stratford residents crammed into the town center. The Four were coming; I could feel their power moving along the wind.

Then they were there, standing atop the lip on the fountain, heads above the crowd. I couldn't stop the gasp that fell from my lips. Thankfully, I was just one of many who either gasped, screamed, or coughed at their appearance. No attention was drawn in my direction.

Unlike the Compasses, these quads were identical, from their dark-red hair right down to their stormy gray eyes. They were dressed similarly, in black military-style clothes and thick shitkicker boots. They wore identical cold, hard expressions. Could their parents even tell them apart? No wonder they were known as the Four; there seemed to be no individuality about them at all.

And they were mutha-effing scary.

They stood there and stared out into the crowd, all four sets of eyes scanning us. Silence echoed around the space, minus the thousands of hearts beating and the rapid-breathing thing that Mischa seemed to be doing. The girl was about five seconds from hyperventilating.

Number Two opened his mouth. "We are here because there have been reports of dragon marked in Stratford." The gray eyes continued to bore into the crowd. "If you are harboring these fugitives, you need to stop. Now." There was a crap ton of force behind that last order.

Three took over the speech. "The council wants to keep from you the fact that the recent prison breakouts were dragon marked. Every single one was a marked. They are free now to bring about the rise of the king. We cannot let this happen."

Angry chatter started around the residents. Now I was seeing where all the rumors had come from. I'd wondered how all the prisoners and guards had seemed to know the breakouts were from a secret room and that they were marked. The Four had been making sure everyone knew; they wanted people to rally against this. They were trying to stir up trouble so no one would keep the marked a secret.

Number Four had a low, strong voice. "You are all probably wondering why the marked are imprisoned and not killed. The simple fact is that we have yet to find a weapon that can kill the marked. For all intents and purposes, they're immortal, which makes it doubly important that they are locked away again."

I choked on my tongue, or something like that. I had to cover my mouth to halt the harsh barking cough trying to flee.

Immortal. Mischa and I exchanged glances. Well, shit, sounds as if I don't have to worry about death anymore. Wish I'd known that when Vlad had me.

Chapter 17

It was time for Number One, who seemed to be the hardest of all, to speak: "There are two female dragon marked, very old and very powerful, freeing marked from prisons worldwide. They're searching for the two to match them. Together these four will mark the points on the compass that will free the king."

Compass points. Was that part of the ritual?

Number One stepped a little in front of his brothers, the first time they had broken rank from their stance. "We cannot let these four join together. We cannot let the king rise. He will have a legion of immortal soldiers at his beck and call, and he will destroy us all."

Shit, he even had me convinced that the dragon marked were going to take over the world, and I was one of them. I continued spinning my head around the zone, trying to find the boys. It was very unlike them not to be with me or their family. Since I could see Jack and Jo close by, I knew they weren't with their parents.

I smiled as I noticed the little boy huddled close to the vampire sorceress's side. Jo had an arm tightly wrapped around his shoulders as if she could keep him safe with her love alone. I was glad that Louis had managed to spell Nash's mark and energy. He was too young to be able to access any of it yet, and for now he was undetectable by the Four. Once this thousand-year thing passed, he might actually have a shot at a decent life. And if no dragon king rose, well, my hope was that the dragon marked would be free from this constant persecution.

I was a dreamer.

Number One stepped back to join his brothers. "You have five minutes." The four of them crossed their arms over their broad chests and raised their chins in unison.

Gah, that was like the freakiest thing ever, robotic almost.

Mischa and I had our hands tightly linked. Jonathon and Lienda were close to us also. The minutes passed in a slow blur of motion. There were no noises, and no one stepped forward to offer up any dragon marked.

I turned my head out into the crowd again. I was starting to jitter on the spot, and I knew I had to stop it. If I continued to act like a guilty dick, the Four were going to find me with absolutely no help from anyone. And where the effing hell were the Compasses? I was going to throat-punch each of them when they appeared, worrying me like this. It was, well, very annoying. Yeah, let's go with annoying.

Then I was going to hug the hell out of them. So the order of actions was clear: throat-punch, then hug.

As I was spinning back to the fountain, my eyes widened and I felt more shivers caress my body. Where the hell had the Four gone? There was space where they'd been standing, and I had not heard or sensed them move at all. My fidgeting was getting worse. Something told me they were searching the crowd. They were going to find us. I just knew it.

"Stay calm, Jessa." Jonathon loaned me some of his power, easing my nerves. "You will be fine. I would never let anything happen to you or Mischa."

His words were low and calming, and yet I was not calmed at all. If anything, my nerves were increasing. Freeing my hands, I spun around and started to blindly push my way through the crowd. I knew drawing attention to myself in this manner was dangerous, but the fear was choking me. I needed to shift into my wolf. Problem being, my dragon was also stirring. She'd unfurled herself and was nudging at the thin, flimsy barrier that surrounded her now. I could almost scent the smoke from her nostrils, the shimmer from the scales and fur that coated her skin. She was just under my skin the way my wolf often was. If I lost control of her now, the Four would be on me faster than Maximus when he scented a sexy vamp girl.

People got out of my way, and finally I made it to the edge of the crowd, which, thankfully, was close to the forest. I was going to be able to run, shed the human skin and be a wolf for a while. I hoped, too, that would ease the tumult of my dragon. I sighed as the cool dark of the forest canopy surrounded me. The earthy scent, a mix of dirt, plants, and flowers flowed over me, and in itself this was soothing.

"Going somewhere?"

The low voice came from the shadows and froze me to the spot. I straightened as I prepared for them to emerge. Sure enough, the Four stepped free from where they had been hidden in my forest. My beautiful forest now tainted by them.

One of them, no idea which, came at me from the east. The others fanned out to the other points. North, south, and west.

East started speaking. "We sent out a little energy. It stirs the dragon mark, causes fear and unease." They seemed so casual as they closed in on me. "You're a strong girl. We can feel the power under your skin. You could have resisted had you known." He tilted his head to the side, sizing me up like a predator. "Which is why we like to minimize the information on dragon marked. Knowledge is power."

"I'm not dragon marked," I said, and I was grateful that my voice didn't shake.

The west one bared his teeth at me. "There's no point in lying. We have no doubt you're the one we're hunting."

I was screwed, but there was no way I was going to let them take me without a fight. I would end up buried in some prison somewhere, never to be found again. I knew this time they would not risk anyone breaking out the dragon marked. We would be locked in the bowels of the Antarctic. Or even the prison that was rumored to be buried under the ocean.

The east one came at me then. He held no weapons. I guess he thought he didn't need them. I dodged the first swipe of his hands, spinning at the last moment and kicking out. I actually connected, smashing him in the gut and knocking him back a few feet. He staggered for a moment before recovering himself and stepping back into alignment.

The Four paused, their identical faces observing me. They seemed intrigued that I had attempted to fight back.

"You can never beat us. Why do you fight?" This was the one at the west. He seemed genuinely curious.

"I'm a wolf; I won't be caged. My lifetime is long, and I won't live it like that. I will always fight."

My impassioned words rang out through the trees.

"Your life is longer than that. It is eternal. The marked are immortal, but . . ." He broke off. "Don't despair of your long life, there's a weapon that can kill the marked, and we're getting very close to finding it. Then we will end the existence of all dragon marked."

I calmed myself, but didn't lower my hands. "You are evil, more evil than the king you proclaim to be defending the supernaturals from. You've stolen innocents, locked away babies and children, tortured and attempted to kill. If there were ever wicked supernaturals that we needed to be protected from, it's you four."

I couldn't understand how they didn't see this, that in their quest to prevent evil they had become evil.

They stopped moving again and spoke as one unit: "Sometimes good men must be ruthless. Sometimes you must sacrifice the few for the many." The four of them repeated this, over and over.

The words were spinning through my mind, and I had to force myself not to vomit. Of course my stomach was empty, which helped with keeping the contents down. They would never be convinced from their path; they were unwavering in their belief. They were crazy as fuck. And it was really hard arguing with an insane person. I knew from my many years fighting with Giselda aka BEF.

"We're going to take you now," the north one said, his voice calm, even kind. "Please do not fight us. We don't want to hurt you any more than we have to."

Oh, I was going to fight.

They came at me again, all of them at the same time. I kicked, screamed, and fought at all angles. But before I could even think about another avenue or call on my wolf, they had me, each holding one of my arms and legs. I was held aloft, suspended above the ground and unable to move. Their strength was apparent. I could not muscle my way out of this. I had just one option left. My dragon. I hadn't called for her because I thought there might have been a chance to talk myself out of being taken. Continue to deny I was marked. But they either knew something or didn't care. They were taking me no matter what.

I reached for my energy, bypassing the wolf and going straight for the dragon. She rose to attention and caressed me. But I couldn't connect to her. Generally, when shifting I'd call for the energy and the change would come. But something was stopping it. I opened my eyes and stared at the hands holding me. Could the Four prevent me from touching that energy? Was that part of their combined power? Okay, well I had only one *other* option.

I screamed, loud, long, and echoing. Surely we were close enough for someone to come and investigate. The Four didn't stop me. They let me scream until I was hoarse. I knew where we were going. They were

Jaymin Eve

moving toward the border of Stratford. Once we got outside of this area, there was no coming back for me. I would disappear.

I still screamed for help, but my voice was barely above a whisper now. The ache in my throat felt permanent. I had done a bit of damage.

Tears were building in my eyes, but I would not give myself the luxury of crying. Or them the satisfaction.

I sniffed a few times, blinking rapidly.

"How did you know?" I whispered hoarsely. "That I was marked."

There was no point denying it now.

"We were in the prison, investigating the breakout," the man on my right arm answered. "Your energy called to us, and we knew there was an active marked in there. For your energy to blast through as it did, you were not in the special marked area with its securities. We set up these secret rooms in all the prisons. We know the five elements that limit the power of the marked, and we thread them through each of the prisons worldwide." His gray eyes flashed down at me. "Since you weren't in the secret room, then you were in the main prison. After that it wasn't hard to figure out who you were. Other than the male, you were the only one to leave the prison, and he is dragon. They are never marked."

"Can you trace the marked energy from anywhere? Will you be able to find all the ones who were freed?"

The same man answered me again. "No, we must be in close proximity, although there is a bit of a pull for the stronger ones. Generally, supernaturals contact us and report a marked. Then we go to that area, and it is pretty easy to find them after that."

So if I actually had run, they might never have been able to find me. I bit my cheek hard enough that I tasted blood. "What did you do to the Compasses?"

"Nothing," he said. And that was all I got from them.

We reached the edge of Stratford. I could see the shimmery dome that prevented the outside world from just walking into our town. Of

248

course, humans couldn't see these protections, but they still worked on keeping them out. This dome was supposed to keep me safe . . . yet, in the end, nothing had kept me safe. The man holding my left leg halted, he reached out with a hand to touch the barrier. About an inch from connecting, he stopped . . . or froze. *What the hell?* My eyes flicked up between all of them. None of them was moving.

What was going on? Had the barrier done something to them?

I started to wiggle, to see if I could free myself. Sure enough, as I started to move and squirm, I managed to wrench my left leg free, followed by my arm on the opposite side. Then with a huge intake of breath, I closed my eyes and jerked the remaining arm and leg clear.

I hit the ground hard, jarring up my body and into my brain. But I didn't stop for a second. I had to get away before whatever had halted the Four lifted.

Just as I was springing forward, my arms pumping, ready to sprint, a familiar figure stepped into view. I ground to a halt before throwing myself into his arms. "Louis," I gasped. "You saved me."

I should have known. Only a sorcerer as powerful as he could have done this.

He hugged me back hard before pulling away to stare down at me. "Listen to me, Jessa, I can only hold them for a short time. They're joined, and they're very powerful." There was strain on his face. "You need to run. Go now, out of the dome and into the car I have waiting for you at the end of the road. Do not hesitate. Get to the private supernatural airport and onto the plane that's waiting there ready to take off. The Four will come after you. This is our one chance to get you to a safe place. Wait for me there, and I will come once I make sure your family is protected."

"I'm going to have to run forever?" I cried.

He shook his head. "No, we will make you safe. We will find a way. But for now there is no time. If they take you, they will be able to hide you from me. Instead, I beat them at that game and I will hide you from them."

He shoved a bag into my hands, a heavy knapsack.

"Go now, Jessa. I have learned much this night, but there is no more time." He pretty much picked me up then and tossed me through the portal.

I closed my eyes, bracing for whatever protections to attack me. But there was nothing, just a weird sucking sensation. Then with a diving roll on the ground, I was on the other side. I was in the human world.

Holy shitballs.

I took off along the long, winding dirt road, nothing on either side but trees and fields. I didn't slow until the black Range Rover came into view, just sitting there in the center of the dirt path as if Louis had dropped it out of the sky. Skidding to the side, I wrenched open the driver's door and without hesitation jumped into the black leather seat. I didn't take any time to remove the bag; it clanked at my side as I hit the button to start the powerful machine. I knew there would be keys inside somewhere, and sure enough, at the touch of my fingertips the V8 engine roared to life.

As I slammed the stick into drive and pushed my foot flat to the floor, I silently thanked Braxton for my multitude of driving lessons. The four tires skidded on the dirt road before finding traction, and then I was off. In the rearview mirror, dust blew up behind me, and I swore, in the far distance, I saw the Four dive out of the dome. Shit. They were already after me.

I decided not to look back again. I focused on trying to recall where the airport was. We all had to memorize the map. It was part of the evacuation route, should it ever be required. But looking at a map and being there in real life, not to mention being chased, was spazzing out my mind a little.

I stayed on the road until I reached a fork; I was starting to get my bearings. I knew the first turn was left, then there was another long road. It was definitely hard to orientate myself; everything looked the same. I was surrounded by huge fields of corn. I continued to take the turns, three left and two right, and then I sucked in a deep breath as the familiar supernatural symbol appeared on a small plaque, discreetly placed beneath the human speed-limit sign. *Thank eff.* I sobbed my next few breaths. I was going the right way.

It took thirty minutes, but suddenly the large hangar building appeared on the horizon. I didn't bother to look for a place to park the car; I just continued to drive until I pretty much ended up on the tarmac. There was only one plane out of the hangars, and it looked ready to roll. I screeched to a halt near the back of the wing. A quick glance at all the mirrors—I was still alone for the moment. I threw myself out of the car, leaving the door hanging open, and sprinted for the steps. I clunked my foot on the bottom step and a man appeared at the top.

"Hurry, Miss Lebron, we have to leave now."

I recognized the golden ring he wore on his middle finger. He was a Guild, one of those humans who helped us out. He was going to get me to safety. I really hoped we wouldn't have to kill him afterward. I'm sure Louis just wiped their memories.

I ran up the stairs, taking them three at a time. Once I was inside, the plane door slammed close and was secured. The takeoff procedure started immediately, before I'd even made it past the front entrance. I leaned against that wall—the heavy bag hanging off my side—and took a moment to calm my racing heart. Until we were in the air I wouldn't feel safe. In reality, knowing how crazy powerful the Four were, I wondered how I would ever feel safe again.

"Miss Lebron?" I spun my head to find the Guild man right beside me. "You need to take your seat and buckle up."

The plane was already moving. I lurched a little as I left the wall I was hugging.

Moving down the hall—it was quite large for a private plane—I emerged in a long, open room that seemed to have lots of leather chairs. And as I focused on the scene before me, I froze, and then loud and violent sobs burst from me. Mischa was in the closest chair, and farther back were the Compasses. All four of them. Red hair caught my attention, too. Grace, the healer witch, was off to the side.

Wait, what?

I knew it was weird that she was here, but right now I was focused on the others.

"Jessa." Mischa's arms came around me. "Thank God you're okay."

I lifted my trembling arms, securing them tightly around her, and held on as if my life depended on it.

Jacob, who'd also jumped to his feet when I appeared, swept me away from my sister and carried me back to buckle me in next to him. "Come on, baby girl, we got you now; you can relax."

Mischa was back in her seat, the plane had started rapidly down the runway, and then we were in the air. I managed to get my sobs under control, lifting both hands to wipe at my eyes. I'd never been on a plane and was distracted from my crying fit by the weird sensations of blocked ears and pressure in my head.

Tyson leaned over Jacob. "Open your mouth wide and yawn." He had to speak loudly over the thrusts of the engine.

I followed his instructions and had immediate relief.

"Thank you," I shouted back. A few more sobs shook me, but I had them under control. I wiped away the last of the wetness on my cheeks. "What's wrong with Braxton?" I finally noticed the way his head was lolling to the side. He looked like he was asleep.

Maximus laughed. "Well, let's just say none of us were very happy with Louis's little plan, but Braxton actually had to be, well, convinced. He's having a little nap."

I cast worried eyes at my bestie, but he didn't seem to be in distress. His breathing was nice and even.

We ascended for a long time, and then, finally, as the plane evened out and started to glide, Braxton blinked a few times before his head shot up. He raised a hand and rubbed at his temples.

"Jessa—" he bit out, looking around the space. The relief across his features when he saw me was apparent. "I'm going to kill that fucking wizard. If anything had happened to you . . ."

The light went off for the seat-belt sign, so I clicked myself free and crawled across the boys to hug Braxton. "I'm fine," I said. "Louis saved me."

Braxton didn't look convinced. "Tell me what happened."

I quickly went through everything, touching briefly on the Four and the power they'd had to halt my shift to wolf. Only Braxton knew of my dual-shifting abilities, so I didn't mention that my dragon had been cut off also.

Then it was their turn. Tyson started. He explained how Louis had come to them and decided to put this contingency plan into place. He said that if the Four decided to attack, it was better to be prepared, and if they didn't, he would return and fetch the boys. He'd grabbed Mischa at the last minute while I'd been occupied with the Four.

I turned to the witch. "Hi, Grace." She returned my smile. "How did you get roped into this?"

Her very dark doe eyes blinked a few times. "Louis asked me if I was willing to help you all, that you would need a healer." She shrugged. "There was nothing keeping me in Stratford, and I've always envied the closeness of your pack." Her stare was direct. I could see Tyson locking his gaze on her, too. "So . . . here I am."

"Thank you," I said, my tone low.

I didn't even want to know why Louis thought we would need a healer.

Braxton hit the button to free himself from the harness then. "Fucking wizard took us all by surprise. I told him we needed to stay and defend you, but he insisted we had no idea what we were going up against and that we had to be smart. I was on my way to smack him in the face when everything went dark."

Tyson kept a straight face. "He hit Brax straight in the chest with a knockout spell, fastest cast I've ever seen."

Mischa moved across then and squished in with all of us on the large couch. "What is in the bag?"

I reached down and freed the knapsack that was wedged in between me and Maximus. Lifting the lid, I tipped the contents onto the small table. Bundles of cash, passports, and drivers' licenses spilled out. Damn, the sorcerer was like a human Boy Scout, always prepared.

We sifted through the lot, opening each document to find there were new identities for all of us, including Grace, enough paperwork that we would be able to survive in the human world if we needed to. And a crap ton of cash. Lastly, there was a folded piece of paper.

I opened it to find a hand-penned letter.

I didn't recognize the neat writing, but I assumed it was from Louis. I read it aloud to the group.

"Jessa, if you are reading this, then the Four know about your mark. I hoped it wouldn't come to pass, but I always have a contingency plan for these situations. I have included in this bag everything you should need to venture into the human world."

I sucked in deeply before continuing: "New names, new identities, nothing traceable for the Four. You may not need them as I'm sending you to a safe house of a friend, a friend whom I trust with my life. He knows a lot about the marked. He will have answers for you. I, too, have a lot to explain. I have learned many things this day, but there was no time. For now, stay safe."

I glanced down at the rest of the note. It was filled with directions to follow once we got to our new destination. He'd signed his name at the bottom in a flourishing signature.

Mischa leaned over to look. "Does it say where we are going?"

I looked at all of them. "Don't you all know where we are going?" Seriously, I just assumed someone knew.

Heads shaking side to side and grim faces. I scanned the rest of the directions in the note, but there was nothing to indicate our final destination. Rising from my seat, I made my way into that little front alcove, where the man who'd welcomed me on board was preparing food.

"Hello."

He jumped. "Sorry, Miss Lebron, is there anything I can help you with?" He faced me, and I realized he didn't look much older than me.

"Sorry, I didn't catch your name when I first got on the plane . . ."

He dried his hands on a towel. "I'm Craig." I wondered if he was going to shake my hand, but he didn't move, so clearly not. I observed him for a moment. He was my first real human, and I was fascinated by his lack of energy, almost as if he were cloaking it. But I knew that was simply what a human was. He was cute but sort of plain. Mousy brown hair and washed-out blue eyes. Nothing special about him, but maybe his normalness was special all on its own.

"Hi, Craig, you can call me Jessa." I smiled, which he returned, but ten to one he was still going to call me Miss Lebron. The Guild was big on formalities. "Can you tell me where we are going?"

His smile faltered minutely. A sort of blank look crossed his face. "You know, I'm not actually sure. I was called on last minute for this charter." He straightened a little. "I'll go and check with the pilot."

He disappeared, and I knew he was heading to the front of the plane where the pilot and copilot would be sequestered. Probably more Guild members. They were on standby everywhere in the world. Craig was back in a few minutes.

He looked uncomfortable, fidgeting with his white-buttoned shirt. "The pilot said the official flight path is for Japan, but that we're actually heading to Romania. To the Carpathian Mountains."

I could sense his confusion, but humans never questioned supernaturals. I nodded my thanks before I stumbled back into the main cabin. Six sets of eyes were watching me closely. Braxton got to his feet. He had to duck so he wouldn't hit his head in the small area.

"Did you find out where we are going?" He reached my side and took my hand. I blinked rapidly as I stared up into his blue eyes.

My voice was a bit vapid as I tried to catalog my thoughts. "Where in Romania is Mount Drago located?" I'd asked Louis that earlier, but I wanted to check he had the right information.

Braxton paused. I could hear his breath. It had suddenly gone that quiet in the plane.

"I believe it's near the Romanian prison," he said, without inflection. "In the Carpathian Mountains."

Shit.

I locked eyes with him. "According to the pilots, that's where we're heading."

Judging by the expressions around me, we were all thinking the same thing: *What the hell was the sorcerer up to, sending us straight into the mouth of the beast?*

About the Author

Jaymin Eve is the author of the Walker Saga, a young adult paranormal series, as well as the Supernatural Prison series. She lives on the beautiful Gold Coast of Australia with her family and spends most of her time on the beach. When she isn't trying to wrangle two daughters, a puppy, and her husband, she can be found hiding in a corner writing her stories. Visit her online at www.jaymineve.com.